Bernard F. Conners is the author of two previous bestselling novels, *Dancehall* and *Don't Embarrass The Bureau*. *Dancehall* has become one of the most perennially popular and bestselling novels in recent years, and has been published in every major country in the world. Mr Conners is also the former publisher of the *Paris Review* and is currently at work on a new novel. He lives in Loudonville, New York.

D1343400

By the same author

Dancehall
Don't Embarrass the Bureau

BERNARD F. CONNERS

The Hampton Sisters

GRAFTON BOOKS

A Division of the Collins Publishing Group

LONDON GLASGOW
TORONTO SYDNEY AUCKLAND

Grafton Books
A Division of the Collins Publishing Group
8 Grafton Street, London W1X 3LA

A Grafton UK Paperback Original 1989

Copyright © Bernard F. Conners 1987

ISBN 0-586-20263-3

Printed and bound in Great Britain by
Collins, Glasgow

Set in Times

For C.C.C.

Acknowledgements

The author wishes to thank the following persons who furnished technical assistance with portions of this novel:

John T. DeGraff, Jr., Esq., Loudonville, New York

Joseph L. Glenn, PhD, Professor of Biochemistry, Albany Medical College

Kenneth A. Handcock, MD, PC, Albany, New York

William A. Petersen, MD, Latham, New York

Robin B. Tassinari, MD, PC, Albany Medical Center, Albany, New York

Old Hampton, Long Island

April

It was a quiet place deep in the wild. By day, a cheerful spot where birds sang and sunbeams pierced the leaves of tall trees, falling in golden patterns on the green moss; where wildflowers swayed in a gentle breeze, and ducks paddled among lily pads on a shimmering pond.

But with nightfall, the dual character of the place was evident. It changed into a gloomy spot where strange images reflected in the mist. The pond was then a steaming black pool, and surrounding objects took on an eerie bluish cast in the moonlight.

The scene was especially forbidding at the moment. Although the forest was still, far above in the pines a light breeze moaned at intervals, as if lamenting the madness unfolding below.

A solitary figure leaned over a bulging trash bag at the edge of the pond. In one hand was a slender surgical instrument, its keen blue steel glistening in the moonlight. With one deft stroke the person made a long neat slit in the swelling pouch. Visceral remains tumbled out onto the ground.

After meticulously emptying the contents, the figure weighted the sack with a rock, and pitched it into the pond. It disappeared in a burst of bubbles amid dispersing lily pads, which tugged at their roots as if repelled by the odious ingredients that washed from the bag.

The figure backed off several yards and remained motionless, looking towards the perimeter of trees that encircled the pond. There in the darkness voracious creatures followed every movement with quiet anticipation. Then, one by one, they emerged from the blackness. Well-fed carnivores the size of small dogs. They approached the feast cautiously, their features turning slowly from side to side, surveying the terrain. Like most nocturnal creatures of the forest, they knew well the dangers of exposure. The difference between eating and being eaten was marginal.

The figure waited for a moment, observing the animals devouring the remains, and then turning, disappeared into the darkness towards one of Old Hampton's best-known homesteads.

Soon the creatures completed their meal. One by one the bloated bodies returned to the trees, leaving behind only the blood-soaked ground – the vestige of what had once been a young woman.

Once again the forest was still. Except for the witnessing spirits that danced in the vapours steaming from the pond.

PART ONE

Old Hampton,
Long Island

June

Chapter 1

An oily-green serpentine object emerged from the upper corner of a partially opened second-storey window. It paused for a moment, dangling in the darkness, its glistening shape blending with the English ivy that covered the walls of the house. After hanging indeterminately for several seconds, it made its way stealthily down alongside a drainpipe near the corner of the dwelling, twisting slowly towards the ground.

Midway in its descent, the lights of an approaching car pierced the darkness. The object hesitated, waiting silently. When the car had passed, it continued its sinuous descent, its curved tip oscillating as though probing the darkness below. Finally it came to rest, folding into a slick, soft pile near the base of the drainpipe. Here it coiled, motionless, concealed in the tall grass.

It was a warm evening, the kind that induce nocturnal creatures to forage. A hard pale moon rode high in a black-ocean sky, sailing far out where its reflection did not inhibit the creeping organisms of darkness. An occasional breeze blew from the ocean, rustling leaves, causing branches to groan. Beyond the dunes behind the house could be heard the intermittent muffled rumbling of the surf.

But sounds of the elements were muted this night. It was the utterances of living things that filled the air. From the Sanctuary across the road came a relentless cadence, the eternal song of life in the forest. Now and then it was broken by the bark of a predator, or the wail of prey, as millions of creatures vied for survival. For all, death was always near.

The green shape coiled at the base of the drainpipe had been designed to kill. It was two garden hoses, joined together and fashioned into an instrument for murder.

Later that night the end of the length of hose would be taken from the grass and drawn around the corner of the house to a large attached garage where it would be inserted into the exhaust pipe of an old station wagon. The hose would be plugged in with rags to provide a sealed conduit. A check would be made of the gas tank to ensure it was full, and then the engine would be started. Between the footbrake and the accelerator a small book would be wedged to make certain that the motor continued to run smoothly.

From the exhaust pipe, fumes containing deadly carbon monoxide would fill the hose. Slowly at first, then more quickly, the fumes would be transmitted through the hose to the upstairs bedroom.

The environs of Old Hampton were a moist, lush region where life flourished. But many creatures were marked for extinction this night – including an illusive one that dwelled in the strange mind of one of Old Hampton's most fetching residents.

Chapter 2

Dawn came softly on Forsythia Lane. From the ocean close by, a light mist drifted over the dunes and settled quietly on the luxuriant estates that lined the road. A faint breeze nudged the yachting flags atop the Bayrock Club – a curious configuration of steeples, spires and banners outlined against the sky, like a battleline drawn to defend Bayrock against un-Christian encroachments. From the Sanctuary on the other side of the road came sounds of awakening birds, muted cheeps respectful of distinguished neighbours still sleeping in nearby mansions. Morning, like everything, arrived gently in Old Hampton.

Sounds of stirring birds were welcome in one of the houses. Number 12 Forsythia Lane was a great, sprawling, grey-shingled structure with white shutters; a tatterdemalion in its well-kept surroundings. Whereas neighbouring lawns and shrubbery were immaculately groomed and represented the finest in landscape architecture, Number 12 had almost completely reverted to the plants that flourished in the moist Long Island atmosphere. Its untended gardens were of concern to staid neighbours, but there was little they could do. For this was the home of Emily and Lydia Morrow, known as the Hampton sisters; daughters of the late Louis Morrow, real estate tycoon and philanthropist who had established much of Old Hampton, including the Sanctuary on Forsythia Lane.

It was Lydia who heard the awakening birds and they prompted her to move quickly. She was preparing for her

15

morning bird walk in the Sanctuary. Birds were important to her. She had written two books on the species that inhabited the eastern environs of Long Island, and the last, *A Field Guide to Birds in the Hamptons*, had been duly acknowledged by ornithologists. Now, dressed in walking togs, equipped with field glasses and clipboard, she headed towards the door.

Suddenly she stopped, her hand on the doorknob, as the sound of a dog barking came from outside. Earlier, younger sister Emily had been awakened by the barking, and had asked her to close the window near her bedroom so she could sleep. Lydia had forgotten, and rather than going back upstairs, she considered ignoring the request. But then, with a sigh of resignation, she placed the binoculars and clipboard on the table and headed back to the stairs. She had learned long ago to accede to Emily's wishes rather than endure the alternative.

In her late twenties, with blond hair, smooth features and a lovely figure, she possessed considerable beauty, but managed to camouflage much of it beneath heavy granny glasses, frumpish hairdos and dowdy clothes. There was no way of concealing her fresh clean complexion, however, and when she smiled, which was often, she revealed a ribbon of beautiful teeth as white as cotton.

She was a happy person whose expression reflected an inner serenity that was most appealing. Her large eyes addressed one in a manner suggesting they had been spared the sight of serious misfortune. Indeed, it seemed worldly troubles seldom invaded her haven at Number 12.

'Sounds like Bart,' Lydia said as she mounted the stairs and moved towards the window at the end of the hall. 'Henry must be up early today.'

Bart was the Newfoundland belonging to Henry Todd, the elderly custodian of the Sanctuary who lived in a small tenant house on the Morrow property. The dog's barking was a constant annoyance to Emily.

'I thought I smelled gas fumes,' Lydia continued. 'That's why I opened the window. I had the worst headache when I woke up. Did you turn off my air conditioner? I could have sworn it was on when I went to bed.'

There was no response from the bedroom. Lydia suspected her sister was awake, but was ignoring her. That was all right. Lydia was accustomed to such discourtesies from Emily.

After closing the window she moved back down the hall towards the stairs. 'Don't forget, the cleaning people come today.' The sisters retained a local maid service to clean their downstairs. Concern for privacy precluded full-time domestics in the country residence. 'Make sure they launder those clothes I left in the back hall. That reminds me, you left your things in my room again.'

Descending the stairs, she went to the front door and picked up her binoculars and clipboard. It was then that she noticed the note that her sister had left on the hall table the previous night: 'DON'T FORGET TO CALL THE PUBLISHER.'

Lydia had been promising for several days to follow up on Emily's manuscript, a first novel entitled *The Sanctuary*, that Lydia had submitted to her publisher the previous month.

Lydia had reason for procrastination. Emily had been working for some time on the book, and had guarded the contents as one would guard a diary. Lydia had given it little chance of completion. She was surprised, therefore, when several weeks previously her sister had asked her to submit the finished novel to Richard Fox, Lydia's publisher. Lydia's surprise turned to stunned disbelief when she read it and found Emily's protagonist was a near-

17

nymphomaniac and ornithologist on Long Island. The work contained a number of sexual scenes so bizarre and explicit that the reading triggered a mild attack of Lydia's tachycardia.

What had particularly unnerved her was a passage containing material similar to an entry – an innermost secret – in Lydia's own private journal. Perhaps it was a coincidence. Still, she no longer left the journal on her desk in the study, but rather kept it under some books on one of the shelves.

After repeated attempts to dissuade her sister from pursuing publication, Lydia had reluctantly agreed to send the manuscript to her publisher, quietly resolving to remove certain portions. Chapters 6, 14, 26 and 32 would never leave the Morrow house if Lydia could prevent it. Although embarrassing, should Richard Fox read the manuscript, at least the problem was under control and delayed the multiple submission that Emily contemplated as an alternative.

'I still think I should go in to see Mr Fox myself,' Emily had said at one point. 'There are things I should probably explain to him. Like Chapter 26. He might think it's a little . . . well, you know, peculiar.'

'I don't think so,' Lydia had replied. 'It might make him uneasy. Publishers prefer to work through agents. I'm sort of acting as your agent.'

Leaving the house, Lydia crossed the lane and entered the Sanctuary. She rarely ventured from the house except to come here or to the beach. Most of her time was spent at home writing her books, making entries in her diary, and handling household chores.

Inside the Sanctuary, she felt the comfort and relaxation the trees and heavy plant life invariably engendered. As she proceeded down a crooked path, a catbird popped its dark head from a branch and watched her quietly. She

18

gave it only casual attention as her thoughts returned to her younger sister's note reminding her to call the publisher. Emily had been pressing her all week to follow up on the manuscript and would be intolerant of further delay.

Lydia had already made a call to the publisher, unbeknownst to her sister, describing the novel when it had been first submitted: a distorted, thinly-camouflaged account of life in Old Hampton, particularly the Bayrock Club, containing no redeeming literary value whatever. Even if publishable, which it was not, it contained enough libellous material to keep the Morrow sisters in court for the rest of their days. Would Richard be kind enough to pretend to have read it, and send Emily a firm letter discouraging her from pursuing publication?

To her dismay, the call had piqued the publisher's curiosity and, perhaps with an eye on the market potential of a Morrow sister's memoir, he had expressed an interest. 'Would Emily care to come in for a visit?'

Lydia was quick to see the disadvantages of such a meeting. She had a secret fondness for Richard Fox, and her sister was not only manipulative, she was beautiful. Although Lydia's contacts with her publisher had been few – her books were handled by one of the editors – the brief encounters had given rise to expectations.

In more pragmatic moments, she realized that probably nothing would come of the relationship. Richard had never displayed any interest in her beyond his professional duties. Still, she was considering asking him to review an outline she had done for a new book in ornithology. Perhaps it would lead to lunch. In view of the possibility, however remote, she was determined that the publisher should not meet Emily. Her feelings in this regard derived from bitter experience.

A voice on the path interrupted her thoughts. 'Mornin', Miss Emily.' It was Henry Todd.

'Oh, hello, Henry. It's Lydia.'

'So it is. Sorry, I'm forever mixin' you up.'

'Early for you, isn't it?'

'Yes, ma'am. Thought I'd come in and look around a bit.' As he removed his cap deferentially, a shock of snow-white hair tumbled down on his leathered brow. He pushed it back with a gnarled hand, and screwed his kindly features into a frown. 'Found some more back there in the bogs yesterday.' He pursed his lips as though reluctant to tell more. 'Long-billed curlews this time.'

'Oh no.' Lydia's face clouded as her eyes searched his face.

'Yep, just like the others.'

'What in the world is going on?' The long eyelashes fluttered. 'I mean, why . . .? Why would anyone do such horrible things?'

'Beats me.' Henry shook his head and the white hair fell down over his eyes. 'Third time this summer. Their beaks was taped shut. Probably some kids from the city, out for the weekend.'

'My, my.' Lydia was about to move on down the path when she noticed a small bandage on the caretaker's forehead. 'Did you hurt yourself, Henry?'

'No, it's nothin',' he said, raising a hand to the injured spot. 'Actually I bumped my head on the station wagon. I went by the house late last night and heard it runnin'. Someone left the motor on. Stuck my head in the window to turn it off. Couldn't see nothin' and a piece of that lumber I left in the back caught me square on the side of the head. Gotta watch those cars. Could be dangerous. Door was closed too.'

'Then that's where the odour of gas came from,' said Lydia. 'Emily must have forgotten to turn it off. She's

20

always forgetting things. But I didn't see her in the station wagon. She usually drives the Mercedes. Oh, well . . . Should be a lovely day, Henry.'

Lydia moved on down the path, reflecting for an instant on the birds that Henry had found, but soon forgetting the caretaker's comments. Henry occasionally alluded to happenings far back in the forest, but she showed little concern. Her interest in the Sanctuary was confined to the familiar surroundings of the path leading back to a pond, which constituted her bird walk. There was something about the dark, heavy vegetation beyond that was forbidding. But she rarely thought about it. Troubling things found little refuge in her mind.

Completing her walk, she returned to the house. Waiting for her inside the front door was Rusty, her golden retriever. He was holding a yellow tennis ball in his mouth. Next to spareribs, a tennis ball was the most prized item in Rusty's life. He would sit for long periods, the ball between his forepaws, waiting for someone to throw it for him.

As Lydia entered the house and placed her clipboard and binoculars on the hall table, Rusty followed. He dropped the ball at her feet, gave a short bark, and looked up at her expectantly.

'Not in the house, Rusty.' Lydia patted the dog affectionately, and moved on into the kitchen where she prepared breakfast: orange juice, croissant with jam, and coffee. She opened a screen on a kitchen window and shooed a housefly from the premises. It was against Lydia's values to kill anything, even plants – the reason for the rampaging vegetation outside.

Such concern for the sanctity of life was not shared by her sister. That same morning Emily Morrow reclined languidly in her bathtub contemplating the tips of her two large breasts – two pink icebergs pointing from the water. Atop the two tips, crawling about frantically to escape the water since Emily had detached their wings, were two houseflies.

Chapter 3

'That miserable worm.'

Outside the office of Richard Fox, whence the exclamation had come, Moseley Parrish, senior editor at Hollard House, shifted uncomfortably at his desk. He had reason to assume that his boss was referring to him. He was wrong. This time the publisher was directing his vehemence at Arnold Seigler, a critic who reviewed books for *The New York Chronicle*.

Richard steamed from his office, a newspaper containing a review of a Hollard book crushed in one fist. 'Helen. Where the hell is that woman? Helen?'

'I think she may have gone out, Richard . . . to the ladies room,' Moseley added respectfully.

'Go get her.'

'But – '

'Tell her I want her. Now.'

Moseley rose from his desk and shuffled towards the outer office. In his early forties, he was a short, bald man, as were almost all of Richard's staff. It was rumoured that to work for Hollard House one had to be shorter and balder than Richard, who was five feet nine inches and had thinning hair. He claimed to be five feet eleven inches, but this would have been standing on the one book he had written – a four-hundred-page tome about the publishing industry that had flopped, after having been summed up in a review by Arnold Seigler: 'Flatulent and errant. . . like a fizzling balloon.'

Moseley returned shortly leading Helen Rushmore, a

small pale-faced woman who was Richard's third secretary in the space of eighteen months.

'Take a letter to Seigler at the *Chronicle*.'

'Helen.' A voice from the intercom interrupted the dictation. 'Miss Morrow calling for Mr Fox.'

'Oh, no.' Pain on Richard's face. 'I just talked to her last week, didn't I?'

It was not that Richard disliked talking to Lydia. Despite his natural aversion to the importunings of authors, he rather liked Lydia Morrow. During their brief meetings he had found her pleasant, sincere, quite attractive actually. He suspected that she might even have a nice figure, although it was hard to tell with those Old Hampton woollies she seemed so fond of wearing. It was only that his day was not going well, his mood had deteriorated and, well . . . it just wasn't a good day for talking to authors.

'Hold it. Stay there,' he said to his secretary, who had started to leave when he reached for the phone. 'I'll only be a minute. I want that illiterate creep to get this letter as soon as possible.'

'Lydia, how nice to hear from you. I was just asking Charlotte about you.'

Despite Richard's modest stature and thinning brown hair, he was quite handsome. He had dark eyes and features reminiscent of old photographs of matinee idols in the thirties. This, plus his ready smile, made him at thirty-nine attractive to most women.

His especially affable manner with Lydia was understandable. Although her bird books were not exactly high on the Hollard backlist, the Morrow name was much respected. Moreover, Charlotte Butterfield, the Hollard editor who handled Lydia's books had mentioned only recently that Lydia had made a generous donation to the Authors Guild. If there were a quality, in addition to

24

genuine talent, that Richard respected, it was wealth and wealth well used.

'Richard, I uh . . . I was calling about my sister's manuscript, which I submitted recently. You'll recall that I mentioned that there was no need to read it. If you would just send a nice letter to Emily telling her that – '

'Oh, we'll be glad to look it over. It's just that I've been busy the last few weeks. Who knows? Maybe it's better than you think. You may be too close to it to – '

'I'm not close to it at all,' Lydia said firmly, putting distance between herself and the manuscript. 'I hope you understand that, Richard. I've had nothing whatever to do with it. *Nothing*. It's Emily's creation. How she ever thought of such things is beyond me. People in Old Hampton would be shocked. There are things in there that – '

'Well, we'll look it over and send it back to Emily, as you suggested. Give us some time to – '

'Ah, excuse me, Richard. Perhaps it would be better if you sent it to me.' Lydia knew that if the manuscript were returned directly to Emily she would learn that Lydia had removed the offensive chapters.

'Of course, whatever you'd prefer.' With an eye on his watch, he changed the subject to Lydia's own books and gradually concluded their conversation. 'I'll tell Charlotte we were chatting . . .'

Richard hung up the phone and turned to his secretary. 'Pull that manuscript we received from the Morrow sisters. It came in a few weeks ago.' Then raising his voice, he called for Moseley.

Moseley came in just as Helen returned and handed Richard *The Sanctuary* manuscript.

'You called me, Richard?'

'Look this over.' Richard handed him the box containing the manuscript.

Moseley adjusted thick glasses over eyes dulled from thousands of manuscripts. 'What is it?'

'That's what I'd like *you* to tell me,' Richard said.

It took Moseley only three hours to evaluate the manuscript. 'It's not publishable,' he said, 'but it's very unusual. It must have been difficult to do. It's a combination of prose and poetry. There are almost a thousand lines of verse scattered throughout the narrative, every few syllables of which are rhymed. No mean feat. It's a satire of contemporary life in the Hamptons – mostly the Bayrock Club in Old Hampton. The poetry, believe it or not, is patterned after *Beowulf*.'

'Baywulf?'

'*Be-o-wulf,*' Moseley repeated slowly. 'You know, the epic poem written in Old English.'

'I've heard of *Beowulf*,' said Richard caustically.

'Yes, well, I just looked it up myself. I'd forgotten most of it. Anyway, *Beowulf* as you know, personified the things the Anglo-Saxons thought were proper in life. *The Sanctuary* is a spoof – more of a lampoon, I suppose – on the white Anglo-Saxon Protestant establishment at Bayrock. The author calls it the Baywolf Club. The poetry, like *Beowulf*, is alliterative. Here, read these opening lines.'

Richard took the page Moseley handed across the desk and read the first few lines of opening verse:

> Come discover, callow lover,
> Sordid secrets I uncover
> From a dreaded dark and dreary mere.

> Down unending, dark portending,
> Far off forests we'll go wending
> Through uncertain sanctums fraught with fear.

Listen, lovers, brooding brothers,
Heavy hearts and unwed mothers,
Those of you who tried at love and lost.

Here related, unabated,
Lurid lines unexpurgated,
Learn of what illicit love has cost.

'Interesting, sort of,' said Richard, his eyes lingering on the page as he handed it back to Moseley.

'But it's all very abstract, dealing with spirits and apparitions in this forest. Not our kind of book. And there are some really bizarre sexual passages. My God, if Mrs Hollard ever saw it – '

'All right, just leave it,' Richard said, returning to some papers on his desk.

'The author, though, must be pretty strange,' Moseley persisted. 'I would like to have seen Chapter 26. Chapters 6, 14, 26 and 32 are missing.' He handed the manuscript a bit reluctantly across the desk to Richard. 'Yes,' he repeated. 'I certainly would like to have read Chapter 26, just for the hell of it. She has quite an imagination. For example, her female protagonist gets these long-billed birds and inserts their bills into – '

'Would you *please* just leave it there on the desk,' Richard interrupted, not looking up. 'I'm busy.'

Richard was, indeed, busy, as well as testy, though with reason. He was in the process of compiling a list of 'friends' he would contact in the event that a large conglomerate, which was negotiating an acquisition of Hollard House, was successful in its bid. The recent history of the publishing business demonstrated that such acquisitions could make a publisher's position highly vulnerable.

He glanced up as Moseley moved towards the door.

Realizing he had been too abrupt with his editor, he called after him, voice softening, 'How's your mother?'

'Oh, about the same,' Moseley began, turning, brightening. 'She had a – '

'Good, good,' said Richard, quickly returning his attention to his desk. 'Please tell her I said hello.'

It was near closing time when the publisher dictated a hurried letter of rejection to Emily:

Dear Ms Morrow:

It is with regret that I return your novel, *The Sanctuary*. This in no way reflects on the manuscript – indeed, the work shows writing skills and considerable imagination – but I'm afraid it is not quite right for the Hollard House list. We have reduced the number of novels we are bringing out, as have most houses, and are publishing only books of the most compelling interest. Alas, it is not a good time for fiction. I wish I could be more encouraging, and I trust you will find success with another publisher.

> With best wishes, I remain
> Sincerely,
>
> Richard C. Fox
> Publisher

P.S. Please note the absence of Chapters 6, 14, 26 and 32, which were not included in the original submission.

Chapter 4

It was another pleasant day on Forsythia Lane, but inside Number 12 a storm was raging. Emily Morrow had just returned from a trip to Manhattan and had opened her mail. 'How could you, Lydia?' Emily, her dark eyes smouldering, stood outside her sister's bedroom the Hollard House letter held tightly in one hand.

'The whole story revolves around Chapter 26. You never even sent it to him. It says so right here.' She shook Fox's letter, her strong pointed nails sinking into the paper. 'You censored my book. And this nonsense about the Morrow name and reputation. What does the Morrow name have to do with it? *The Sanctuary* is fiction, Lydia. *Fiction*. Besides, it makes no difference. You had no right to remove those chapters. You gave him a story that makes no sense. No wonder he rejected it. Acting as my agent! I should've known better. What if someone cut the heart out of one of your stupid bird books?'

Emily had positioned herself outside her sister's room so that she would not slip away. She knew Lydia wanted to leave, to go to the Sanctuary. Her sister often took refuge in the Sanctuary when they had a spat.

Emily, although remarkably similar in her features to Lydia, was also very different. Almost three years younger, she was stunningly beautiful, with black hair and wide dark eyes that flashed ominously when she was angered. There were times when she awed Old Hampton's gentry by her erratic social behaviour. Although capable of dissembling much of Lydia's sweetness and warmth when it was to her advantage, her independence towards men often put off would-be suitors. Some five feet nine inches, she was strong and athletic, with a biting wit. Most of the charm and graciousness in the Morrow genes had, it seemed, gone to Lydia. Emily had a personality that had led a former beau to remark, 'Emily would make one helluva guerrilla fighter.'

The severe side of her personality was clearly in evidence at the moment. 'I'm calling Mr Fox. Going to see him,' she continued. 'I don't give a damn if you like it or not. And I'm warning you, Lydia, you'd better not interfere.'

Emily waited outside the door, listening for a response. Her sister, stretched out on a chaise on the far side of the room, was silent. 'Go ahead on your stupid walk,' Emily called out, giving the door a sharp kick. 'I hope you fall in the pond.' She would have liked to say quicksand pit instead of pond, but Lydia was unaware of the pit, which was back in the bogs. Indeed, no one was aware of the pit, as far as Emily knew. It was her own private place – somewhere she could be alone to think, to do her research, to dispose of things . . .

Emily strode from the hallway into her bedroom and slammed the door shut. She realized why Lydia hadn't wanted her to send the novel to the other publishers. She wanted to keep it from being published. Lydia had started a novel once. Never finished. Couldn't write anything except bird books and that silly journal. Envy. But Emily had succeeded. Perseverance. She'd worked hard on the bloody thing. Have it end up in the closet? Never. It would be published no matter what Lydia or anyone else thought. She slumped into a chair considering what to do.

Suddenly she stood and walked into a nearby study where the telephone was located. Looking through a rotary file, she found Richard Fox's number. She'd call him, get to know him. Maybe have lunch. Yes, that was it, lunch. At '21'. Men liked '21'. Upstairs in the rear. More privacy there. A few cocktails. His office was on Madison Avenue. They could pass her apartment going back and pick up the missing chapters. Become friends. Men . . . all the same . . .

She dialled the number and waited as it rang. Lydia, damn her. Acting as her agent. Some agent.

'Hello, Mr Fox, please. Miss Morrow calling.'

Delay. He wasn't going to take her call. Well, she'd call until he did. Maybe just go to his office. Unannounced. She wasn't going to be put off by –

'Hello, Lydia.' It was a man's voice, pleasant.

'Hello, Mr Fox. It's not Lydia. It's her sister Emily.'

'Oh, oh, yes.'

'I'm afraid there was some confusion regarding my manuscript, *The Sanctuary*. I'd like to drop by and talk about it.'

Silence. Then, 'Why, yes, of course. Ah, have you . . . that is, have you discussed this with Lydia?'

'I can come tomorrow.'

'Well, yes. I'd be delighted to see you. Perhaps Lydia – '

'I'll be there at noon.'

As she hung up the phone she sensed the early signs of a headache. Tension, she thought. She raised her hand to her forehead. Her hand felt cool and provided a moment of relief. Leaving the study she walked to a bath adjoining her bedroom. Here she took a pill from a bottle in the medicine cabinet and swallowed it with water, then entered her room and lay down on the bed. Soon she was asleep.

It was almost dark when she woke up, feeling the disorientation that often accompanied daytime napping. Had someone called her? Lydia, probably. She glanced towards the door. It was open. On a bureau nearby she noticed Lydia's jacket. Apparently her sister had come in while she was sleeping.

She sat up on the edge of the bed, her earlier feelings of resentment towards her elder sister rekindled. Standing, she walked across the room, slumped into an easy chair and lit a cigarette, inhaling deeply. Oh, oh, a feather. Was it a feather? Yes. On the floor leading to the hall. How could it be? She'd cleaned meticulously. But they floated so. Everywhere. She'd have to be more careful. Her sister found her interest in taxidermy repugnant.

Through the coil of smoke drifting from her cigarette, she focused on a large silver-framed photograph resting on a bureau. It was a picture of a man in his early forties, handsome, with dark eyes and hair and a wide smile, leaning against the fender of a vintage Rolls-Royce convertible. He was wearing a white cardigan sweater with a large collar and white flannel trousers. Under one arm were two tennis racquets. As she looked at the picture there was a subtle change in her expression: a softening of the eyes, a mellowing of the features, a trace of unaccustomed gentleness.

Emily looked at the photograph infrequently, but when she did it invariably produced the same reaction. This was Louis Morrow, her father, and probably the only person who had ever evoked such tender feelings in her. Having lost his wife in an auto accident shortly after Emily's birth, her father had tried to make up for the mother's loss by concentrating on his younger daughter. With Lydia away at boarding school, Emily had come to depend heavily on her father during the early years and a kinship had developed that transcended and submerged the usual father-daughter relationship. From her schoolwork, where teachers marvelled at her academic brilliance, to the tennis court, Emily reflected the talent and tutelage of Louis Morrow.

Sounds of the ocean floated through a nearby window, breaking her reminiscence, a surf washing relentlessly against the shore; long, rolling rushes of water that rose to a crescendo, followed by intervals of silence. Emily stood up and walked to the rear window, which looked out towards the sea. A large yellow moon had surfaced in the ocean sky far out beyond the dunes. It reminded her of the yellow-striped balloon in which her father had taken her for a ride when she was a child. Was he perhaps out there now with the sailing moon, communicating through the sound of the waves? The thought was not uncommon . . . she often sensed his presence through the aural qualities in nature – especially, it seemed, in the Sanctuary at night.

She stood there leaning against the windowsill, transfixed by the bright yellow sphere as the repetitive swishing of the waves carried her back to that day many years before. The day that had led one prominent psychiatrist to comment that Emily Morrow would probably never be quite like any other little girl again.

A great wave erupted offshore in a shower of white spray sending green water flooding on to the beach, engulfing the sand castle that Emily and her father had been building. Reaching its peak, the invading force held for a moment and then retreated, carrying with it much of what had once been a magnificent castle.

Emily was dismayed. 'Oh, Daddy,' she wailed, looking wistfully at the remains. She sat down, legs outstretched, supporting her small body on her arms. 'It's *ruined*.'

Her father sat down beside her and gathered her on his lap. 'Come now, darling.' He brushed sand from the front of her bathing suit. 'I told you it would happen. You can't build things with sand and expect them to last. We'll build another one next Saturday. We'll make it even bigger than – '

'But, Daddy, that's my birthday. We're going for our balloon ride, remember?'

A few weeks before, they had gone to a fair in Amagansett and ridden in a large yellow-striped balloon. The balloon, though, had been tethered to the ground, providing only a brief rise above the fair. But it had been so thrilling for Emily that her father had hired the balloon owner to take them across the Old Hampton countryside on her upcoming birthday.

'Oh, that's right,' her father said. 'I keep forgetting.'

'Daddy, why is it you always forget important things like balloon rides?'

'It just slipped my mind, honey.'

Emily dusted the sand off her hands and turned so she was looking into his eyes. They were brown with large black pupils. Soft, loving eyes.

'I can't wait till Saturday,' she said, the trauma of the demolished castle gone with the tide. 'Will we sail over the Sanctuary?'

'The whole length of it.'

'Just think, Daddy. I'm going to be nine years old. I wonder what it will be like to be nine? Are you going to get me a birthday present?'

'Birthday present?' He pretended surprise. 'What do you think the balloon ride is?'

'But that doesn't count.' Her eyes clouded. 'You would've done that anyway.'

'Of course I'm getting you a present,' he said quickly, unwilling to endure even her momentary disappointment. 'But don't ask what it is.'

'Oh, come on, Daddy. I hope it's a puppy. Sadie said she wouldn't mind.'

'We'll see.'

'I know it's a puppy. Tell me it's a puppy, please.'

'Don't ask me anything else. It's a surprise.'

'Oh, it *is* a puppy. I can tell.' She threw her arms about his neck and hugged him tightly. 'I love you so much, Daddy.'

His arms came about her and he drew her close. She liked the feeling of the soft hair on his chest when he hugged her. But it was moments such as this that sometimes gave her a funny, unsettling feeling; a vague premonition that her young mind could not comprehend. She knew her father was ill. He had lost weight. And earlier in the summer he had had something taken from his leg. And her father's sister Aunt Kate had come to stay for a while. Emily had overheard her talking on the phone to a relative. Her father had something called cars aroma.

Emily had stunned them later when she mentioned it at dinner. She always surprised grown-ups with words she knew. Hadn't her third-grade teacher said that she had the vocabulary of a sixth grader? It hadn't taken her long to figure out cars aroma. Sadie had told her that aroma meant something like smell, and, of course, everyone knew what a car was. So it followed, naturally, that it was the smell of the Rolls that made her father sick.

When she mentioned it at dinner, after his initial surprise, her father had smiled. 'Sure, that's why we keep the top down on the Rolls, right, Kate?'

Aunt Kate hadn't thought it funny. In fact, Emily hadn't seen her laugh the whole time she was there. She was nice, but Emily was kind of glad when Aunt Kate finally went home.

But now, cuddled on his lap, his thin arms about her, she *sensed* his illness and it worried her. Her classmate Gretchen's father had been killed the previous year in an aeroplane crash. But Gretchen had a mother . . . What if

35

something happened to her father? There was no one.
Would she have to go to live with Aunt Kate?

'Shall we make up a poem?' her father asked.

'Oh, yes,' Emily said. 'Let's finish the one we started in
the Sanctuary.'

When shadows creep across the . . .

She hesitated, looking at her father with a puzzled
expression. 'I kind of forget it now.'

'Let's do it together,' he said.

She joined him as he recited the verse:

When shadows creep across the kill
And darkness dulls the daffodil,
The saturn scene is soft and still
As whispered wind, on Hampton Hill.

'There, now you know it,' he said. 'We overdid the
alliteration some but – '

'Alliteration?'

'Yes, don't you remember how we talked about conso-
nance and assonance? Alliteration is repeating the first
consonant of syllables or words. Like when we read
Beowulf. Anglo-Saxon poetry didn't have rhyme, but they
repeated consonantal sounds the way we did in our verse.'

'I don't know, Daddy.' Emily looked at him dubiously.
'I'm getting mixed up again.'

'Well, look at the first line. When sha-dows creep a-
cross the kill. See, we've repeated the consonants in *creep*
a-*cross* the *kill*. We may have used a little too much here.
On the other hand, a really good example of assonance is
the opening line of *Kubla Khan*, we read it a few weeks
ago, remember? "In Xanadu did Kubla Khan . . ." I'm
going to have to find some poems for you by Emily
Dickinson and Charles Swinburne, they did wonderful

36

things with the sounds of words. You have a talent we need to develop. Someday you'll be a poet.'

He punctuated his praise with a kiss on her forehead. Then, looking at his watch, he said, 'It's getting late.' He lifted her off his lap and stood up. 'I told Sadie we'd be home an hour ago.'

They gathered up their beach equipment and walked over the dunes to the club parking lot beyond the terrace. Parked near the entrance was a sleek vintage Rolls-Royce convertible with a grey body and chrome fixtures that glistened in the afternoon sun. Two large headlamps mounted on long black fenders stared at them owlishly as they approached.

'Careful getting in,' her father said after stowing the beach regalia and occupying the seat behind a large spoked steering wheel. 'These seats get hot in the sun.'

'Don't worry, Daddy.' She climbed in and assumed her usual position, standing beside him, hands grasping the top of the windshield. 'I never sit down in the Rolls.'

They left the parking area and proceeded past the clubhouse down the long winding drive to Forsythia Lane. Emily was looking forward to going home. Sadie most likely had baked some chocolate chip cookies, or maybe brownies with walnuts, or a blueberry pie with brown sugar crumbs on top. She glanced at her father behind the wheel. He seemed to be deep in his thoughts. Fathers were like that. She guessed he was thinking about business.

Tonight they were going to see a repeat of *The Wizard* at the local theatre. Then they'd go to Farrow's Ice Cream Parlour for an ice cream cone. She thought of the coming balloon ride, the puppy . . . The breeze felt good blowing through her hair. 'Shall we sing, Daddy?'

'All right, you start.'

She began singing, her squeaky voice straining to be

heard over the wind and the motor. It was a song her father had composed for Lydia and her:

Oh, we're a happy three
And we, are we . . .

Sadie was sitting in the shade on the terrace when they arrived at 12 Forsythia Lane.

'Hi, Sadie,' Emily called over the top of the windshield. 'Any calls?' This was always the first thing her father asked when he got back home.

'Dr Pattison called while you was gone, said for you to call his office soon's you got in.'

Her father eased the car past the tall trim hedgerows that lined the drive, bringing it to a stop in front of the large well-groomed dwelling. Quickly, he left the car and entered the house.

Emily followed Sadie to the kitchen and emerged a moment later with an egg salad sandwich. Tucked under one arm was her stuffed teddy bear, Pushkin. Choosing a grassy spot in the shade of an elm tree, she sat down and ate the sandwich. When she finished she wiped her mouth on a paper napkin and did the same for Pushkin, then stood up and began dancing. She imagined herself a ballerina – one of her favourite fantasies. She was in a great hall under glittering chandeliers, dancing in front of a big audience. A changement royale, a grand jeté, and then a pirouette. Round and round she turned until she became dizzy and toppled on the grass like an expiring top. Then, standing, she picked up Pushkin and went into the house to look for her father.

As she approached his study she heard him on the telephone talking in low tones. She sat on the floor outside the door, playing with the teddy bear, waiting for him to finish.

'I understand . . . yes, well actually . . . well, I was rather expecting it . . . I understand . . . all right, I'll see you Monday, Doctor.'

Hearing him hang up the phone, Emily stood and entered the study. Her father was sitting in a black leather chair behind a large desk, staring through a window.

'Was that Dr Pattison?' she asked, walking towards him.

There was no answer. Reaching his chair, she tried unsuccessfully to balance Pushkin on his knee. She took one of his hands and put it on the teddy bear to steady it, then crawled up on to his lap. 'What's the matter, Daddy? You don't seem happy.'

'Nothing, honey.' He bounced her idly on his knee, continuing to gaze through the window.

She made some attempts at conversation but after a few minutes she tired of his preoccupation and went in search of Sadie.

It was late in the afternoon and she and Sadie were playing checkers in the kitchen when she heard her father leaving the house. She ran to the window and crawled up on the counter so she could see out.

'Where you going, Daddy?' she called.

'Just for a walk.'

'Wait. I'll come.'

'*No*. No, you stay there with Sadie.'

She watched from the window, disappointed, as her father crossed the road and disappeared into the Sanctuary. For a moment she considered following him. But he had sounded firm. She went back to Sadie and the checkers.

Later, after a nap in the playroom, Emily went into the kitchen and found Sadie fretting. 'Your daddy's still not home. I'm gettin' worried about him.'

'But we're supposed to go to the movies,' Emily said,

rubbing the sleep from her eyes, then walking to the window and crawling up on the counter to look across at the Sanctuary. 'He's probably back by the pond. He likes to sit there and watch the ducks. I'll go get him.'

'You'll do nothin' of the sort. Your father don't want you walkin' in there 'lone.'

'But I'm sure that's where he is. I saw him go. Come on, Sadie, we'll be late for the movie.' She jumped from the counter, picked up the remains of a brownie, and headed towards the door, scooping up Pushkin from his place on top of a highchair in the corner.

'Here, you wait for me,' Sadie shouted. 'Leave that teddy bear. You're goin' leave him in them woods for sure, then I gotta go get – '

Ignoring her, Emily skipped out the door.

The sun was well below the treeline as they crossed the road. Inside the Sanctuary grey shadows settled over the plant life, muting all colour. Wildflowers that had shone brilliantly in the sunlight were now indistinguishable from other plants.

Moving down the path, Sadie called after her, 'Not so fast, child. You're gonna to fall, sure as can be. Hear me?' But Emily, a bloodhound on the scent, paid little attention.

There was a closeness, a heaviness, in the air as they proceeded deep into the woods. Dusk in the Sanctuary was particularly gloomy. A time when birds and other daytime wildlife had come to rest, and night creatures had yet to start their prowl. A sombre interlude when all was colourless and lifeless in the enveloping mist. The only sounds that broke the stillness were those of a little girl's feet skipping along the crooked path.

Emily was well in front of Sadie when she rounded a turn and came to the pond, a pool of still, black water that stretched off into the forest. She felt a rush of satisfaction when, just as expected, there was her father sitting on a bench, his head resting against a large elm.

'Here you are, Daddy,' she said. 'We were getting worried about you.'

But he hadn't heard. She walked up to him. No wonder. He was asleep. But his eyes . . . open. Soft and dark, staring up at her through the twilight. 'Daddy, are you all right?' What? A *gun*. And then, oh. The back of his head . . . *Oh*.

Later, Sadie was to relate the scene: 'She wasn't doin' nothin' when I come up. Just standin' there. Those black eyes of hers starin' down at him. No cryin' . . . *nothin'*. Just starin' . . . chewin' on that teddy bear's ear.'

Chapter 5

'What do you mean he's in Europe? He passed me in his car this morning . . . All right, all right, I understand. Just tell him his friend Richard Fox called.'

Richard slammed the phone down just as his secretary slipped a note in front of him: 'EMILY MORROW HERE TO SEE YOU.'

Richard glanced up. 'You told her I was here? My God, it's lunch time. Moseley! Come *in* here.'

Richard Fox considered himself a decent enough person. Indeed, he was fond of most of his staff. But in business matters he demanded much of himself and made similar demands on those around him – a style different from his social manner, which was considerate and urbane. During office hours, however, amenities were rare, and a 'How're you doing?' from Richard could induce acute anxiety in an employee.

But if Richard's professional incivility were legendary, so was his talent for marketing books, and Hollard House had benefited handsomely during his tenure as publisher. So much so that right now the firm was the target of British American, a conglomerate eager to add a publishing firm to its empire.

For Richard, who had operated with full rein under the Hollard family, the impending change was a source of anxiety not shared by others. Where rumours of a take-over would send shudders through many houses, not so at Hollard. The whisperings in the hallways on the tenth, eleventh and twelfth floors occupied by the firm on

Madison Avenue were at least understandably ambivalent.

But the mood of his staff was not of concern to Richard. He was busy trying to resurrect old acquaintances in the industry, and he was finding his 'friends' slow to return his calls. He had been on the phone with the secretary of one of them when Emily Morrow was announced.

'Moseley,' Richard repeated. 'Where is that – '

Moseley Parrish appeared suddenly in front of his boss' desk. 'Yes, Richard?'

'One of the Morrow sisters just came in. Helen told her I was here. Please explain to Helen that she should never tell an author I'm here at lunch time. Now, give me five minutes with her, and then come in and say we're going to be late for lunch.'

'You're going to lunch with *me*?' Moseley's eyes widened behind his thick lenses, as he glanced at the secretary apprehensively.

'Of course I'm not going to lunch with you,' Richard said. 'I have to get rid of the Morrow sister. I may act as if I want to spend some time with her but don't leave no matter what I say.' He turned to his secretary. 'All right, bring her in.'

Moseley departed and Helen was on her way to collect the visitor when the phone rang on her desk. She stopped to answer it and then called Richard. 'Mr Fox, Miss Fielding on line three.'

Worry lines wrinkled Richard's brow. He reached for the phone, hesitated, reached again and then paused, his hand resting on the receiver. Should he have Helen tell her that he'd stepped out? No, she might know he was there. She had an uncanny ability to know where he was.

He picked up the phone. 'Hello, Sheila. I was just thinking about you. How are you this morning?'

'I'm fine, Richard. Just sitting here . . . like always. I

get so bored . . . just sitting here.' Although the voice was that of a woman, there was a childish petulance to it.

Richard rolled his eyes but his voice gave no hint of his exasperation. 'Why don't you pull a few manuscripts off the slush pile and skim them? You could be a big help to – '

'They're so boring. Are we going to lunch?'

'Not today, Sheila. I'm sorry, I was about to call you to tell – '

'But Saturday you said – '

'I know, I know, but something came up. This publisher from Munich . . . here unexpectedly. I have to meet him for lunch.' Richard ran his fingers through his hair and glanced nervously towards Helen in the other office. 'In fact, he's waiting on the other line right now. I'll explain everything tomorrow night, okay?'

Richard replaced the receiver and leaned back in his chair, tapping his fingers against the arm. The calls were increasing from the tenth floor. He would have to do something about Sheila. But now wasn't the time – not with Hollard House under scrutiny by a potential buyer. Everything in the publishing business was going public these days. Sheila would have little difficulty joining the trend.

His thoughts were interrupted by Helen asking if he were ready to see Miss Morrow.

'Yes, yes, bring her in.'

But Richard was distinctly not ready for what entered his office moments later. Emily had prepared carefully, and the result turned every head in the outer office towards Richard's door. She was wearing a light-grey summer suit tailored at the waist and hips, with a scarf as jet black as her hair tied at her neck, the ends cascading down and over her breasts.

When the wide dark eyes and beautiful teeth smiled

44

across his desk, it was a phantom of sensuality that tingled down through Richard's frame to his neglected prostate. 'Miss Morrow . . . what a *great* pleasure,' barely conveyed his feelings.

'How-do-you-do, Mr Fox?' said Emily, extending her hand. 'Lydia has told me so much about you.' The tone suggested that it had all been splendid.

Richard rose quickly, hands darting from hair to tie to jacket. 'Well, well, what a pleasure,' he repeated, brain temporarily stunned as he guided Emily towards a chair-couch ensemble by the windows in the corner. En route he noted strong athletic calves emerging from black high-heeled shoes that carried his guest nearly two inches above him.

'We're fortunate to have an aspiring novelist express interest in Hollard House.' His composure regained, gracious comments flowed. So much so that five minutes passed and Richard was barely beyond expressing his delight that Emily had come, when Moseley entered.

'Excuse me, Richard. We're going to be late for lunch.'

'Thank you, Moseley. I'm going to be delayed a bit. You go ahead.'

The withering gaze that Richard communicated might have stopped things right there, had not Moseley been inured to them. Instead he wandered over and stationed himself above Richard's shoulder, wondering why anyone would want to disengage from Emily. 'It's a pretty important lunch,' he added firmly.

Richard, juggling graciousness with Emily and irritation with Moseley, stood quickly, excused himself and marched his assistant towards the door. 'Are you *non compos mentis*?' he hissed into Moseley's ear. 'Get out of here.'

A bemused Moseley promptly complied.

'Now, this novel of yours . . .' Richard said, returning

to the corner. 'Actually, there's talent there. Have you thought about collaborating on a bird book with Lydia? Charlotte was saying only recently that . . .' – though his visitor's expression remained serene, her black eyes took on a hard look – 'that is, of course, if you decide not to pursue your novel.'

'I'm committed to the novel,' Emily said firmly. 'I hope you'll read the *whole* manuscript. I'm sure it made little sense without all the chapters.'

'Certainly, of course. That's our business, reading manuscripts.' Then, with a wag of his head, a gesture he reserved for his more gallant moments, he violated his most basic rule. 'Perhaps we could talk about it at lunch. Do you have any plans? There's a nice spot across the – '

'How about "21"?' Emily said. 'I like their upstairs in the back. It's not as crowded.'

'Excellent,' Richard said, standing. 'Shall we go?'

They were standing in the hallway waiting for the elevator when Moseley reappeared, decidedly gun-shy. After a hurried consultation with Helen he had decided better to be safe than sorry. 'Excuse me, Richard,' – he adjusted his glasses nervously – 'you sure we're not going to lunch?'

This time the look was sufficient. Moseley moved back inside.

'Wasn't that sweet?' said Emily. 'I think he's disappointed you're not going to lunch with him. You apparently have a good rapport with your people.'

He shrugged modestly and ushered her into the elevator. As they started down he saw the light come on indicating a stop at the tenth floor. Just his luck to have *her* there waiting when the door opened. It had happened before. She had been standing directly in front of the elevators talking to the receptionist. He shrank towards a corner of the car . . . Now, the elevator coming to a stop, he held his breath as the door opened. No one was there except the receptionist working at her desk off to the right. The door stayed open interminably, at last started to close. Suddenly from down the hall came the rapid clicking of high-heeled shoes.

Emily, who was next to the operating panel, reached for the button to hold the elevator. Richard quickly reached past her and pushed the CLOSE DOOR button. The door slid firmly shut as the approaching heels reached the entrance.

'You pushed the wrong one,' said Emily.

'Oh, too bad,' Richard said. 'It's okay, there'll be another one right along.'

True, the odds were against its having been Sheila – it would take a fire to make her move that fast to catch an elevator – but why take chances? The way his luck was going he might have found himself standing between the two of them trying to figure out how to pass off Emily as the publisher from Munich.

But it was not over. Although Lady Luck had not joined him on the elevator, she was waiting downstairs. There were the breasts, the tight skirt, the spiked heels, the green eyes peering from under the honey-blond hair . . .

To fill the vacuum caused by her aborted lunch date, Sheila had gone to the small stand in the lobby to pick up a sandwich. She saw Richard at the same time that he spotted her.

Caught with his hand on Emily's elbow as he ushered her from the elevator, Richard didn't know what to do, and so did nothing. He chose to ignore Sheila.

The eyes that followed him from the elevator, down the corridor and out the door to the street, narrowed, from boredom to green fire.

Chapter 6

A lioness, they say, is a pertinacious hunter. She approaches a herd of animals stealthily, selects a victim and pursues that animal relentlessly, disregarding other prey. Such was Emily Morrow. Once the dark eyes focused on a target, little deterred her. The target now was Richard Fox.

Few approached their affairs with more precision than Emily. Louis Morrow had been a punctilious engineer and his penchant for detail had been passed on to his daughter. In this instance, a tactical part of her plan was to take Richard to the 21 Club. His efforts to divert her elsewhere – Sheila might hear about the lunch through the grapevine if he went to '21' – had been skilfully averted.

Richard was quiet as their cab stopped in front of the black wrought-iron entrance to the club, his thoughts flitting from Emily to Sheila. Sheila was like a defective grenade which, having its pin pulled, remained dormant for a period, only to explode unexpectedly. She was capable of brooding over the event in the lobby, and then trying to arrange an appointment with Mrs Hollard to discuss her career plans . . .

'21' is, of course, the popular establishment frequented by the rich and famous and those who aspire to such status. The atmosphere is genteel – particularly in the upstairs dining room, where it would be gauche to stare at celebrities or take undue notice of one's surroundings. Yet when Emily and Richard filed into the dining room behind Jacob, the maître d', although no one appeared to notice, there was scarcely an eye in the room that did not follow them to their table in the rear. Even to a place as accustomed to beautiful women as '21', Emily's entrance was noteworthy. Richard sensed the attention. For one who had been coming to the club for years with little recognition, it was invigorating.

'I trust this is satisfactory. Your waiter will be here shortly.' With a silent bow, the maitre d' departed.

Lunch at '21' could be expensive, and though he had an expense account, Richard still winced at the cost. His usual misgivings quickly melted, however, as his knee inadvertently came in contact with Emily's leg.

'Would madam care for a drink?' asked Julius, a waiter with whom Richard was acquainted.

'Do I dare have a martini?' asked Emily, smiling demurely.

'Why not?' Richard shifted his buttocks, settling himself into his chair. It was a rapid rocking motion he often made when anticipating something pleasant. 'It's sort of a special occasion, right?'

'Are you joining me?' she asked.

'What?'

'A martini?' she said. 'Is that what you're having?'

Richard prided himself on his physical condition, a fact he attributed in some degree to his spartan lunches. Besides, alcohol affected him, loosened his tongue and affected his judgement, not a good idea at lunch.

'Ginger ale,' he said to Julius.

Emily looked at him, eyes wide. Her plan was in jeopardy. 'Well, I'm certainly not having a martini if you're drinking soda pop,' she said, a bit of the real Emily slipping from its cage.

Her bluntness, in marked contrast with the sweet and demure manner she had shown to this point, momentarily startled Richard. 'Make that two martinis, Julius.'

When the waiter left, Richard focused on Emily, screwing his buttocks into the seat. They were seated side by side at one of the lounge tables, as Emily had planned. When he turned towards her she also turned, facing him. They were very close. He was aware of a light perfume. What features, he thought. Even her ears seemed perfectly formed, with tiny pearls piercing the lobes. Suddenly, he was fantasizing, nuzzling close, nibbling the pearls and soft lobes – only the beginning of the imagined feast as his eyes moved down her lovely neck . . .

'What was that? Oh, no, actually I love martinis. Incidentally, why don't you call me Richard. Mr Fox makes me sound like your father.' He forced a laugh, sorry he had even made the father reference. He wondered about her age. Twenty-six, maybe twenty-seven. What a contrast to her sister, except for the similar features. And mature, polished. 'Martinis are my favourite. It's just that I may play some tennis later on.'

'I might've known you were a tennis player.' Emily's gaze moved admiringly over his body. 'You look like a tennis player. I like to play myself.'

'Really? Where do you play?'

'On the island. Mostly the Bayrock Club in Old Hampton.'

'Oh, sure, Bayrock,' said Richard. 'Beautiful place. Grass courts.'

'That's right. Have you played there?'

Was she kidding? She probably surmised he was Jewish. If Bayrock had its way they wouldn't let Jews drive past the place, let alone play tennis. 'No, I've never played there.'

'Perhaps we could play sometime. Lydia said you have a place in Southampton. That's not far from Bayrock.' She shifted slightly and her hip came against him.

'I'd like to. Or maybe sometime we could play here in town. Come to the city much?'

'Yes. Quite often. We have an apartment at 901 Fifth. My father's old *pied-à-terre*.' Again her hip brushed against his.

'That's just crosstown from our office.'

'That's right. Lydia met her editor there once – Charlotte, is it? – to work on a manuscript.'

'Yes, Charlotte.' Richard managed a rapid shift of his buttocks and reached for his water glass. Lord . . . his hand was shaking.

The next fifteen minutes saw Richard Fox make the transition to lunchtime drinker. Not only did he consume the first martini but, inspired by Emily, was into a second when the waiter appeared with a note.

'For you, madam, from the gentleman in the corner.'

Richard followed the waiter's line of direction to a table at the far end where a youngish sandy-haired man waved.

'It's Steve,' Emily said. She opened the note, glanced at it, smiled and nodded at the man. 'A friend,' she told Richard lightly.

Richard fingered his napkin uneasily; it was, against house rules at '21' to send notes. He was relieved when the man stood up, waved to Emily and left.

'Steve Sawyer.' Emily closed out the encounter with a final wave towards the departing figure. Taking note of Richard's pique, she quickly folded the paper and slipped it into her handbag. 'He's a tennis player too, plays at Bayrock.' Then she focused on Richard with a brilliant smile, making clear *he* was the most important man in her life at the moment.

After lunch and most of a bottle of wine, Emily brought up *The Sanctuary*. She had mentioned it casually earlier but Richard had avoided the subject. He had not read the manuscript, something Emily would quickly discover if she pressed the matter. And judging from Moseley's report, it had no chance of being published, at least not at Hollard House. Ultimately, he would have to tell her, but realizing that the only way he was going to establish any relationship with her was through her manuscript and wanted to delay the rejection for as long as possible.

'I know, of course, that it needs work,' Emily said with becoming, if dubious, modesty. 'I need some direction.' Her eyes turned on him, dark and intense. 'I guess what I need most is a truly good editor . . .'

He realized the ball was in his court, but it had been a drop shot – something he had never handled well on – or off-court. And the martinis and wine were having their effect. Still, there was nothing more sobering to him than the prospect of working on an unpublishable manuscript.

'Well, first . . . first we have to read your manuscript carefully to see if it's . . . well, reasonably publishable.' He had at least returned the ball, kept the point going.

'But didn't you say that you'd already read it?' she asked softly, hesitantly. 'That there was potehtial?' She was controlling the game. 'Your letter mentioned something about . . . I forget now . . . writing skills?'

'Yes, I think I did say that and I meant every word. There's potential there . . .' He had to change the game, needed time to relieve the pressure. 'What I meant was that we need to take a close look at those missing chapters . . .' A lob – short, weak. 'You know, the chapters we never received. Then we'll – '

Emily, anticipating this response, cut him off and moved in for the kill. 'I'm afraid I forgot to bring the chapters with me,' she said, shaking her head and smiling winsomely. Richard could almost feel her warm breath against his face as she put away the winning shot. 'Perhaps on the way back to your office we could stop and pick them up at my apartment?' Her dark eyes danced intimately.

Chapter 7

'Ask Ray Bullock, he'll tell you. He tried to make out with her and she almost turned him into a eunuch.'

Having returned to his office following lunch with Emily, Richard was on the phone listening to an assessment of her by a friend.

'Forget her, Richard. A lot of the big boys have been there ahead of you and they *all* got burned. She's beautiful all right, but she's more than meets the eye. You say you had lunch with her? I'd be careful. She must want something.'

'She was in town and they asked me to have lunch with her.' Richard replied quickly. 'We've done a few books with her sister . . . So what do you hear about British American?' he asked, changing the subject.

'I hear what everyone else hears. They're in the process of buying you out. Good luck. They'll suck all the cash out of Hollard, hit you with parent company overhead, present you with a P and L each month that shows you're going bankrupt and then can you.'

It was an appraisal Richard was too familiar with. Fortunately another 'friend' was returning his call on an incoming line, and he wound up the conversation quickly, pushing the button for the incoming call. After some trade talk he asked casually, 'Allan, do you still have your place in Old Hampton?'

'Sure do. It keeps appreciating so much I can't afford to sell it.'

'Right. Do you by chance know Emily and Lydia Morrow?'

'The Hampton sisters? Sure. Who doesn't out there? They live near the club on Forsythia Lane. Why?'

'We've published a few of Lydia's books. But what's her sister like? Emily?'

'Emily Morrow? Now there's a woman. Beautiful. Have you met her?'

'Yes, through Lydia. I hear she's kind of unusual.'

'Independent, for sure. She has the old guard out there up in arms most of the time. She doesn't conform. Men go for her, women don't, for obvious reasons. She's a hell of a tennis player.'

'I've heard she's a bit eccentric?'

'Eccentric? Well . . . I don't really know them that well. I believe Lydia's something of a recluse. People out there think they're odd because they don't cut their hedges. They're all growing out of control. I understand they inherited a ton of dough from their old man. But Emily is something. Smart as hell. She plays quite a lot of tennis with one guy. A doctor. Steve something. I'm not sure what their relationship is. Hey, you thinking of asking her out?'

'No, no. As I said, we publish her sister Lydia. Emily was in town and they asked me to take her to lunch. I just wanted to get a line on her . . . By the way, could you use an editorial assistant over there? I'm trying to help a young lady get relocated. Sheila Fielding. Very talented. Actually, she's over-qualified for the job here. It's sort of boring for her. And with the rumours about our being bought out . . . She's getting a bit nervous.'

'Have her call George Barry in the trade division. He may have an opening.'

Following the call, Richard sat assessing what he had heard. He had difficulty reconciling the Emily he'd just met with the independent nonconformist described by his friends. At lunch she had been warm, gracious and accommodating. Indeed, they were the same traits he associated with her sister Lydia, except Lydia was not vivacious, dynamic, stimulating . . .

Of course, he reminded himself, much of her interest in him probably had to do with her novel. Whatever, Emily Morrow was someone he wanted to know better. He was a little shorter than she, but some women preferred shorter men. Gave them a sense of power. Look at that little queer Arnold Seigler. He was often with beautiful women – and Arnold no more than eye level with their pussies.

Enough of that. His immediate problem was *The Sanctuary* manuscript. After lunch at '21' he and Emily had gone to the Morrows' Fifth Avenue apartment, which turned out to be considerably more than the *pied-à-terre* she had mentioned. The late Louis Morrow had done much of his business in Manhattan, and had left a well-staffed penthouse atop one of New York's most prestigious cooperatives.

They had been served tea on the terrace overlooking Central Park, Emily crossing and uncrossing her long shapely legs while asking him about publishing. She had given him the complete manuscript of *The Sanctuary* and allowed as how she would really enjoy working with a publisher who was also an editor with a track record . . .

As he was leaving he had noted among some memorabilia a spectacular photograph of Emily sailing in a bikini. Less stimulating had been another photograph of a young man in tennis clothes. Richard wasn't sure but thought it might be the person who had sent the note at '21'.

The interlude at the penthouse had been almost as stimulating as their lunch, and Richard was pleased when she suggested that she call him to arrange a meeting at her apartment the next week to discuss *The Sanctuary*.

Now at his desk, the martinis and wine wearing thin,

looking down at the manuscript, he was having misgivings. Maybe he'd talked too much about the importance of a good editor, how much he enjoyed personally working on manuscripts . . .

'Moseley, come in here please.'

Moseley, in the process of transporting several unsolicited manuscripts from the mailroom slush pile to his desk via a hand truck, stopped abruptly. In a moment he stood before his boss.

'Why don't you sit down, Moseley?' Richard's voice was unusually solicitous as he motioned Moseley towards a chair. 'Helen, bring Moseley and me some coffee.'

Moseley hesitated. A chair? Coffee?

'Go ahead,' Richard said. 'Sit down. I thought we might take a minute to talk about this *Sanctuary* manuscript. We have all the chapters now and I'm sure it will make a good deal more sense now that it's intact.' He avoided Moseley's eyes as he spoke.

'I don't think anyone could make any sense out of it with or without the missing chapters,' Moseley said, settling into a chair, glad for his boss' apparent willingness to listen to his opinion. 'I thought we decided to reject – '

'Why don't we let me decide what's to be rejected,' Richard said with a wry smile.

'Well, it's so convoluted . . .' Moseley said. 'You'd have to be a cryptographer to know what the author had in mind.'

'Tell me about it.' Richard slumped in his chair. 'You say it's a satire about the Bayrock Club? What's the storyline?'

'Well, that's part of the problem. There really is no story. The protagonist is a woman who writes a bird book, okay? So what is the bird book about? It's about a woman who writes a bird book, about a woman who writes a bird book . . . And on and on like that. Add in several hundred lines of poetry, some of which is altogether abstract, and . . . well, you don't exactly have a page-turner.'

Richard picked up a paperclip and began twisting it. 'There must be more to it than that. There are over five hundred pages here – '

'Oh, sure, there's more. But it's . . . it's outrageous.' Moseley hunched forward in his chair, placing his elbows on Richard's desk. 'There's this Sanctuary, a lugubrious sort of place filled with all kinds of spectral images. It's supposed to be a refuge for wildlife, but actually it's just the opposite. Everything is killing everything else, which for all I know is how it is in sanctuaries. But the way it's done it's almost apocalyptic. She tried to show through these indelicate analogies how the people in the Hamptons prey on each other the way wildlife does in the Sanctuary. As I said, it's a sort of satire on summer life in the Hamptons, and the Bayrock Club in particular.'

'What's wrong with that?'

'What's wrong is – ' Moseley paused as Helen brought in two containers of coffee. When she left he lowered his voice. 'I guess it's supposed to show the commercial exploitations of the Hamptons. She has her protagonist, who's something of a taxidermist, take these long-billed birds from the Sanctuary and set up a business selling them as female vibrators. You know, dildos . . . erotic devices where the birds flap their wings. *That* sort of thing. I'm not kidding. Anyway, the business is a big success and the protagonist uses the money to buy this small publishing company that she relocates in the Hamptons and starts publishing porno books. Well, one of the books is this bird book I told you about.'

'Bird book?' Richard said between sips of his coffee. 'What bird book?'

'I told you, it's a bird book about a bird book about a

bird book. And throughout the thing ... I mean, throughout the book within the book, *if* you follow me, is all this poetry – a poem entitled *The Balloon* that describes psychedelic drug trips while sailing through the Sanctuary in a balloon. No wonder the author warns the reader – '

'Warns?'

'At the beginning. Here, look at the first page.' Moseley reached for the manuscript on Richard's desk. 'Listen to this.' He began reading from the opening verse:

> If acceding to this reading,
> Be forewarned before proceeding,
> Fiction oft offends the faint of heart.

'Believe me, that's no overstatement,' said Moseley, '*and* you know there's no fainter of heart than Mrs H. It makes you wonder about the author, though. And what about her sister? The protagonist seems to resemble Lydia Morrow, what little I know of her. For example there's this scene ... you won't believe this ... where the protagonist takes a pelican ... you know, the bird with the enormous beak ... well, she takes it and puts it ...'

'Never *mind*.' Richard slumped further into his chair, hands over his eyes. He sat quietly for a moment, and then said, 'It does sound strong, but you're taking things out of context, and besides, delicate and sensitive women have often written this sort of Gothic material. It's allegory, you said so yourself. Anyway, see if you can fix it up, tighten it a bit and – '

'Tighten it? Richard, how do you *tighten* a thousand lines of verse? It isn't that kind of book. This thing is weird.'

'Moseley,' Richard broke in, his voice rising. 'Would you like to be publisher of this house?' The martinis and wine had worn off; his nerves now raw.

Moseley backed off. He had no aspirations whatever to be publisher. Moreover it was moments such as these when his senior editor's job was not all that attractive either. 'I'm sorry, Richard, I only meant that I don't think it's our kind of book, it's not even publishable in its – '

'I'll decide that. Now, as I said, please take this manuscript and *fix it up*. Talk to Grace Miller. She's a poetry expert. We'll discuss it further at our editorial meeting.' Having finished his coffee, he took Moseley's and poured it into his own cup.

Moseley, sensing the coffee break at an end, picked up the manuscript and slipped away. At the doorway he hesitated, and was about to speak when Helen's voice came over the intercom.

'Mr Fox, Miss Fielding on line two.'

Moseley waited, but only for a moment. His boss' expression told him not to linger.

His editor gone, Richard picked up the phone. 'Hello Sheila, I was just about to call you.' His voice was hushed, as though speaking in a confessional. 'No, of course I didn't see you in the lobby . . . Woman? What woman? . . . Oh, *that* woman . . .'

It took nearly fifteen minutes for Richard to solve his credibility problem on the tenth floor: no, the attractive lady he had been escorting through the lobby was not the publisher from Munich (even Sheila wouldn't have swallowed that), it was . . . Mrs Hollard's niece, who had just arrived unexpectedly from California . . . Mrs Hollard had asked him to show her around New York, or actually St Patrick's Cathedral – she was a devout Catholic – and Mrs Hollard was too busy, needing to spend time with the publisher from Munich who demanded he see her personally about the Hollard House backlist . . . And, no, really, he hadn't seen Sheila in the lobby. The way the sun was blazing in the front window it was impossible to recognize anyone standing in that dark corner where the sandwich bar was . . .

Richard had found that the longer and more outlandish the excuse the better when it came to Sheila. Her mind tended to wander following details.

It was nearing five o'clock when he finally was able to hang up. Then, realizing it was late, he swung quickly around in his chair to the credenza behind his desk and withdrew from a cabinet a small stuffed toy duck. He started towards the door, and abruptly stopped. It wouldn't do to be seen carrying the duck.

He went to a file cabinet and found a large manila envelope to cover the toy. It did not fit completely, but he managed to conceal all but the head. Then, duck in hand – and with a goodnight to Helen – he left for what was the only thing in his life more precious to him than his job at Hollard House.

Chapter 8

It was late afternoon. An orange sun had slipped below the jagged range of Manhattan skyline. A slender edge of the burning disc still showed behind a line of tall apartment buildings, casting long shadows down the concrete canyon that formed East Seventy-fifth Street. A delivery truck had just double-parked in front of one of the buildings, blocking traffic. Immediately motorists began sounding their horns, the blasts echoing from the walls that towered on each side.

From a sixth-storey window in one of these buildings a small boy grimaced as he watched the cars backing up behind the truck. The traffic jam could delay the event to which he had been looking forward most of the afternoon.

The boy scrutinized each vehicle as it joined the lengthening line. Far down the block he saw a yellow cab come to a stop at the end of the chain of cars; a door opened and a man stepped out on to the sidewalk. The boy could not be certain because of the distance . . . When the figure started walking towards him, he gave a squeal of delight. There was no question now. He knew every detail of the gait, every mannerism.

'Grams, here he comes!'

Jared Fox was the same every day at this time. Unless his father called to say that he would not be coming home or that there had been an unavoidable delay, at precisely 5:30 Jared would take his position at the window and examine every vehicle until a door finally opened and his father emerged.

He was a handsome boy with blond hair that fell in soft

curls over his ears. His eyes were most unusual, a striking grey, deep-set and focused in a lingering, contemplative way that seemed mature for his six years. 'Like Lois,' his father would say. 'Yes, his mother's eyes.'

The eyes now gleamed with expectation as Jared watched his father proceed towards his building. When he disappeared into the doorway below, Jared pulled back on the lever of his electric wheelchair, driving himself back from the window, bumping into a small table and knocking it over. Turning the chair, he moved quickly through the living room into an alcove and the entrance to the apartment, where he stationed himself in front of the door, waiting for his father to appear.

Soon there was a low rumble of the elevator stopping at the end of the hall, the door clanking open, then closing with a thud. Jared knew all the sounds. Although he was confined physically, his senses were especially acute.

He waited impatiently for the insertion of the key, the bolt to move, the doorknob to turn. Then the door swung inward, and standing in the entrance was the centre of Jared Fox's world.

'Hi, Daddy,' stretching his arms towards Richard. 'I saw you walking down from the corner.'

'Hello, Tank.' Richard put the envelope with the duck on a table inside the door, then reached down and lifted the boy from the chair. Jared wrapped his arms around his father's neck and hugged him, burying his face in his collar. There was the strong odour of tobacco, always there when his father came from the office, and his beard felt rough this time of day. Jared cherished the smell, the feeling. He squeezed his father's neck as tightly as his small arms would permit.

'Hey, easy, Tank,' Richard said, gently disengaging, 'you're strangling me.'

'What's that?' Jared asked, drawing back and pointing a finger.

'It's a duck. See his head? He walks, quacks, everything. First, we have to wind him up.'

Cradling his son against his hip with one arm, he picked up the package and walked into the living room. 'Where's Grams?'

A diminutive woman in her early sixties appeared from the kitchen.

'Hello, Mom,' Richard said, meeting his mother midway in the room and kissing her lightly. 'Any calls?'

'Only one. A woman named Morrow. I think she said her name was Emily.'

Richard put the package on a coffee table and sat down on a nearby sofa. Gently he lifted his son from his lap to a sitting position next to him. 'What did she say?'

'She wants you to call her tonight after seven. She left her number. Who is she? She seemed a bit uppity, I must say.'

Jared listened as his father said that the caller was a sister of a Hollard House author, also a first novelist. It seemed his grandmother had already decided she didn't like the woman, but Grams didn't like any of his father's lady friends. Especially the one with the big front that his father had invited home from the office the other night. He'd heard Grams once say that there would never be anyone like Lois.

'Isn't that unusual, Richard?'

'What?'

'An author . . . calling you at home?'

'Not really. She's working on some revisions. I told her she could call me . . .'

Tank sensed that his father didn't want to talk any more about the woman. He was glad. He wished his grandmother would go back to the kitchen.

'How did it go today at the Centre?' Richard asked. 'Did Dr Wilson see Jared?'

'Tank, Daddy. *Tank*.' Jared liked the name Tank. His father had happened on the name one evening after Jared had accidentally demolished a potted plant with his chair. Shortly thereafter Richard had bought him a T-shirt with *TANK* in large block letters across the back; a shirt that except for when he was persuaded to surrender it to the washing machine was always on his back. Even some of his teachers at the Centre now called him 'Tank'.

'Dr Wilson wasn't there,' said his grandmother. 'I talked to Miss Pearlman. She said his tests were brilliant. We'll talk later.' She disappeared into the kitchen.

'Can we open the present, Daddy?' Tank asked, relieved that his grandmother was gone.

Richard leaned forward and removed the duck from the envelope. After winding a key that protruded from its back, he placed it on the coffee table, where it commenced walking in small circles while quacking loudly.

Tank watched delightedly as the toy wound down and finally stopped.

Suddenly there was a sound from the hall.

'Someone at the door?' Richard asked, turning toward the alcove.

'No, it's just Mrs Baker,' Tank said, referring to one of the neighbours. 'She's going to the store. She always goes to the store about now.'

Richard looked at his son, always amazed at his ability to sense the comings and goings of the building occupants.

Jared leaned back, snuggling under his father's arm, but his father seemed preoccupied. There was something about him that Tank found vaguely upsetting . . . ever since Grams had mentioned the phone call from that woman.

64

Chapter 9

'But you've even taken out the chapter about the pelican!' Emily Morrow's dark eyes narrowed as she spoke. She was lounging on a chaise on her Fifth Avenue terrace, her legs drawn up beneath her. It was a clear morning and the sun reflected brightly off her white, gold-trimmed jumpsuit. Her black hair was drawn back revealing small gold earrings that matched the trim on her clothing. In her lap was *The Sanctuary* manuscript.

The object of her black eyes shifted in his chair and reached for an appropriate answer. Richard was honouring the commitment he had made the previous week when he had returned Emily's phone call and had agreed to meet with her to discuss her novel. Now, in his double-breasted navy-blue suit, sitting under a canopy on the luxurious terrace, he was finding the going every bit as hot as the coffee he was sipping.

The previous weekend he had skimmed through the original manuscript, which reading had led him to concur with Moseley. It *was* obscure, disjointed and probably libellous.

When Moseley presented him with the edited version the previous day, he had been surprised. The manuscript had been cut markedly. He had sent it immediately by messenger to Emily's apartment so that she could review it for their meeting. He had anticipated a reaction from her and he had been right. Now, struggling for answers, it was apparent that he had to make Moseley the heavy.

'I thought it best to let one of our senior editors look at it, do some line editing. I guess maybe he has been a bit heavy-handed. I understand how you feel. It's your baby, and you don't want someone tampering with it – '

'*Tampering?*' she interrupted. 'The baby's been dismembered, Richard.'

Richard hesitated, finding himself increasingly defensive. Her blunt comments were in sharp contrast with the winning personality he had seen at lunch.

She riffled through the manuscript. 'Look, every other page he writes, "This must go *in toto*. This must go *in toto*." I must say, if I owned Hollard House, *he'd* go *in toto*.' She smiled as though to soften the comment. It was a strange smile.

'I wouldn't let it bother you, it's the first cut – first draft, rather. A manuscript often goes through a variety of shapes before it's done. I haven't had time to review his editing but I'm sure – '

'Look at this,' Emily said, her tone now turned plaintive, less hostile. 'He cut all of Chapter 26. And here, see what he wrote here . . .' Her long red nail dug into the paper next to one of Moseley's notes. 'He says, "No pelican would ever do *this*. Pelicans must go *in toto*." Well I happen to know that the *pelecanus occidentalis* will do *just* that. What does your editor know about pelicans?'

'Probably nothing,' Richard said. 'Well, we try to let the author have the deciding word in these matters . . . Why don't you give me a few days to look it over? I'm sure I'll have some suggestions . . . Now, what about lunch? Would you like to go to – '

'I thought we could lunch here. I told Brenda to make something for us.' She set the manuscript aside and smiled ingenuously. 'I hope you'll forgive me, Richard, if I seem. . . well, testy. It's just that I've become so frustrated about this manuscript.'

Richard, surprised at the abrupt change in her manner,

settled back in his chair. 'Of course, it's only natural for you to feel that way.' He felt better.

'What about your tennis?' she said. 'Are you going to the Hamptons this weekend? Perhaps we could play.'

Richard felt a rush of excitement. 'Yes, that'd be great . . .'

'Where do you play?'

'New Hampton Tennis Club, near Bridgehampton.'

'I played a tournament there once.' Emily straightened her legs and reached for a pot of coffee close by. 'More?'

Richard offered his cup. As she leaned over to pour he noted her tanned breasts in the decolletage of her jumpsuit.

'Why don't we play at Bayrock?' she suggested. 'Have you played on grass?'

'Not too much.' Not at all, would have been more truthful. Although he had often volleyed on the regular grass in Central Park while waiting for one of the public courts to open up, it was, he knew, hardly lawn tennis.

'Are you busy Sunday morning?'

Richard's spirits dropped. He had told his son that he would take him on a fishing trip to Montauk Sunday morning. Tank would be disappointed if the trip were cancelled. Yet there might not be another opportunity with Emily . . . and he could make it up to Tank . . .

'No . . . I'm free.' Immediately there were visions: the intense grey eyes looking up at him . . . the disappointment . . . 'Ah . . . actually, now that I think of it, Emily, I do have something planned Sunday morning.' Should he mention his son? No, it wasn't the time. 'I'm really sorry. I would have liked – '

'How about Saturday morning?' she said quickly.

Richard had invited Harvey Metzger, a friend, and Harvey's wife to his club Saturday morning to play mixed doubles. They were excellent players and there had been a note of condescension in Harvey's acceptance. ('Who would Richard's partner be?') For a moment Richard toyed with the idea of inviting Emily to play with them but quickly discarded the thought. No point wasting Emily on the Metzgers.

'Saturday would be fine.' He had much less trouble cancelling the Metzgers. 'You may be out of my league, though. I have the feeling you're very good.'

'Don't be silly. We'll just have a good match . . .' She looked at him a moment as though not seeing him, then raising her hand to her forehead said, 'I have a terrible headache, I'm afraid. How about a drink? A martini?'

Oh, no, not again, Richard thought. 'Maybe a white wine. I may take another look at *The Sanctuary* after lunch, and I don't drink when I'm editing.'

His answer appeared to sit well with her. Getting up, she said, 'I'll have Brenda start our lunch. Be right back.'

Richard watched her disappear inside, savouring the way she walked. Her bearing, like everything about her, was distinctive, commanding attention. There was a rolling motion to her gait, a nonchalance, a suggestion of the athlete . . .

His thoughts turned to problems back at the Hollard House offices. Only that morning there had been some upsetting calls – one from a friend at another publishing house to the effect that the acquisition of Hollard House by British American was imminent; more immediately disturbing, a call from the tenth floor. Sheila, it seemed, had complained about an assignment from a superior. During the exchange she had said something about seeing her lawyer about alleged harassment by male executives in the firm. What type of harassment? Well, the caller hadn't pressed the point but thought Richard should be

68

aware of the remark, office rumours being what they were –

He stood and walked to the edge of the terrace over-looking Fifth Avenue, avoiding looking directly down – peering from heights made him queasy. Instead, he glanced out over Central Park at the New York skyline, a lovely view that inspired a feeling of well-being in spite of his problems. Things could be worse, he thought. After all, here he was developing a relationship with a fascinating woman.

The romantic side of his life had always been conservative. He had dated his former wife since high school, their marriage a foregone conclusion that at least had made their families happy. His wife's death from cancer had come only months after their son had fallen from a ledge and been paralysed. The double tragedy had left him devastated. In the following years there had been little in his life other than Jared and book publishing. The very gradual resumption of a social life had proved less than satisfying – mostly affairs like the rather foolish one with Sheila, an employee.

But now with Emily there was the prospect of a dramatic change. She was *different*. But how would she react to Jared? People were unpredictable when it came to the disabled, especially a disabled child. Yet with Emily's intelligence, sensitivity, background . . . He took a deep breath of the morning air, his emotions building.

Inside the apartment were less romantic deliberations. From behind the blinds a pair of dark eyes focused on Richard. They were cool, calculating, dispassionate eyes. The kind found in the wild where interests were pursued with deadly purpose.

Chapter 10

Footsteps broke the quiet darkness of Forsythia Lane. The steady footfall was a solitary beat of life that contrasted with the deep stillness from the Sanctuary.

It was a clear June evening. A small white moon sailed high in the ocean sky off Old Hampton, its beams reflecting across the water, sparkling from silver dunes and casting long shadows down Forsythia Lane.

The footsteps slowed as they neared Number 12, and then came to a halt. Henry Todd stood in the road looking towards the Morrow entranceway, where a tall figure waited, it seemed, to be admitted. The custodian resumed walking, and nearing the house recognized Steve Sawyer, a friend of Emily's. He continued slowly, waiting for the man to go inside before passing the house. He was not avoiding Steve but felt it might be awkward if Steve had to wait to greet him as he was entering.

No one answered the door, however, and after waiting a few more seconds, Steve walked around the side of the house and disappeared down a path leading to the beach.

Henry continued, and as he drew abreast of the house he looked in the windows. Lights were on in several rooms. Lydia was probably at home, just didn't want to come to the door. Nice person, but like him she kept to herself. He hardly ever saw her except when he ran into her on one of her bird-walks. Just as well. His job was the Sanctuary. The less he got involved with the Morrow sisters, the better.

Particularly Emily. Odd duck. Why a fellow like Steve Sawyer would bother so much with her, he didn't know.

Beautiful, sure, but sort of nutty too. He knew for a fact that she'd killed the parrot, then stuffed it. 'Else, where'd the stuffed parrot come from that was found in the trash? She'd said it got out of the house and disappeared. Disappeared, all right. Most of it right down the shitter. Of course Steve Sawyer knew nothing about such things. Nice young fella. His father Al had owned a small tree-service business in Amagansett. Fell off a roof working at the Morrow property. Shouldn't have been up there in the first place. Almost killed him. Probably better if it had, instead of being all crippled up that way. He remembered going to see him a few months after the accident. Young Steve had been there . . .

He'd been at the wheel of the Morrow station wagon, a dark-green antique Ford with a brightly polished wooden body. Although old, the car had been kept in mint condition and had been used by the Morrows for local shopping and transporting guests from the railroad station. Behind him was his dog, Sam, a brown-and-white collie. Next to the dog, a crate of fruit, a Christmas remembrance for Al Sawyer from Louis Morrow.

At Number 60 Henry eased the car to a halt in front of a small grey frame house, took the crate from the back seat and started up the narrow walk. A bitter wind swept down Virginia Street, stirring up swirls of light snow that had fallen earlier in the day. Henry mounted the steps to a small porch and rang the bell. Several seconds passed and the cold had begun to penetrate his work clothes when the door opened wide. Standing in the entrance was an adolescent boy with sandy hair.

'Henry Todd, son. I got somethin' here for your father.'

'I'm Steve. Come on in. Here, let me help you,' he said, taking the crate. 'My Dad's back here.'

Henry followed him through a living room to a kitchen

in the rear. Al Sawyer, a husky man in his late forties with rugged features and strong blue eyes, sat in a wheelchair near a wood-burning stove. On his lap was a dinner tray.

'Have a chair, Henry. Merry Christmas.'

'Merry Christmas, Al. Mr Morrow sends his best. Asked me to drop off that fruit. Don't want to keep you, your dinner's gonna get cold.'

'Don't worry about that. Lots of time to eat, that's for sure.'

'I'll put it back in the oven,' Steve said quickly, picking up the tray from his father's lap.

Henry nodded towards Steve. 'Nice boy you got there.'

'Yes, Steve's been a big help these last few months. Don't know what I would've done without him. We're making it, though, right, Steve?'

Steve nodded, listened with some embarrassment as the father told how he was near the top of his class and how Mr Whitney had given him a job after school helping to take down the brightwork on the Whitney yacht at the shipyard. It was apparent that what was left of Al Sawyer's life centred on his son.

Finally Henry rose, preparing to leave. 'Anything I can do, Al, give me a call,' he said shaking hands. 'Anything at all.'

Steve walked with him to the front door. 'Thanks for coming, Mr Todd.'

'Glad to stop by. Haven't seen your father much the last few years. I got that new job in the Sanctuary, you know. Don't spend as much time at the Morrows' anymore. Used to see your father there now and then when he come to trim the trees. Terrible thing,' he said, shaking his head. 'I was over in the Sanctuary when it happened.'

Henry took hold of the doorknob, paused. 'You been mighty good to your father.'

Steve shifted self-consciously. 'Well, I'm just glad he's here.'

'Let me know if I can help out. G'night, son.'

Outside, Henry descended the steps to the station wagon. Virginia Street seemed colder, even more forlorn. As he drove away, thoughts of the visit lay heavy on his mind. Hard to see a man all crippled up that way. Still, it might've been worse . . . At least the accident happened on the Morrow property. There were rumours around town – Al didn't have to worry about money. Something about a trust or stock . . . his kid's education . . . Pretty rough, though, seeing him there in that chair . . .

Henry's reverie was interrupted when a car's headlights appeared in the distance, heading towards him. He stepped to the side of the road and waited as it raced by, then continued his walk.

Having completed his nightly stroll on the beach, he had come up to Forsythia Lane to make a brief check of the Sanctuary. As he passed Number 12 he looked down the path that led to the beach. There was no sign of Steve. Approaching a dark opening in the heavy foliage along the other side of the road, he carefully descended a small slope into the Sanctuary.

Inside it was cool and a light mist drifted through the forest. As he proceeded down the familiar path he wondered about Bart, a friendly Newfoundland he had acquired after his dog Sam's death a few years before. Bart accompanied him on nightly trips, and since he generally fed Bart before their walk, it was unusual that the dog was gone.

Henry walked leisurely, contented with the remains of some roast duck digesting in his stomach. In the pocket of his jacket was a flashlight, which he did not use, choosing to keep unseen on his nightly patrols. Recently there had been signs of teenagers congregating at night. Evidence of bonfires, beer cans and other refuse from parties had been uncovered. Also, and what was more upsetting, were things he had noticed farther back past the pond: footprints in the soft sand; feathers – from struggling birds? Damn kids, he thought. But it was strange. Kids, or anyone for that matter, never went that far into the woods.

Henry had not reported his findings other than in a few remarks to Lydia. The less people knew about his job, the fewer problems he would have.

He was well into the Sanctuary, not far from the pond, when he heard a dog bark. Bart? He pushed ahead quietly, carefully. He had an abiding respect for the unpredictable nature of the Sanctuary, particularly at night. Not the least of his concerns were the bogs: wet, spongy ground with soil made up mostly of decayed vegetable matter you could sink in. Even worse was quicksand.

He had discovered a pit of quicksand back in the Sanctuary, and was well aware of its treacherous nature. It was not easy to make out, especially at night. When it was dry it looked like powder, the grains round or jagged. Water forced upward through the sand pushed the grains apart and the sand swelled, lost firmness and would not support weight. For anyone caught in its grasp the only hope of survival was to keep very calm – not easy, when being buried alive.

He had come on the pit a few years earlier when he strayed from the path near the pond. Confused, he had wandered back into the bogs, where he had come to a clearing and found a doe mired in a bed of quicksand. Helpless, he had witnessed the agony of its final moments.

He had tried to put the incident from his mind. The pit was far back, where it posed little threat to human life.

74

Besides, it was not unlike other things that preyed in the Sanctuary. They were there, waiting, ready to swallow victims that stumbled into their grasp.

It was from the direction of the pit that the barking now came. Fearing for the safety of his dog, he pressed ahead through a thick fog deeper into the forest and soon came to the open area that surrounded the pit. Standing in the darkness at the edge of the woods he peered out into the clearing.

As his eyes adjusted to the light he made out what appeared to be someone feeding a dog from a bag near the pit. Was the dog Bart? Henry was about to step into the clearing when the figure suddenly threw the bag out into the quicksand. The animal ran to the edge, where it hesitated and began barking. Distracted by the food, it did not see the person move up behind. Suddenly the individual shoved the dog into the quicksand.

Henry stood transfixed. Terrified yelps came from the struggling animal, and then an awful quiet. Henry shrank back under the cover of the trees, trying to recover his stunned senses.

Then, footsteps coming towards him. The person would probably pass him to reach the path leading out of the Sanctuary. Should he move out? Confront him? No, a criminal act had been committed. Who knew what such a person would do if challenged. Better to leave before he was seen.

He turned quickly but lost his balance. Down he went, crashing into the brush. A short cry escaped from his lips as a sharp pain shot through his back and down one leg. He lay still, listening as the heavy silence of the forest closed about him. Had the person heard him? He tried to sit up but was overtaken by pain.

Again the footsteps. Approaching. Cautiously. And then, silhouetted above him in the vapours, a form. He was about to speak when suddenly it crouched. It had him by the ankles. Dragging him. Out into the clearing.

'Wait, stop! I'm the custodian – '

The pain in his back and legs was excruciating. He was being pulled towards the pit. He tried to turn, clawing at the ground. He was at the edge, being shoved towards the quicksand. He grabbed wildly for the form. And then the pit had him, sucking him into its maw. He struggled feebly, unable to breathe, his screams now muffled bleats as the pit slowly swallowed him.

It was still then. The Sanctuary slept, digesting its latest victim.

PART TWO
Old Hampton
June

Chapter 11

It was an American twist, a soft second serve that kicked up high and away on his backhand. Richard had difficulty returning the shot. American twists were rare at his level of play, and his backhand was not a strong part of his game. As he had done with previous serves, he drove the ball back into the net.

It was the fourth game of his match at Bayrock with Emily Morrow, and he had yet to score a single point. The stark spectre of a golden set, losing twenty-four straight points, was staring at him. If Emily won the next eight points in a row he would join the ignominious ranks of the 'goldies'.

Richard was sweating, although not from physical exertion. Emily had won the points deftly and quickly, making running unnecessary. Adding to his embarrassment was the presence of the club pro and a few Bayrock members watching the match from a veranda overlooking the courts.

Richard had come to Bayrock on schedule over an hour before. He had been nervous as he drove his freshly washed BMW up the club's winding drive, which was resplendent with blooming rhododendrons. He had left the car in the parking lot and, avoiding the cold massive stone clubhouse, had gone directly to the tennis courts in the rear where Emily was waiting. She was radiant, her tan contrasting with her white tennis dress, but he had immediately sensed something wrong as she eyed his array of white and navy blue.

She was diplomatic. 'We may have some . . . problems,' she had said. 'We're supposed to wear all white. Club rules, so damn *silly*. Well, let's see what happens.'

They had barely stepped on to the court when Ron, the tennis pro, tall and blond, had joined them to invoke the all-white rule. A moment of tension had ensued as Emily threatened to inveigh against *all* Bayrock rules. Ron had defused things quickly by suggesting that he loan her guest some of his own whites. Moments later Richard had emerged self-consciously from the locker room in shorts that were clearly too large.

The shorts had added to the discomfort of his debut, and now as he double faulted to start the fifth game, his composure was cracking.

'Are you okay?' Emily asked.

'Never complain, never explain,' he said with a stoic smile. 'I think I'm just outclassed.'

'Nonsense,' declared Emily, smiling winningly. She managed to miss two shots before ending the set with a final American twist to Richard's backhand.

They adjourned to the veranda, and Richard was relieved when Emily continued walking to a table with two large wicker chairs at the far end.

There was concern on her face as she said, 'I hope you didn't overdo it.'

'No, but I'm afraid I didn't give you much of a game.'

'I think you did very well,' she said graciously. 'You just have to get used to grass. It won't take you long. Maybe we could line up some doubles. Ron will play, I could ask him to get a fourth – '

'Ah . . .' Richard hesitated, having no desire to resume the spectacle. 'Could we hold off just a bit? I thought we might discuss *The Sanctuary*.' He actually had no desire to bring up the manuscript but it was the only delaying manoeuvre that came to mind.

'Certainly,' Emily said quickly. 'How about a drink?'

She motioned to a waitress. 'Why don't you try a Mimosa? Orange juice and champagne.'

'Great,' Richard said, relieved she hadn't suggested a martini.

After ordering the drinks she pursed her lips, and two tiny vertical lines formed between her eyes. Richard could almost anticipate her words. 'I read that man Moseley's edited version again and I must say, Richard, I think he's just plain missing the point of my novel. The book depends on the minutiae of life here in the Hamptons. He's cut whole passages. I honestly wonder whether he understands the metaphysical approach . . .'

Emily's strong, graceful body interested Richard considerably more than what she was saying. She was as lovely in her tennis clothes as he had expected – and what an athlete. . . ran like an Olympic sprinter. Probably the result of being chased after by every male in the Hamptons.

'Did you have a chance to read it?' she asked. 'The edited version?'

'What? Oh, sure . . .' He thought the edited work was improved over the original, mainly shortened, but it still wasn't a Hollard book. Not by a long shot. The writing was literate, but it was often obscure and confusing. He wasn't prepared to tell her any of this, though. Not now. Not here . . . 'Yes, I read it and, well, I tend to agree with you that Moseley's maybe tightened it too much. But remember what I said, in the final – '

'Tightened it? Moseley strangled it. You can't cut the heart out of it and expect it to survive.' Emily moved forward in her chair, her eyes now hard and black.

Richard, startled by the abrupt change, glanced towards the group at the other end of the veranda. They did not appear to be listening, but someone was approaching. 'Hello, Emily.'

81

He turned and looked up at the tall light-haired man who had sent the note to Emily at '21'. He was wearing the obligatory white tennis clothes and under his arm were two tennis racquets.

'Hi, Steve.' Emily's voice softened and a bright smile masked the irritation of moments before. 'Come and join us. Bring one of those chairs over there. Richard Fox, Steve Sawyer.'

'Nice meeting you,' said Steve.

Richard stood up for the introduction but his spirits dropped. Here was competition: thick sandy hair bleached by the sun, blond eyebrows shading deep blue eyes, wide youthful smile.

'Glad to meet you.' Richard extended his hand but Sawyer didn't appear to notice as he turned and drew up a chair from an adjoining table.

'I hope I'm not intruding,' he said.

'Don't be silly.' Emily patted Steve's arm as he sat down.

Her familiar gesture with the man caused Richard's confidence to drop another notch.

'Sorry I had to cancel, Steve,' Emily said. Then turning to Richard, 'Steve and I were supposed to play some mixed doubles this morning.'

'Oh, I hope I didn't – '

'No, it's okay,' Emily said, again patting Sawyer's arm. 'Steve doesn't mind, do you?'

'Would it make any difference if I did?' he said, smiling at her.

It was obvious the two were more than casually acquainted. 'You must be a very good player if she's any indication,' Richard said, nodding towards Emily.

'Oh, he is,' Emily said. 'He used to be our club champion.'

'Well, I'm sitting here between two pros.' Richard

82

feigned enthusiasm. 'Emily just gave me a lesson out there.'

'I was watching from the clubhouse.' Steve kept his eyes on Emily as he spoke.

'Richard isn't used to grass,' Emily put in.

'I doubt it would make any difference if I were,' Richard said.

An awkward silence was broken by Ron, the pro, from the other table. 'Steve.' He nodded towards a figure on a nearby court. 'Mr Harder's calling you.'

The man on the court waved. 'Care to hit some, Steve?'

'Be right down.' Steve got up and turned to Emily. 'Are you going to be here later?'

'Sure. Why don't we have lunch? Richard, you can stay, can't you?'

Richard nodded. What else could he do?

'We'll meet you around one over there, Steve.' She nodded towards the terrace beyond the veranda.

'See you then. Nice meeting you,' Steve said.

'Yes, sure . . .' Richard held out his hand. Steve responded, but with his left hand, turning it over so the palm came in contact with Richard's. It was then that Richard noticed his other hand – the fingers were missing.

'Yes, nice meeting you,' Steve repeated with little conviction. With a final smile at Emily, he was gone.

Richard sat down. 'Isn't that the fellow we saw at '21'?'

'Yes. Steve's an old friend,' Emily said, picking up her glass

Her intonation indicated nothing special in the relationship, but Richard received the distinct impression that Steve felt otherwise, and was less than pleased to see him with Emily. 'Does he live in the Hamptons?'

'He has a house in Amagansett, works in Manhattan. He's a doctor, a pediatrician.'

'An attractive guy.'

'I told him about my manuscript,' Emily said. 'He wants to help me with it.' She smiled pleasantly.

An image of Steve, *Sanctuary* manuscript close by, lounging with Emily on the Fifth Avenue terrace shot through Richard's mind.

Looking at him carefully, Emily said, 'I didn't mean edit it or anything like that. He just offered to talk about it with me. We have similar ideas on things. He felt he understood what I said I was trying to do . . . the analogies between the Sanctuary and life in the Hamptons, social relationships, the *nature* of the place – '

'Place?'

'The Sanctuary . . . it's like the whole universe. No conscience . . . something makes a mistake in there and it's gone . . .'

The popping sound of a tennis ball drew Richard's attention to the courts, where Steve and his opponent had begun to play. It was evident immediately that Steve was an excellent player. He moved gracefully about the court, smoothly stroking the ball, driving it deeply and consistently to the other baseline. He used a two-handed forehand as well as backhand. Compensating for the deficiency in his hand, thought Richard. He was curious about the impairment, and was tempted to ask. Perhaps it would lead to a discussion of his own son's disability. Although maybe she already knew about Jared. Lydia could have heard about him from one of the editors and mentioned it to her. Instead, he said, 'What about this club? I get the impression from your manuscript that you aren't too enamoured of Bayrock?'

'It's an awful place,' Emily said. 'It hasn't changed for three generations.'

'But aren't you worried . . .?' Richard paused. 'I mean, aren't you concerned what people here might think? Some of the members may be offended by – '

'I don't give a *damn*. Richard, you're beginning to sound like Lydia. Who *cares* what they think?' She took a sip from her glass and then, as though realizing her words might have been too severe, her face softened and she smiled nicely. 'You probably think I'm just awful . . .'

'Hardly.' Richard leaned back in his chair, marvelling at the changes in her disposition. Her personality puzzled him. She had such an extraordinarily winsome air, and yet there were moments when she could be almost scary in her directness and intensity. The mood shifts in no way diminished her appeal. If anything, they made her even more fascinating.

He looked out over the parking lot and tennis courts to the rolling countryside, and in the distance to Old Hampton with its stately houses and opulent grounds. 'Where is the Sanctuary?'

'Over there. See where all the vegetation is?' She raised her arm and pointed to the stretch of forest beyond Forsythia Lane. It was then that Richard noted the marks on the underside of her upper arm. Four long, deep scratches.

'That's the Sanctuary,' she said quietly. 'A lot happens in there.'

Chapter 12

'Lydia, the painting is divine. Everyone's been raving about it. You've been so generous.'

Lydia smiled appreciatively. She was in her upstairs sitting room, talking on the telephone to a Bayrock matron about one of her father's oils – a handsome wildlife painting she had uncovered while rummaging in the Morrow attic and had donated for the club drawing room.

Lydia's support of club activities was well known among the membership, and her sunny disposition shown during her gracious, if infrequent, visits had endeared her to all with whom she had come in contact. She valued her popularity, and the comments from the woman helped overcome the despondency resulting from an earlier clash with Emily.

Following the call, Lydia returned to work at a large oak desk by a window that looked out the rear of the house to the ocean. Lying nearby, breathing deeply, enjoying a mid-afternoon nap, was Rusty. On the desk was her diary, a large heavy ledger bound in garnet and black leather in which she was making notes. The diary was important to her. Although recent entries had been spasmodic, the diary provided insight into Lydia Morrow's life.

After she had completed her notes she paused to gaze out the window where the bright afternoon sun reflected off a blue sea tufted with whitecaps. Far out a few puffy white clouds sailed on the horizon. Like spinnakers on a sailboat, she thought, running with the wind.

She had enjoyed sailing, but she rarely thought about that time in her life. It was too confusing, too painful.

From the end of the hall a solitary chime announced the half-hour on a grandfather clock. It was a tall-case English clock, a replica of the antique located in the library downstairs. The sound echoed through the room, leaving a deep silence in its wake. It reminded her of the lonely knell from the navigational buoys at sea. Her dark eyes filled as she focused on the white clouds in the distance. They had been there, she thought, those same clouds . . . She returned to the diary, staring at it pensively. Then, slowly, her fingers turned back the pages to another summer's day . . .

It was a summer ago, a glorious time in the life of Lydia Morrow. She was in love. Everywhere was the marvel of summertime. Long sunny afternoons, moonlit nights . . . all filled with endless romance. As she lay sunning herself on the foredeck of the sailboat her happiness seemed to billow up and fill the great white mainsail above her.

It was a perfect day for sailing, with a strong steady breeze that sent the *Tempest*, a forty-six-foot sloop with handsome lines, cutting rapidly through a whitecapped sea. Lydia was lying back with her head resting against the forecastle, the breeze on her tanned face, smelling the clear ocean air. She enjoyed watching the rhythmic action of the bow as it plunged into the waves, then rose like a blowing whale, showering the deck with light salty foam.

Off the starboard bow on the distant shore she saw the colourful yachting flags on top of the Bayrock Club. To the east, barely discernible beyond the dunes, was the roof of 12 Forsythia.

The sight of her house added to her good feeling. She wondered if Emily were home yet. Her sister had called earlier from Kennedy Airport to announce her arrival from Paris, where she had been working at the university. Lydia had not seen her for more than six months and was looking forward to their reunion. In anticipation she had purchased a tennis dress for her as a present. She thought it particularly attractive – a design that only someone with Emily's figure could wear – and was anxious to surprise her with it.

Suddenly from the port side there was the sound of young people's laughter. She turned to see a large ketch under full sail that overtook the *Tempest* and passed on, its crew shouting and waving.

Lydia sat up quickly and waved back, her blue eyes wide with excitement. She found the exchange exhilarating and she continued to wave at the boat as it drew away. 'I wish it would never end,' she said, speaking into the wind.

'What's that?' asked a voice from the stern.

'Our day.' She turned and looked at a young man sitting in the open cockpit piloting the vessel. 'It's so wonderful out here, I wish we could go on sailing forever, just the two of us . . .'

'I can arrange that,' he said. 'Look, I'm getting lonesome here by myself. Come on back.'

Lydia laughed, her teeth gleaming in the afternoon sun. 'You'll start at me again.'

'No, I won't. I promise.'

'That's what you said last time. I don't trust you.'

'As the skipper I can order you back.'

'Go ahead and order. You can't let go of the boat.'

'I can't, huh.' He started to get up as though coming towards her.

'All right, *all right*, I'm coming.' She took a navy-blue bandana that matched her one-piece bathing suit and tied it around her hair, then made her way to the stern, where she nestled in beside him.

'This is the way a skipper and his mate should always be.' He shifted the tiller to his other hand so that he could hug her with his free arm. 'We can spend our honeymoon on the *Tempest*.'

'I don't know about that,' Lydia said. 'I heard of a couple who honeymooned on a sailboat. The first thing they did when they got back to port was get divorced.'

'I'd spend my life with you on the *Tempest* . . .'

'I wonder how the Whitneys would feel about our appropriating their sailboat.' She squeezed his hand, listening to the sea exploding against the sturdy bow. She luxuriated in having his strong arm around her shoulders. She had known him only a few months, yet she was deeply in love. Never had she met anyone so kind, so wonderfully attractive. She stretched upward, kissing him lightly. 'I love you so much.'

He squeezed her gently, then looking out to sea said, 'I don't like the looks of that sky. There's a line of dark clouds moving this way. I think maybe we should head in.'

'What happened to the person who was going to take me through the hurricanes?'

'Don't worry, our marriage will be a long calm voyage. No storms, I guarantee it. Here, take this sheet, Mate.' He handed her a line attached to the jib. 'Prepare to come about.'

There was a loud cracking and flapping of the sails as he brought the *Tempest* into the wind and set a course towards shore. Aided by the strong breeze they were soon at the yacht basin and approaching their slip. As they docked they saw someone waving from the porch of the yacht club.

'It's *Emily*,' Lydia said exuberantly. 'Hi, Emily,' she shouted, waving her arm.

89

Her sister returned the wave as she came down the steps and along the pier towards them.

'It's wonderful to have you back,' Lydia said, climbing on to the dock and embracing her sister. After a brief exchange about Emily's trip, Lydia turned to the young man standing in the cockpit. '*This* is the one I've been telling you about,' she said proudly, happily. 'Meet Steve Sawyer.'

Chapter 13

'You can put the pelican back in or leave him out, Richard. It makes no difference. *The Sanctuary* isn't publishable.'

Richard was only half-listening to Moseley. Feet propped on his desk, he was looking out at the small patch of blue sky visible from his office window. It would be lovely in the Hamptons, he thought. And what was Emily doing at this moment? She had told him that she usually got up early and jogged along the beach. The exercise was evident – thighs firm and shapely tapering where they disappeared into her tennis panties . . .

It was Monday morning, and Richard had come to the office preoccupied with Emily. In fact she had been on his mind ever since Saturday at Bayrock. After tennis they had talked about her manuscript over lunch, and Steve Sawyer had joined them and said supportive things about her novel. His manner towards Richard had been proper and reserved.

Emily had passed him off as a friend, but Richard was sure that at least from Steve's viewpoint there was a good deal more.

Richard had left Bayrock after making suggestions for revisions that Emily could do during the week. They'd agreed to meet at Bayrock the next weekend for more tennis and more editorial discussion.

His first order of business on arriving at the office this morning had been to assign Moseley the problem of reassembling *The Sanctuary*. The pelican was to be stetted, as were most of the chapters that had gone.

'Even if I were to rewrite it completely it still wouldn't – '

'I'm not asking you to rewrite it,' Richard said in a mild tone. 'I just want you to shape what's already there.'

Moseley was puzzled by Richard's unaccustomed restraint, sitting there calmly, speaking softly, gazing at the sky.

'Actually, Moseley, *The Sanctuary* is a good deal more than we originally thought. Underneath there, somewhere, is a tour de force of sorts. I'd like you to find it, develop it. And remember, as we both have said, there's nothing wrong with making the reader work a little, challenge him. I know, I know, the protagonist being ravished in the Sanctuary by the five snakes is pretty strong stuff, but it can be helped by being put in the perspective of allegory, at least metaphor. The Bible has some pretty strong stuff too.'

'Richard, think of Mrs Holl – '

Richard lifted his feet from the desk and swung away from the window, the dreaminess gone. 'You see, Moseley, that's your problem, that's why we missed out on *Fired Forests* and lost a bestseller. You can't be so *literal*. You have to get below the surface. It's not the five-snakes doing that. Emily – that is, the author – made clear it's actually a kind of totemism. You know, where primitive beings associate themselves with animals and birds. That's how the author leads the reader into the passage about taxidermy. It's the kind of challenge . . . well, the kind of thing readers can sink their teeth into. Right?'

'Sure, whatever you say, Richard.' Moseley took up the manuscript and started to leave. 'But if we ever do publish this I know one reader who'll *really* sink his teeth into it.'

'Who's that?'

'Arnold Seigler.'

With the mention of critic Seigler's name, a string of

invectives formed in Richard's mind. Before he could express them, though, Helen Rushmore's voice came over the intercom.

'Mr Fox, Miss Fielding on line one.'

Richard hesitated, struggling to balance his hatred of Seigler with frustration with Moseley and anxiety over Sheila. But Sheila was away . . . she'd gone to New Jersey to visit her parents.

Recovering, he took the phone. 'Tell her I'm in conference, I'll call her later.'

'I can step out, Richard,' Moseley offered, starting to leave. 'Actually we're all done with – '

'Stay,' Richard commanded, holding up his hand. 'I don't give a damn what that illiterate faggot Seigler thinks . . .' He embarked on a denunciation of Seigler that Moseley suspected may have been touched off by the call from Miss Fielding. He paused when Helen Rushmore came back on the line.

'Miss Fielding says it's urgent, Mr Fox. She's calling long distance . . . collect.'

Richard ran his fingers through his hair, reached for the phone, hesitated . . .

Moseley took the hint. 'Excuse me, Richard. I'll be going.'

'My mother baked some of those fruit cookies you like,' Richard said, nodding towards a paper bag on the corner of his desk. 'Give some to the people in the office.'

'That's very nice of her,' Moseley said, 'please tell her how much I appreciate – '

'Yes, sure,' Richard interrupted. He waited for Moseley to leave and then pushed a button connecting the incoming call. 'Hello, Sheila. Look, I'm in the middle of a – '

'Richard, I have to talk to you. You were supposed to call me last night.'

'I know, I was in the Hamptons, I didn't get home until . . .'

'Richard, I think we have a problem.'

'. . . almost midnight. I was going to call you when . . . what's that? You have a what?'

'A problem. *We* have a problem,' Sheila interjected in a sobering tone.

Richard stretched his neck in rotating fashion as though attempting to unscrew it from his collar. 'Really?'

'Yes, *really*.'

'What kind of problem?' Richard formed the words with difficulty.

'Well . . . I can't be absolutely sure yet, but . . .'

Richard lowered his head and closed his eyes.

'Are you there, Richard?'

'Yes. Yes, I'm here.'

'Well, I won't know for sure for a while yet, but – '

'What *is* the problem?' Richard erupted.

'Richard, don't shout at me. You have no right to yell at me that way. It isn't my fault. You started it all.' Sniffling sounds came, barely audible.

'Look, Sheila, for God's sake, pull yourself together. Where are you?'

'With (sniff) my mother.'

'Does, ah . . . does your mother know about the problem?'

'(Sniff) no.'

'Good. When are you coming back?'

'I was going to come back Friday. Maybe I should come sooner – '

'Look, everything's going to be all right. Understand? . . . Sheila?'

'Yes.' A weak voice.

Richard switched the phone to his other ear. 'Don't talk to anyone until you see me. Okay?'

'Yes, okay.'

'The main thing is *not* to panic. Everything's going to be just fine. Right?'

'Yes.'

'All right then. I'll call you back tonight, okay?'

'Yes. Richard, do you love – '

'Yes, yes, I do. I'll call you tonight.'

He replaced the phone, setting it down gently with both hands. Then, standing he began pacing behind his desk, his mind racing. Was it possible? Could anyone in this day and age be that careless? Not to take the *pill*? The answer resounded in his mind. *Yes*.

Chapter 14

It was a cool midsummer night. A yellow moon striped by wisps of long slender clouds rode high in the heavens over Old Hampton. Most residents of Forsythia Lane had long since retired as a form slipped quietly into the Sanctuary.

Abruptly the silence was shattered by the roar of an engine as a car with five youngsters rocketed down the road.

Inside the Sanctuary enthusiasm of a different order was brewing, Emily, inspired by the full moon, was on one of her walks, wearing her favourite light-green warm-up suit and white tennis shoes. A green-and-white band encircled her head, holding her dark hair in place. In one hand she carried a small canvas bag. Inside the bag was a cat.

Lydia had adopted the cat. As a result of Henry Todd's apparent drowning – he had been last observed walking on the beach – his cat had been taken to the local pound where it faced an uncertain future. Lydia had seen fit to claim it out of her affection for Henry. That afternoon it had been delivered to Forsythia Lane and had cried loudly ever since. It had taken Emily little time to decide its fate. If the animal's future had been uncertain at the pound, it was no longer.

Inside the Sanctuary Emily rested the bag on the ground and sat down, her back against a large tree. From her pocket she took a small kit containing a razor, a mirror, a glass vial resembling a straw and a small packet of white powder. With the razor she arranged the powder on the mirror into two narrow lines about an inch long. Then, taking the glass tube, she inserted one end into her nostril and sniffed sixty milligrams of cocaine.

After replacing the kit in her pocket she rested her head back against the tree. Quickly the narcotic entered her bloodstream and brain from mucous membranes, and within minutes she began to experience a feeling of exhilaration and well-being. The effects of the 'lines' would last for almost half an hour, but she would augment this with additional 'lines'. On some evenings she enhanced the experience with Thai sticks that she also had with her – a strong form of marijuana that prolonged her high and lightened the descent.

Lately she had become concerned about the quality of her cocaine. Recently, during 'trips' she had experienced both visual and auditory hallucinations and suspected that her present supply might have been laced with amphetamine variants.

As the initial exhilaration came over her she stood, picked up the bag and ambled into the woods. The air was alive with high-pitched creaking noises – that steady cadence of nocturnal life in the forest. Emily loved the sounds. When she was a child, during evening strolls with her father they had made up verses, using syllables that went with the meter and musical tones from the woods. The sounds were particularly vibrant when she was on a trip.

Walking through the darkness, she listened closely to the tempo of the forest. Sometimes the meter was a soft beat followed by a strong one in iambic form. Tonight it was trochaic, the stressed or accented beat coming first. To her it sounded like Dad-dy, Dad-dy. The word pulsated relentlessly through the night air as she pushed into the inner part of the Sanctuary.

Suddenly from far down the road came a great crash,

splintering metal and shattering glass. Was it the youngsters who had sped past as she entered the Sanctuary? At
the time she had thought that they were travelling too fast
to negotiate the hairpin turn near the golf course. But
they would have reached the curve before this. Still, they
could have stopped for some reason and then continued
on. Whatever, they were a wild bunch who'd tempted
fate and were now probably dead, victims of their
mistake.

Shifting the bag to her other hand, she continued into
the Sanctuary, wrapped in a euphoric world. The sounds
of the forest grew louder. From the darkness around her
exotic beings of the night lifted their beat into an alliterative chorus, a requiem, she thought, admonishing those
who had perished in the car.

> Spirits soaring, laws ignoring,
> Down the roadway they went roaring,
> Reeling, squealing wheels and whistling wind.

> Lads caressing, gals undressing,
> All the righteous rules repressing,
> Here repose remains of souls who sinned.

Soon she came to the pond. She stopped, as always,
and looked towards the bench beneath the tree where her
father had died. Emily had no recollection of having
found him that day. She remembered leaving the house
with Sadie and walking through the woods looking for
him, but the actual discovery had been blotted from her
mind.

It was not the only amnesiac period she had experienced. Indeed, fuguelike states accompanied by headaches were relatively common in her life; inexplicable
periods when time was simply lost. Such episodes
occurred mostly at home or in the Sanctuary, when she

would suddenly find herself unexpectedly in a different location, or discover strange articles in her possession. Although the episodes had been frightening during childhood, she had become used to them and had guarded her secret. After all, Aunt Kate had hardly been the sort to whom one would confide such strange things.

As she looked towards the bench she thought of her father, as she often did, sitting on the bench in his white cardigan, staring out at the pond. He looked towards her now as the refrain from the woods called up memories from long ago . . .

'Dad-dy, Dad-dy!'

Louis Morrow glanced up from the bench where he was sitting, feeding bread crumbs to a mother duck and her five ducklings. 'Shh, don't shout so, honey. You'll scare them away.'

'But look, Daddy,' she said, calling his attention to a large mallard she was feeding bread. 'He takes it right out of my hand, *see.*' She stood, rubbed her small hands together, dusting off the crumbs, then began turning in a little dance. Round and round she turned until the forest became a green blur. The twirling brought her dangerously close to the edge of the pond. She stopped, collecting herself, and then ran to a wicker picnic basket on a blue plaid blanket nearby. Taking a piece of bread from the basket, she quickly returned to where the duck was treading water expectantly a few feet from shore.

It was spring, a day when shafts of sunlight pierced the heavy foliage of tall trees and fell in bright patterns on the green moss below. Along the edge of the pond a profusion of wildflowers shook their heads, a chorus of slender figures that danced gaily in the breeze rippling across the surface of the water. It was a day that promised continuous happiness for a little girl and her father.

'When are we having lunch, Daddy?' Emily had watched Sadie pack the picnic basket before they left. In addition to chicken salad sandwiches, potato salad and milk, there were two large brownies with walnut fudge topping, Emily's favourite dessert.

'Anytime now, honey. First let me get a few of those flowers on the bank. We'll make a centrepiece for the blanket like your mother used to do.' He put down the teddy bear, which Emily had tucked in beside him, next to the bench and walked down the bank to the flowers.

Meanwhile Emily had enticed the duck close to shore. As it took the bread from her hand she suddenly grabbed it by the neck and forced its head under water. Her father, hearing the splashing, turned quickly.

'What the devil . . . ?' He ran back and freed the terrified bird, slapping his daughter's hand in the process. 'Emily, for God's sake, what were you doing to the poor thing?'

For a moment she seemed about to cry. Realizing he had frightened her, he gathered her in his arms and carried her to the bench, and sat down.

'Honey, you have to be careful with birds,' he said, balancing her on his knee and looking into her eyes. 'They're very fragile. You wouldn't want to hurt the duck, would you?'

'But, Daddy, they do it to each other.' She looked up at him with dark-eyed innocence. 'I've seen them. One duck will take the other by the neck with its bill and hold him under till he drowns.'

Her father nodded. 'I know, dolly. But . . . well, that's part of their way of life. But *you* wouldn't want to hurt a little duck, would you?'

Emily shook her head. But if a little thing like holding a duck's head under had made him so mad, well, she wondered what he'd say about the other things . . . ?

After a moment she climbed down from his knee and walked to the edge of the pond. A patch of white water lilies floated nearby, a vivid contrast with the black water. She leaned over and gazed at her image amid the tall trees and sky reflected inversely around her. She took a small pebble from the bank and dropped it into the water, making the image shimmer in the ripples. Then she straightened up and began to dance again. Round and round she whirled, her small form reflecting among the lily pads in the dark upside-down world of the pond.

Recollections from the past were interrupted by the sound of sirens in the distance. Officials en route to salvage what was left of the teenagers, Emily thought.

She walked to the bench at the edge of the pond and sat down, placing the bag with the cat next to her. Reaching into a pocket, she brought out the Thai stick. Lighting it, she inhaled deeply and leaned back against the bench, looking up at the yellow moon that sailed in the clearing above the pond.

The effect of the Thai was quick – a feeling of relaxation followed by buoyancy, a sense of levitation that carried her towards the sky. She was floating . . . a yellow balloon . . . From the heavens drifted a choir of magnificent voices as she sailed through a countryside of radiant colour. Mountain masses, plunging passes, gaping gorges, purple grasses . . . to an enchanting world of palaces, cathedrals, castles.

> Here were towers, fragrant flowers,
> Priests imparting papal powers,
> Fairylands where gods would entertain.
>
> Friendly friars, candled choirs,
> Spirits interspersing spires,
> Brilliant kingdoms conjured by cocaine.

But with the flight came the descent, and soon Emily found herself crashing on the bench by the pond.

Her head ached as she reached into the bag next to her and took out the cat. Holding it on her lap, she groped in the bag and produced a small can of lighter fluid. She stood, held the animal by its collar and doused it with the fluid. Then holding it at arm's length, she ignited it with her cigarette lighter and tossed it away. With a frenzied scream the animal shot off, a bolt of wildfire bounding through the black forest.

For Emily, always fascinated by pyrotechnics, the experience was only moderately stimulating. Actually, she had found flaming birds more spectacular.

As time passed her headache lessened. The moon was now covered by a thin veil of clouds, and a blue haze drifted lightly over the clearing. She looked out over the black pool. In her novel she had compared the pond to the fiery lake in *Beowulf*, so awful that the hunted stag chose death from wolves on the shore rather than seek safety in its depths.

But she loved the pond. It was a quiet place where strange images reflected in the moonlight. Fairies cavorted in a nearby brook, and spirits danced in the vapours steaming from the bogs. She came here often to sit in the darkness, listening to whisperings from the forest. Here, deep in the wild, alone with the phantoms in the blue night, she was at peace.

Chapter 15

It was Saturday. Richard stood on the beach looking up at the massive grey structure beyond the dunes that was the Bayrock Club. It was an impressive sight, a great ship commanding the waters of Old Hampton.

It was the kind of weather Bayrock members had come to expect of their weekends. The sky was clear except for a few grey clouds that sailed far out on the ocean's rim, a proper distance from the Bayrock's channel. Even the surf, which exploded threateningly in showers of foam offshore, was gentle when approaching the Bayrock bathing beach, inching forward respectfully before retiring out to sea.

Richard in white bathing trunks and polo shirt and carrying a white beach blanket, stood near the lifeguard tower waiting for Emily. Perched above his thinning hairline was a pair of new aviator sunglasses. He had come to the club early that afternoon at Emily's invitation. She had called during the week suggesting that after they played tennis they go to the beach to discuss her manuscript.

Richard was particularly happy about the beach part of her invitation. It was a place where he could show the results of his abstemiousness and regular exercising. Although not overly muscular, he was lean and athletic-looking.

Following a mixed doubles match with Ron, the club pro, and a younger girl, they had gone to the locker rooms to change into their bathing suits. Ron had complimented him on his game . . . it had been one of those days when his mishit balls had returned miraculously to the court like homing pigeons.

Now, waiting for Emily, Richard was pondering strategy about her novel. The subject of a contract had come up during their phone conversation . . . Steve Sawyer, it seemed, had suggested that maybe the book ought to be under contract to Hollard House before Emily did revisions. Richard, feeling pressure, had gone along, and so, wrapped inside the beach blanket with the manuscript was a contract providing for a guaranteed, if nominal, advance.

When several minutes passed and Emily still had not come he spread the blanket on the sand, weighting the corners with his sandals, then lay down in a way that he could watch for her. It was a comment from the lifeguard on the tower, though, that alerted him to her arrival. 'Hey, Chuck. Here comes one of the Morrow twins.'

Chuck, an associate lying on the ground nearby, rolled quickly into a kneeling position, looking towards the club. Emily strolled from the entrance-way wearing a straw hat, sunglasses, and little else.

'My God,' Chuck sighed, 'she's coming this way.'

'Sit down, will you,' said the tower voice, 'and quit staring, you animal.'

'Are you nuts? Who isn't staring? Incidentally, they're not twins.'

'Bob said they were twins. They sure look alike.'

'Naw, that's Emily. The other one's Lydia. She's older. Not as bitchy. They used to come down together last summer.'

Sauntering across the sand in a powder blue bikini, Emily seemed indifferent to the eyes on her. At that moment, whatever ambivalence Richard had had about working on *The Sanctuary* disappeared.

'Sorry I took so long,' she said, smiling, her teeth very

white in the shadow beneath her hat. 'Ron wanted to talk to me. Ah . . .' She looked down at the blanket. 'Why don't we go down the beach where it's quieter?'

Richard happily gathered up his things and with a glance towards Chuck, who continued to stare, joined Emily walking towards the water.

'It's easier to walk down here along the shore,' she said.

As she went she raised both arms above her head to adjust a ribbon on her hat, the movement causing her bikini to slip down slightly. Richard, watching closely from behind his aviator glasses, noted a fringe of pubic hair.

'Sorry to have kept you waiting,' she said. 'I got delayed up on the terrace.'

'No problem, I was enjoying the sun. By the way, when you first came down I overheard the lifeguard refer to you as one of the Morrow twins.'

'Happens all the time. People think we look so much alike. I can't imagine why. Lydia's blond, her face is rounder. Frankly, she's heavier too . . .'

'Yes, well, you do sound almost the same on the phone. I can never tell which of you – '

'It's such a lovely day, Richard, and I'm so glad you were able to come.' Clearly, Lydia was not a favoured topic of conversation.

A few hundred yards took them to a sparsely populated area where, amid a flock of disrupted sea gulls, they spread the blanket and lay down. They were just settling themselves when one of the displaced gulls that had come to rest near the water's edge a few yards away began strutting back across the beach towards them. Richard noticed Emily intently following the bird's advance. When it paused a few feet away she carefully removed one of her sandals, and then without warning, lashed out, barely missing the gull.

'I hate those bloody things,' she said through clenched teeth, watching the bird soar off.

Then, as though realizing Richard might have been surprised by her action, she smiled and added, 'They're very dirty . . . scavengers, really.'

Emily commenced busying herself with the clasp on the back of her halter and Richard was immediately transfixed, thoughts of the sea gull banished. Was she going to take off her top? Maybe that was why she had taken him to the remote area.

'Richard, would it . . . bother you if I removed my top?'

My God, had he heard right? No, it wouldn't bother him. He might have a stroke, but it wouldn't bother him. He had difficulty forming the one syllable, 'no.'

She continued as she removed her halter, 'It's such an accepted thing everywhere in Europe. I can't imagine why people make a big fuss about it here . . .'

Richard, stunned by the sudden display of Emily's prodigious breasts, was only half-listening.

'I wear these ridiculous pasties,' she was saying, touching a pair of tiny cup-like objects that covered her nipples, 'just in case. Last year the local gendarmes came down with their pads and started ticketing topless women. Can you imagine anything more *primitive?*'

Richard had no comment. Adjusting the glasses, he noticed his hand was unsteady. He had to get control of himself. His last systolic blood-pressure reading was 155. Unlike his tennis, his cardiovascular rating was a genuine type A.

'Did you enjoy the doubles?' Emily asked, stretching out on the blanket. 'You played much better today.'

'Thanks . . . I guess I was more comfortable with the surface. Also with my own shorts.'

'I'm sorry. I should have told you about the all-white rule . . . Speaking of rules, that's why I kept you waiting. Ron was talking to me. He said he overheard some members say that Emily Morrow was abusing the guest privileges . . .'

'What?' Richard pushed his sunglasses back on the crown of his head.

'Guests are only supposed to play once a month.' She shrugged. 'Ron said that before they had the rule the same guests were coming every weekend – '

'I'm sorry, I didn't realize that – '

'No, no. It's all right. Ron doesn't care. It's just that we have to watch it a bit. Better yet, why don't you become a member and we wouldn't have to worry.'

Richard blinked. A member of Bayrock? The most impenetrable Wasp establishment on Long Island? The reason she was getting pressure about guest privileges, he thought, was probably because her guest was Jewish.

'It's no big thing, Richard. You fill out an application. Lydia and I sponsor you. I'll have Steve Sawyer or someone second it. We introduce you to Mr Rodgers, the membership chairman, then you come to the club for cocktails to meet some of the governors and members. They do their little background check and zingo' – she snapped her long powerful fingers – 'you're in.'

Richard lowered the aviator glasses. 'Frankly, it sounds like it would be easier to get into the KGB. Look, that's very nice of you, Emily, but why don't we think about it . . . Look, I've got the contract here.' He took it out of the box and handed it to her. 'It calls for a five thousand dollar advance, which I know isn't much, but the royalty schedule is standard. If the book does well the advance isn't that important.'

'So this is a publishing contract.' She took the document and began to read.

While she scanned the contract, Richard's eyes returned to her breasts and legs. There must be some flaw. Nothing was that perfect. Some sand on her thigh . . . should he brush it off? What would her reaction be? It would be an intimate gesture . . . but a natural thing to do . . .

Leaning forward, he said, 'Some sand here on your leg.' He began lightly brushing her thigh.

Emily's eyes flashed up from the contract and gripped him in a black stare. He quickly withdrew his hand and lay back on the blanket. Was she angry? Maybe not, he had caught her by surprise. But those eyes . . . who could read them?

And what about her invitation to join the club? He'd worry about that all week. He tended to worry about everything, especially Jared. He'd always been a worrier. Sheila's call the previous Monday had put him on the edge of a nervous collapse, until he called back later and found that her 'problem' was that she was having an interview for another job and might have to leave Hollard House . . . an interview that, in fact, he had helped set up.

And now here he was worrying about Emily's invitation to join Bayrock. Maybe she was just making conversation. No, her offer had seemed genuine enough . . . But a member of Bayrock? It seemed remote. He could just hear the comments at the membership meeting. 'Richard Fox? Did you say *Fox*? Oh, my . . .'

He gazed down the long stretch of shore past the colourful beach umbrellas to the Bayrock Club – the great ship sailing beyond the dunes. On its deck overlooking the ocean was the old guard, standing watch against the ethnic minefields wary of the waves of would-be members

108

crashing against the bow. It was a majestic sight, sailing with authority, providing old-world comfort to those who had gained passage. Above, yachting flags, square patches of colour stretched in the wind, sent their message: All was secure aboard the Bayrock.

Chapter 16

'Emily determined to nominate Richard Fox for membership at Bayrock. Wants me to propose him . . .'

After dinner, Lydia had gone to the upstairs study, where she sat at her desk making notes in her journal. As she made the entry about Richard, she thought about the problems involved in his application. She was aware of the unwritten code about ethnics, a code that in no way reflected her own sentiments. Like many members of prominent old establishments governed by ethnic taboos, she left the disposition of such disquieting matters to the club hierarchy. She didn't really care that much about the club and rarely went there. It was Emily's place. As for Emily's campaign, her reasons were obvious . . . to ingratiate herself with Richard Fox.

It hadn't been a good month. The disappearance and presumed drowning of Henry Todd had left her disconsolate. She'd been fond of the custodian. Now Emily was trying to drag her into something that was, as usual, for Emily's interests. And that involved another and continuing source of anxiety – Emily's so-called novel. She still believed it would be rejected, but she had been watching the developing association between Richard and Emily during the last few weeks. Emily was not to be underestimated.

After making the entry in her diary she turned the pages, perusing her notes at random. An entry caught her eye, one that evoked an episode at the house shortly after Emily had returned from Paris several months ago. She smoothed the page with her fingers as she began reading. Thinking back now, it was hard to understand how she had failed to see what was happening right before her eyes. She had been sitting with Steve in the library when Emily had come into the room . . .

'I thought I'd go over to the club,' Emily said, dropping into an easy chair next to her sister. 'Marion Brown said she and Bill Sadler were going. God knows, there's nothing else to do around here.'

Emily had been home less than a week, but her tone made clear she was already restless with Old Hampton's social life.

'Why don't you stay and have dinner with us?' Lydia said. 'I told Steve I'd cook for him tonight.'

'I should accept your offer,' said Emily, smiling wryly.

'No, really, why don't you? You can regale Steve with some of those stories about Paris. Right, Steve?'

Steve, seated next to Lydia on a couch, hesitated and was about to speak but Emily gave him no chance.

'Look at his face,' she said, laughing. 'He'd just love to have the kid sister hanging around, wouldn't you, Steve? We could make it a family affair.'

'I think it would be fine,' Steve said quickly. 'I'm the one who's probably intruding. You two haven't had a chance to be together – '

'We've never spent that much time together, have we?' Emily said, looking at her sister.

'Not really . . . it seems we were always away at school or somewhere.'

'Everyone in town talked about the beautiful Morrow sisters,' Steve said. 'We were always getting you mixed up. But you were hardly ever around. You haven't seen each other much? Too bad. You seem to get along so well together.'

'Oh, sure,' Emily said drily. 'Tell him, Lydia, how you once hit me with a lamp.'

'She's *kidding*,' Lydia said. 'I told her that when she was little I accidentally knocked a lamp off a table and it hit her on the head. Aunt Kate thought I'd done it on purpose. It was very upsetting . . .'

'Apparently it didn't hurt your head,' Steve said, turning to Emily. 'I hear you're quite a scholar.'

'Oh, she is,' Lydia said with genuine pride. 'Valedictorian, Phi Beta Kappa. A writer, too. She's got prizes for her poetry, and she's writing a novel . . . Oh, now I'm embarrassing her,' she said, noting her sister's arched eyebrow.

'I'm not embarrassed,' Emily said coolly. 'But you are breaching a confidence. Besides, you've no idea what it's about.'

Lydia felt the bite in the remark. 'Well, please stay and have dinner with us,' she said, quickly changing the subject.

'Sure, please do,' Steve said. 'I promise not to ask you anything about your writing, okay?' He smiled at her facetiously.

Emily remained undecided for a moment, but after a look at Steve said, 'All right, if you're sure I'm not intruding.'

Lydia stood and moved towards the door. 'I have to take care of some things in the kitchen. Tell Steve about your trip to Venice. You know, when you went to the Lido and lost your luggage.'

Satisfied that she had involved them in conversation, Lydia went to the kitchen and immersed herself in dinner preparations. She heard occasional laughter drifting from the library. They were getting along well, she thought.

She had been working several minutes when she found

she was almost out of butter. 'Steve,' she called. 'Will you go over to town and pick up some butter?'

'I knew I was getting too comfortable,' he said, climbing slowly to his feet. 'You sure that's all you need?'

'Yes, that should do it . . . Emily, you could set the table. Okay?'

'Well . . . maybe I'll ride over with Steve. I've been in the house all day.'

Back in the kitchen Lydia could hear Steve and Emily talking animatedly as they left. Another burst of laughter. It was vaguely disturbing. She shook her head, trying to dislodge the uneasiness that had begun to creep into her mind.

Lydia's remembrances of the past were interrupted as Rusty came into the study carrying a yellow tennis ball, which he carefully deposited in Lydia's lap. He stood, tail wagging gently, his eyes looking up expectantly.

'Where did you get this, Rusty?' Lydia asked. 'It's new. Did you take it from Emily's tennis bag? I bet you did. She'll be furious.'

With the mention of Emily's name Rusty's ears flattened and his head dropped. He knew his place when it came to Emily.

Lydia put the ball on the desk and patted his head. 'Don't worry, I'll put it back. She won't know the difference.'

Rusty went to a corner and lay down, head resting between forepaws. Much of his existence was spent adjusting to the personalities of the Hampton sisters.

Suddenly the phone on the desk began to ring. It rang several times before Lydia finally relented and lifted the receiver. 'Hello.'

'Hi, this is Leroy.' It was a deep gruff voice that startled Lydia. 'I'm coming out. Need anything?'

113

'I beg your pardon.'

'You want any stuff?'

'I'm sorry, I don't understand,' Lydia said. 'Are you sure you have the right – '

'Is this 516-324-5432?'

'Yes, but – '

'You want somethin' or no?'

'I'm afraid you have the wrong party.'

'You sure as hell *sound* like the right party. What's goin' on?'

'Oh . . . you must want my sister . . . She's not here now. May I take a mess – '

Click. Followed by a dial tone.

'Stuff indeed,' murmured Lydia, replacing the phone. Probably one of those crude taxidermists who occasionally called Emily. With a slight shudder, she returned to the diary.

She continued to marvel at her own naïveté. She had never been a match for Emily when it came to men. The journal was full of instances that confirmed this. Nor had Emily's conquests been limited to boyfriends. In spite of Louis Morrow's efforts to show otherwise, Lydia had always been convinced that Emily was her father's favourite, which perception had contributed to a degree of sibling rivalry. There had been confrontations, some going back to when they had been children. The lamp incident had been particularly traumatic. It had happened one afternoon shortly after lunch. She had been with Sadie in the kitchen . . .

'*Six* children?' Sadie looked down at the five-year-old next to her who was helping her wipe dishes. 'Why you want *six*? Two's plenty, honey. Two's more'n plenty. Yes, ma'am, two can keep you busy as you ever wanna be.'

'No, I'm going to have six,' Lydia said firmly. 'Four girls and two boys. The boys are going to be older.'

'Older?'

'Than the girls. So that the girls will have big brothers. I wish I had a big brother. Someone to play with.'

'You got a lil' sister over there.' Sadie nodded towards the child in the corner. 'Ain't that 'nuf to play with?'

'Well . . . it's not really the same. You see . . . she really doesn't play with you. She just sorta sits there. She justs sits there and looks at you or cries.'

'Well, never you mind. She's your little sister, honey, and you got to be nice to her. Go on now, go sit with her. And here's a cookie. Enjoy it. It's the last one.'

Lydia took it and went to the corner, where she sat down next to her younger sister. Taking a bite of her cookie, she then tried to haul Emily on to her lap, much as she would a rag doll. The manoeuvre brought a loud cry from Emily just as Aunt Kate entered the kitchen.

'What in the world? Lydia, what are you doing?'

'I was only playing with her,' Lydia said, dropping Emily on her face. The crying turned to a shriek.

'Get away from her this instant.' Aunt Kate pulled Lydia from the corner.

Lydia had turned towards the door and almost left the kitchen before she remembered her cookie. She turned just in time to see Emily pick it up and start to stuff it into her mouth. Quickly, she ran back and snatched it away. The wails now reached a crescendo.

'Let her have it,' said a distraught Aunt Kate.

'But it's the last one. Sadie gave it to me – '

'Give it to her,' Aunt Kate repeated. 'I can't stand that crying.'

'But – '

'I said *give* it to her. She's your little sister. You have to be good to her. You just dropped her.'

In a rare moment of defiance, Lydia popped the cookie into her mouth, an act that brought out the temper in Aunt Kate, an ageing maiden lady having difficulty adjusting to the role of mother.

'All right, that does it.' She gave Lydia's bottom a sharp whack. 'Off to your room, young lady.'

'But it was my cookie,' Lydia sobbed. 'Sadie gave it to me for helping her. It was the last one.'

The protestations did little good. Once committed, Aunt Kate had the heart of a drill sergeant. But what might have been a moderate upset turned into a major one when Lydia, flouncing from the room, jarred a table. A lamp toppled from it on to Emily, cutting her forehead. It was an accident, but Aunt Kate, who had turned away, looked back only to see the result.

'My God! What are you *doing* to the poor thing?'

Lydia rushed to her room, terrified, sobbing. But it was later the same day that the full impact of the incident was felt. She was coming down the stairs from her room when she overheard her father and Aunt Kate talking in the library.

Aunt Kate was saying, 'She might very well have seriously injured Emily. I can do just so much, Louis. With all your travelling you're in no position to rear them. You should get that girl in a school as soon as possible. Some place where she'll receive the proper care and training. There's really no alternative . . .'

Her father spoke in soft tones so that Lydia could not make out the words. When a door opened down the hall near Sadie's quarters, Lydia turned quickly and went back to her room. Climbing into bed, she stared at the ceiling, shaken. What did it mean? To live somewhere other than Forsythia Lane? Away from the flowers, the maple tree with the swing, the doll's house her father had built? What about her father? Sadie? From outside her window came the voice of a songbird. What about her birds? Would they have bird-feeders at a school?

It was later that night, well past her bedtime, when she tiptoed down the hall, past Aunt Kate's room, down the stairs to her father's study. He was sitting in his easy chair reading when she slipped into the room.

'Lydia?' her father said, surprised. 'What are you doing up this late?'

'I can't sleep, Daddy.' She crawled up on to his lap and snuggled into his arms. 'I really like it here with you.'

'Why of course. Are you all right, darling? Anything wrong?'

'No, everything's fine. I just like being here with you.' She rested her head back against his chest and closed her eyes as her thumb went involuntarily to her mouth. Remembering Aunt Kate's words about proper training, she quickly removed her thumb. Then there was only the sound of her father's heart beating against her ear. It was a peaceful sound. Strong, rhythmic . . . The soft feeling of sleep closed in. Soon, thumb back in mouth, she was dozing.

Louis Morrow moved carefully in his chair, preparing to stand up and carry his daughter to her room.

Suddenly she sat up, eyes half-closed. 'Daddy, I'm sorry Emily got hurt. You watch, Daddy, I'm going to be good to her. You watch.'

Chapter 17

'Let's be honest, Steve. He's an absolute bigot!' Emily was sitting with Steve Sawyer at a table on the grass next to a Bayrock tennis court, resting between sets of their singles match and complaining about Kenton Rodgers, Bayrock membership chairman.

'He's in the insurance business. Someone buys insurance through him, they have an entry to the club. Why do you think he's kept the chairmanship all these years? But who cares? The problem is he has some crazy hang-up about ethnics and everyone goes along with it.'

Steve had been listening patiently but was now tiring of Emily's one-note litany . . . especially since her indignation seemed to have surfaced mostly on behalf of her campaign for Richard Fox's membership. Since she'd failed to persuade Lydia to nominate Fox, she'd suggested he do it. He'd been as quick as Lydia to see the liabilities and was sparring for time.

'Oh, Kenton isn't that bad,' he said during a pause. 'He's just getting a bit old and – '

'You're such a Pollyanna,' she interrupted. 'I wish you had more backbone.'

'Look, Emily, let's leave my anatomy out of it, all right? Are you sure he even wants to be a member?'

'He likes the tennis here. I'm sure he'd like to be a member. I think you should propose him.'

'But I hardly know him,' Steve said, his irritation beginning to show.

'Please, Steve,' Emily said, her manner shifting abruptly, becoming more solicitous. 'You play tennis with

Rodgers. Besides, he doesn't like me, you know that. I know I've offended him, but he does get to me so . . . Just because he's a retired colonel, or whatever, doesn't give him the right to order people around. Anyway, that's even more reason for you to propose Richard. Okay, Steve? Please . . . ?'

Steve shifted in his chair, avoiding her eyes. 'You're utterly relentless, Emily. But what if he's turned down?'

'They won't turn him down. Not if we stick to our guns. My father did a lot for this club. You once said yourself that they wouldn't have the new golf course if he hadn't donated the land. We'll get Charlie Hastings to support the nomination. He was just elected to the board. Anyway, I already told Richard you'd do it.'

'You what!'

'I didn't think you'd mind. After all, he's being helpful with my novel, and besides . . . Mr Rodgers may already know you're going to propose him.'

'Why would he think I – '

'I just have a feeling.'

'Jesus, you really are something.' He shook his head. His own roots in Bayrock were not that deep, deriving from the good graces of Louis Morrow – a fact he bore in mind when dealing with more established members. 'I wish you'd at least talked it over with me before telling everyone . . . Frankly, I don't like all the time you're spending with him.'

'How can you say that? It's nothing but a *professional* relationship. You know that.'

She had walked behind him as though leaving, and he was about to turn to try to appease her when suddenly he felt his chair being tilted back onto its rear legs.

'What the devil?' In spite of his efforts to regain his equilibrium he found himself immobilized on his back in his seat. Above was the inverted face of Emily smiling down at him as she used the rear legs of the chair as a fulcrum to balance his weight.

'Promise you'll help get Richard into the club?' she said sweetly.

'You nutty – '

She tilted the chair back. 'Promise?'

'Yes, yes, okay.'

She then let the chair tip all the way back to the ground so that he was stretched out. Kneeling beside him, she kissed him, long and passionate, ignoring the members who watched from the veranda. 'You're so sweet, Dr Sawyer. No wonder I'm crazy about you.'

Steve's resistance melted under her warm lips. 'You're crazy as hell, but I love you.'

Suddenly she disengaged from him and climbed to her feet. 'Do you mind if we call it a day, Steve? I think I'll just run along home. I feel a headache coming on . . .'

Startled by the abrupt change in her manner, he did his best to conceal his disappointment and frustration. 'Shall I pick up some medication?'

'No, thanks. I have some.'

'I'll drop over later tonight.'

'I'd rather you didn't, Steve. Not the way I'm feeling. I'll call you later, okay?' She picked up her racquets and started to leave, then paused. 'Steve . . . before I go . . . Mr Rodgers was looking for you earlier. He . . . ah . . . asked me if I saw you to tell you to call him at home tonight.'

Steve glanced up at her quickly, then shook his head. 'I can't imagine what's on his mind,' he said drily.

Emily hesitated as if to respond. Then, as though thinking better about it, she smiled, turned, and walked towards the club parking lot.

Watching her leave, Steve thought about the swings in her moods. They concerned him increasingly. He suspected that she was having some emotional problems, but there was little he could do. Her independence and touchiness asserted itself when he intruded on such personal matters.

His frustration deepened as he watched her move off in the evening light; the seductive sway of her hips; the tanned athletic legs; the soft dark curls bouncing gently above her shoulders as she disappeared over a grassy knoll.

He longed to go with her but had learned to temper his desire. Only a limited amount of Emily Morrow's life was to be shared.

Chapter 18

Fresh blood. Dark red spots, some the size of a half-dollar, glistened on the beige linoleum. They led from the back door, through the laundry room, to the stairs that disappeared into the darkness of the cellar.

Lydia had discovered the trail of blood earlier after hearing her sister leave the house. She assumed it had dripped from a subject of Emily's taxidermy. Now, paper towels in hand, kneeling next to a bucket of water, she had taken on the revolting job of cleaning it up.

Nor was it the first time she had had to perform such a task. A few months before she had managed a similar chore, only then it had been a bigger job. She had speculated from the mass of blood at the time that whatever creature Emily had dragged into the cellar was far larger than any of the relics that she had stuffed previously. Also, that time she had noticed in the shadows beyond the door leading to the cellar a bulging plastic bag.

Lydia cleaned the floor meticulously, stopping at the cellar door. Clearly it was above and beyond for her to go into the cellar. Besides, she could see how the blood had already seeped into the wooden steps, blending with the darker brown stains that marked the blood from earlier in the year.

After she'd finished, she deposited the soiled towels in a trash bag, emptied the bucket of water into a nearby laundry tub, washed her hands and went upstairs to the study.

Here she stood looking out the rear window, undecided

about how to spend the rest of her afternoon. One thing there was no indecision about. She preferred to be out of the house when Emily came back. It was a grey, windy day and the ocean was churning. Not a day for the beach or the Sanctuary. It was times such as this, when she was restricted to her study, that she could become very lonely. Moments when thoughts of Steve and what had been lost pressed into mind.

She glanced towards a coloured photograph on a far wall. It was a gay scene, depicting a family of children picnicking with their parents on a grassy knoll. Lydia loved the picture. It represented all that she had ever hoped for in life . . . a husband and lots of children. She had told Emily that an old friend from Europe had sent it to her. In reality she had clipped it from a calendar and framed it. Emily would have found that silly.

But there would be no home, no children. None of the things she had dreamed of as a child. Her existence was as barren as the desolate shore that stretched out below.

She felt the bittersweet melancholy of self-pity start to close about her. Abruptly she turned away, resolved to fight the feeling. Maybe she should go into the mall near Islip. It had been a while since she'd been shopping there. The stores shouldn't be too crowded. Yes, she'd buy a few clothes. Perhaps a dress, some new shoes . . .

She went into her bathroom, where she quickly undressed to shower. She took a shower cap from a hook on the wall. Then turning to a full-length mirror on the back of the door, she carefully pulled it over her head. Her hair was a perfect mess, she thought as she tucked the strands under the cap. She'd have to borrow one of Emily's turbans for the afternoon so it didn't show. 'Yes, the turban should do it,' she murmured, tucking a few remaining wisps of hair under the cap. 'The beige one with the navy-blue stripes.'

She stood for a moment inspecting herself in the long mirror. Was she getting heavier, she wondered? Emily was forever accusing her of putting on weight. For no reason. Didn't she weigh almost the same as she had in college? Well, a pound or two more, maybe. But her shape was every bit as good as Emily's.

Her clear skin was perennially tan, and even those parts of her body that were not regularly exposed to the sun had a smooth tawny look, the only blemish being a faint birthmark on her lower abdomen just above the dark pubic hair.

Her full breasts were unusually firm for their size, although Lydia always felt they sagged just a trifle. She felt a tremor of anxiety as she focused on her left breast, looking for the tiny nodule. It was not visible but it was there. On the periphery of the lower right side. She lifted her hand to feel it but hesitated, reluctant to touch the round firm lump.

She had detected it a few weeks ago while showering, and had been consoling herself with the thought that it was probably nothing more than a benign tumour. But the spectre of possible breast cancer had been with her from the moment of discovery. And perversely, she had been putting off seeing a doctor, afraid of what he might tell her. She had mentioned it to Emily, though, who had responded predictably – with total indifference. So typical of Emily. She had all the sensitivity of a rhinoceros. But she should really go to the doctor. Maybe next week . . .

She put the thought from her mind as she continued to appraise her figure . . . Her waist narrowed to less than 24 inches, unusual for a woman with her build, and her hips and long graceful legs had the look of an athlete. Yes, she thought, pulling in her stomach and turning sideways to view the round hollows in her lean hips, her figure was every bit as good as Emily's.

She noted her expression change in the mirror as she thought of her sister. It was amazing, she thought, how much she resembled her when she frowned. Particularly when her hair was concealed as it was now. She stood for a moment, mimicking her sister's expression. The eyes cool and distant, the elevated chin, and slightly pouting expression. If she ran into anyone shopping, with her hair tucked under the turban, they'd no doubt mistake her for Emily. They almost always did.

Maybe on her trip she'd sort of pretend she was Emily. She'd done it before. It was fun, exciting. She raised her chin to a haughty angle, narrowed her dark eyes, and looked saucily into the mirror. Ah, yes . . . Emily!

Chapter 19

It was now a month since Emily Morrow had come into Richard Fox's life, and, he was in love.

The previous week at her apartment the contract had been signed with less modification than he had anticipated. He was even more relieved at Emily's willingness to make revisions, and the skill and speed she showed in the rewriting. Assuming that she would continue to make such changes, Richard could foresee a publishable work.

On the other hand, she seemed to be putting him off lately. At their last meeting he'd hinted he would be in the Hamptons on the weekend, hoping she would suggest tennis. She had not. He'd thought of asking her to dinner on Saturday night, but she had alluded vaguely to weekend 'plans'. He suspected they included Steve Sawyer. Her relationship with the pediatrician was a continuing source of speculation.

He wondered about her, where she was, what she was doing. He had left her apartment the previous week with the understanding that she would call him Monday. Now, waiting by the phone on his desk, he thought of little else.

His preoccupation had not gone unnoticed in the Hollard House hallways, 'Have you noticed Richard lately?' . . . 'Yes, seems preoccupied.' . . . 'Not the old Richard.' . . . The only one who suspected his true condition was Helen. Whenever she announced Emily Morrow calling it was as though she had stuck her boss with an electric prod. Indeed, at the moment she was slipping a note in front of him while he was on a call, letting him know that Miss Morrow was calling. Punching a button, he cut off an editor in mid-sentence and connected the incoming call.

'Hello.'

'Good morning, Richard.'

'Hel-lo, Emily.' It was a warm greeting, delivered with enthusiasm. 'I was sitting here thinking about *The Sanctuary*. Must be beautiful out your way this morn – '

'It's Lydia, Richard . . . I hope I'm not interrupting.'

'Oh . . . oh, yes. Good morning, Lydia. You sound so much like Emily on the phone.' The melody vanished from Richard's voice. 'How are you this morning?'

'Fine, thank you. Ah . . . Emily tells me she's signed a contract with Hollard House; that you're actually going to publish her novel.'

'Yes, that's right.' Richard was guarded. 'She's making a number of revisions, as you probably know – '

'Richard, I'm very disappointed. 'Why, the libel aspects alone are enough to . . .'

'I wouldn't be too concerned, Lydia,' he said quickly. 'We're changing some of the characters. The protagonist, for example. You know, the ah . . . the writer of bird books? We're making a number of excisions, changing the locale to a more – '

'But, Richard, don't you understand? It won't really change anything. The setting could be Albuquerque but it wouldn't make any difference. The book . . . well, it's simply not fair. She's destroying reputations. All of the petty rumours that are part of any community . . . well, she's given them life. Even if you change the locale it would still be I, Lydia Morrow, writing a book and selling those *horrid* bird devices. Arlene Morris and Jim Bartel are still the ones having the affair in the Sanctuary – '

'I understand, Lydia, but I think you may be overreacting. To you, it's very personal, but other people won't necessarily view it the same way . . . Why don't we wait a bit. You may be surprised. A finished manuscript often bears little resemblance to the original.'

'My God, I *hope* so,' Lydia blurted. 'Well, I have confidence in your judgment, Richard . . .'

'Please don't worry, Lydia, I think the situation is under control.'

'Very well, . . . I truly hope so.'

Richard had just hung up when Helen announced that Mrs Hollard was calling.

He reached quickly for the phone. 'Good morning, Edna.'

'Richard, would you come up to my office, please.'

'Be right there, Edna.' He straightened his tie, smoothed his hair and headed for the door.

A call from Edna was unusual on Monday. She rarely began her week before Tuesday, preferring long weekends at the Jersey Shore. Heightening his concern was her voice. It was definitely down beat.

As Mrs Hollard's male secretary, with whom Richard had never been on good terms, ushered him into the president's office, his heart was heavy with foreboding. Edna was sitting at her desk, a small oval fruitwood table, and her remorseful expression confirmed his fears.

She was a diminutive woman who looked her seventy-four years. Endless confrontation with the sun at the Jersey Shore had added its toll. Her face was the colour and texture of a worn chamois. Compounding the problem was strawberry-coloured hair arranged in a cone-shaped coiffure that gave her head the appearance of having been pulled from a pencil sharpener. Perched behind the miniature desk, she resembled a figurine from a doll's house more than the president of a publishing company.

'Please sit down, Richard.' She motioned to a chair between two large plants.

The ambiance of her office reflected Edna's interest in horticulture. She had done her best to turn the room into a greenhouse. Everywhere was a plant, hanging from the ceiling, peering from behind furniture, leaning from a corner. Edna wasted little time on amenities. 'Hollard House has been sold, Richard. We signed the papers with British American.'

Although he had expected the announcement, it was a major blow. His plans for new authors, new titles, his backlist, pending projects; it was as though he had been told he was being separated from his family. He lowered his eyes.

Edna stiffened in her chair uncomfortably. 'They want you to stay on as publisher, Richard,' she added quickly. 'They're very impressed with your accomplishments and have assured the board of your continued position. However, I must tell you something in confidence. They're bringing in Norman Kaplin as associate publisher.'

Had the two plants on either side of Richard suddenly grabbed him, he could not have been more shocked. Twelve years earlier he and Kaplin had worked together at another publishing company. A conflict had developed and Richard had finally left in frustration. His memories of Norman Kaplin were all bitter. The man had repeatedly tried to undermine him with the president of the company. Not the least of his offensive traits, from Richard's viewpoint, was his choice of friends – a close associate was Arnold Seigler.

'I can imagine what you're thinking, Richard, and I'm sure you know how I feel. I've been opposed to selling from the beginning but I have only one vote on the board . . .'

Richard was only half-listening, trying to sort out the implications for his future. He'd been under no illusions. He realized that any change in management would have serious consequences, but considering his achievements he'd been reasonably confident he would retain a good deal of flexibility in his office, at least for the foreseeable future. Now, with a snake of Norman's stripe on-board, anything was possible. And he could hardly afford to be out of a job . . .

After a while Edna had run out of assurances. She thanked her publisher for his loyalty and the contributions he'd made to the Hollard family fortunes. Richard left graciously but with a feeling of having been exploited. What a fool he'd been, operating with a sense of security as though he owned the company. His books, editors, authors, his most productive years . . . all now part of a conglomerate ready to be sold again at the whim of a new board of directors.

He returned to his office to see Moseley and Helen having a tête-à-tête at the secretary's desk. They looked up quickly as he approached, and Richard sensed they had already heard about the acquisition. Such news would travel fast.

'Any calls?'

'No, Mr Fox,' Helen said. 'Things are pretty quiet.'

'I can imagine,' he sighed, entering his office.

'Should I call your home?' Helen asked. 'It's almost four.'

'Yes, but let me know if any calls come in while I'm on the phone,' he said, thinking of Emily.

He closed the door and went to his desk, waiting for the call to his home. He reached for the phone as Helen announced that Jared was on the line.

'Hello, Tank . . . Yes, five-thirty. How were things at school? Good for you. Sure we can, if not Saturday, we'll do it Sunday. Don't worry, five-thirty . . .'

The call completed, Richard's thoughts reverted to Mrs

Hollard . . . Norman Kaplin . . . Emily . . . Emily still hadn't called . . . And then an image of Jared, the grey eyes looking through the window, waiting for him . . . He slumped back in his chair, enveloped in uncertainty.

Chapter 20

'Excuse me, Richard, are you busy?'

The voice startled Richard, who was sitting at his desk absorbed in a memo from Mrs Hollard about the sale of the company. He glanced up to see Moseley's bald head and glasses in the entranceway. The rest of his senior editor was concealed behind the door as though shielding himself from something about to strike.

Richard's first inclination was to say, Of course I'm busy you idiot. You think this whole goddamn company is coming to a halt just because it's been sold? Instead, he exercised restraint. 'Of course, I'm busy, who isn't?'

'Well, could you spare a minute to talk about these last revisions of *The Sanctuary*?'

'All right, make it quick, though. I've got a lot on my mind.' . . . the acquisition by British American . . . the appointment of Norman Kaplin as associate publisher . . . still no call from Emily . . .

'I talked to Grace Miller about the poetry as you suggested,' Moseley began. 'She feels the stanzas are consistent and in a traditional metric form.'

'She likes it, good. What else?'

'The dominant line is trochaic tetrameter,' continued Moseley, scanning his notes. 'This accounts for the first two lines in all of the stanzas. The last line scans out to three trochaic feet, and the last foot is a dactylic foot. One well-known example of trochaic tetrameter is Shakespeare's "Fear No More the Heat of the Sun" – '

'Moseley!' Richard interrupted, dropping his pencil on the desk exasperatedly. 'Do you see that pile over there?'

He nodded towards a large stack of incoming mail. 'I've got enough to do without – '

'Yes, of course, Richard. But that's not really what I wanted to talk about . . . It's these latest revisions I'm troubled about. There's one here in particular . . .' Moseley started leafing through the manuscript. 'It's really pretty extreme . . .'

'The ghosts screwing in the Sanctuary?'

'No.'

'The verse about the lesbians?'

'No.'

'The homosexual raping the – '

'No, not that,' Moseley said, continuing to leaf through the pages.

'Well, what *is* it?'

'You know the part about the editor.'

'The editor?'

'Yes, you know . . . where the editor in the pornographic publishing firm is mutilated . . .'

'You mean where the protagonist has the editor strapped to the tree in the Sanctuary and cuts off his – '

'*Yes*.' Moseley's eyes lowered.

'And then shaves herself and fixes it on to her – '

'Yes.' Moseley shifted uneasily.

'Well, what's wrong with that?'

'What's wrong with it?' Moseley exclaimed, his expression incredulous.

'The protagonist is a lesbian taxidermist. It's logical for her to do this as an expression of her violent feelings. She doesn't like the editor, right?'

'But Richard, I take personal offence at – '

'You think it's you, right?'

'Well, of course it is. Who else could it be? The publishing firm in the novel is beginning to look more and more like Hollard House. It's a *roman à clef*. And the protagonist parading around with that penis hanging like a trophy from her – '

'You're too sensitive.'

'Why Mrs H. will be fit to – '

'Forget about Mrs Hollard,' Richard interrupted. 'And try not to be so involved with personal sensibilities. This one has a chance at some commercial success. We could use that around here, especially now – '

The buzzer sounded on the intercom. 'Mr Fox, Miss Morrow calling.'

'Which *one*?'

'It sounds like *Emily* Morrow,' Helen said. 'Should I ask? I can never tell for sure.'

Richard picked up the phone as Moseley quickly exited. 'Good morning,' the music back in his voice.

'Hello, Richard. It's Emily. I'm in L A.'

'Oh? Where?'

'Beverly Hills Hotel. I just came out. A friend invites me every year to play tennis with her.'

'Did you take your manuscript?'

'It's right here beside me. In fact, I'm almost finished. I should have it done by this weekend. Which brings me to the reason for the call. Would you be free to go with me to a dance at Bayrock Saturday night?'

'Sounds good.'

'It's our summer gala. Do you like to dance?'

'Yes, matter of fact I do, although I haven't done much recently.'

'Well, I *love* it,' she said. 'When I was a little girl I used to dream about being a ballerina. They'll have a big band, everyone will be there. It'll give me a chance to introduce you around. All right, so Saturday night. It's black tie. Could you pick me up at seven-thirty?'

'I'll look forward to it. When are you coming back?'

'Tomorrow. That is, if I don't stay here and go into the

movies. Don't laugh. I met a producer at the pool here. He wants to put me in one of his movies.'

'Really.' Richard tried to sound enthusiastic. A picture of Emily lounging in her bikini at poolside flashed through his mind. Film producer, indeed. One look at her in her bikini and they all wanted to put her somewhere. 'Well, I'd be careful. Lots of strange ducks in Beverly Hills. One career is enough at a time.'

'Don't worry, Richard. Nothing's going to interfere with my novel.'

He hesitated, then said, 'Lydia called. She's very worried about your book, as you know. She thinks it's libellous, that the people in Old Hampton will think – '

'Don't you worry about her . . .' interrupted Emily, her voice drifting off.

'What's that? I didn't hear what you – '

'Oh, nothing,' Emily said, raising her voice. 'I'll take care of Lydia!'

Chapter 21

It was dark on Forsythia Lane. A steady rain had fallen throughout the evening, filling gutters and pouring down the drainspouts at Number 12. A pool of water had collected by the base of one of the spouts at the rear corner of the house, saturating the ground and seeping into the cellar, as it tended to do during prolonged rains.

'Gotta do somethin' about that water,' Henry Todd used to say. 'Should lay some pipe an' carry it off'n the house. That wall's breakin' up down cellar. Gonna ruin the foundation, for sure.'

Such admonitions had generated little interest from the Hampton sisters. They paid little attention to the visible part of Number 12, to say nothing of what was underground.

This evening Lydia was in the Morrow library not far from where the water was collecting. The soft steady sound of the rain falling on the heavy vegetation outside came through a partially opened window nearby. It was a comforting sound that added to her feeling of relaxation. She had paused to rest, having been occupied during the evening dusting and rearranging the section of the library that comprised her research books on ornithology.

Suddenly there was a noise from the rear of the house. A door opening? Was Emily coming home? But she hadn't heard her car. She waited, listening. It was quiet. Just another creaking sound, she decided. Indeed, the ageing timbers at Number 12 were continually groaning about their timeless burden.

As she sat gazing at the volumes that lined the dark

panelled walls, she took satisfaction from her work. An earlier comment by Emily had prompted her to undertake the chore. Emily, still resentful over Lydia's interference with her novel, had remarked, that all Lydia's bird books had ever done were collect dust. Lydia had taken the comment to heart, and after her sister had left in a huff, she'd gone to the library, where she proceeded to dust off her many research volumes.

The Morrow library was a large rectangular room furnished with sofas, easy chairs, antiques and oil paintings. A visitor would find it typical of the drawing rooms found in Old Hampton estates – except for the area next to the fireplace in a far corner. Here, partially concealed by two large wing chairs, not readily apparent to the casual observer, were shelves containing rows of stuffed birds and other small animals – Emily's collection. A few of the creatures had been suspended from the ceiling on thin strands of wire, simulating birds in flight.

Lydia rarely went near them. Indeed, she avoided even looking at them. But she always felt their presence, staring down at her with those unblinking black eyes.

She was about to resume her work when lights flashed in the front windows signalling a car entering the drive. Emily, she thought, coming back from the club or wherever.

She walked to one of the windows and looked out, not at Emily but at Steve who left his car and came towards the entrance. Immediately she pulled back behind the drapery, her pulse quickening. She stood quietly as the doorbell rang once, then twice more. Her hand moved instinctively to her head, smoothing her hair as she considered answering the door. She restrained herself from doing so, as always, and Steve finally returned to his car and drove away. She stayed at the window, watching the lights fade in the distance, a feeling of gloom displacing her previous mood.

Such near-encounters, evoked memories of the times Steve Sawyer had come calling on *her* . . . They would sit for hours on the large sofa there in the library, talking, drinking, making love. The same sofa on which he now spent time with her sister. She often heard them from her bedroom, which was directly overhead. Nights when she lay awake listening to the low murmur of conversation, followed by long periods of silence. It was the silence that was most agonizing.

Slowly she crossed the room to a spiral wooden ladder set in casters used to reach higher shelves. She rolled the ladder to the area where she had been working, climbed the steps and resumed her dusting.

She was gently sliding one of the volumes from its slot when suddenly the lights went out. Startled, she let go of the book and clutched the brass railing at the side of the ladder. When she saw the dim light spilling from the hallway she realized that the upstairs lights were still on. A fuse must have blown, she thought. Fuses often blew at Number 12, mostly downstairs when the old wiring became overloaded from excessive use of appliances.

Carefully she descended the ladder, dismayed at the thought that she would have to go to the cellar to change the fuse. Ever since childhood she had been afraid of the cellar. And for good reason. Once, while foraging there with her father among old trunks, she had been bitten by a rat. This, added to the fact that it was the scene of her sister's offensive taxidermic endeavours, kept her from trips to the cellar except in emergencies.

When her eyes had adjusted to the darkness, she made her way slowly across the room to a desk in the corner where candles were kept. It was near Emily's mounted specimens, and as she lighted the candle, rows of black eyes flickered. Holding the candle in front of her, she made her way from the room, through the kitchen and laundry to the door leading to the cellar.

She opened the door, and peered down the steep dark passageway, tempted to go to bed and leave the fuses until morning. That's what she would have done if not for the thought of Emily returning to a darkened house. Almost certainly her sister would wake her up and attack her for not having changed the fuse.

As she started down the creaking stairs there was a noticeable cooling of the air and a sense of dampness. When she reached the basement she paused, looking into the blackness. There was the usual dank, musty smell, but another more powerful odour – the stench of something dead. A rodent, she suspected. But then another, more upsetting thought. One of Emily's projects? Steeling herself, she started forward.

The fusebox was located on a wall midway down the cellar. Near it was a cord attached to a light bulb in the ceiling. The light was on a different circuit from the one that had blown. Once she reached it she could turn it on and extinguish the candle.

Reaching the fusebox would not have been difficult if not for the oddments strewn about the cement floor; objects that had accumulated during the eighty years since the house had been built.

She picked her way through the litter, ever mindful of the large grey water spiders that inhabited the area. Although she was not unduly concerned about insects, the spiders were something else. Some, Henry Todd had once said, approached the size of a human hand. Their movements were unpredictable. One moment they were resting motionless, their huge grey bodies blending unde-tected in the shadows, only to dart off abruptly when disturbed. It was an unnerving sight that had made even her father queasy. But as he used to say, although not altogether convincingly, 'Don't worry, they always go the other way. They're as afraid of us as we are of them.'

As she pushed ahead, a current of air caused the candle to flicker, enlivening shadows amid the debris. She stopped abruptly, cupping her hand around the flame, afraid it would go out. As she stood watching the flickering light, she heard a sound far back in the cellar. Something was moving. Chilled she stood motionless, her hand protecting the flame.

Almost immediately she recognized that the steady continuous sound was only water dripping, probably coming from the corner of the house where water collected and seeped into the foundation.

Relieved, she pressed ahead. On a far wall she saw the outline of the fusebox. Soon she could turn on the light. She stepped around a large trunk and paused, looking up for the light cord. As she was about to step forward she glanced downward and saw, directly in front of her, a gaping black hole. The cistern. A square wooden lid that usually covered the abandoned well had been removed, leaving exposed a hole some three feet wide and almost fifteen feet deep. One more step and she would have plunged down the shaft.

Shaken, she stood for a moment to collect herself. Henry Todd must have removed the lid for some reason and never replaced it. A careless mistake that could have been fatal for her.

Recovering, she carefully stepped around the hole and proceeded to the fusebox. Locating the light cord, she pulled it and a dim yellow light came on. Quickly she replaced the burned-out fuse from one of the spares in a box alongside. From above in the laundry room came the start-up sound of the clothes dryer. That must have been part of the problem, she decided . . . Emily, before she went out, probably turned on another appliance while the dryer was still going. If so, after a sustained period the old wiring would have become overloaded and broken the circuit for that section of the house.

Leaving the light on, she started back towards the stairs. As she stepped around the cistern she saw the wooden top leaning against the wall a few yards away and considered trying to drag the lid over to cover the well. No, it was too heavy, and she'd already been through enough for one night. Better to wait until morning and have Emily help her. Perhaps when she realized what had almost happened she'd be more careful.

Once up in the laundry room she saw what had triggered the blown fuse. Not only had Emily turned on the dryer, she had left on the air-conditioning unit, the lights, and an iron. 'So stupid . . .' she muttered, turning off the appliances.

As she went up the hall steps to her bedroom she thought about her near-tragedy, her resentment of her sister building. Emily certainly should have known that overloading the system would blow a fuse. It had happened enough times in the past. It was so thoughtless. So typical of Emily . . .

Chapter 22

'I can knock that price down if you wanna take a little walk back in them woods.'

It was not the first time Leroy Taylor had propositioned Emily. Indeed, he made overtures every time they met. And they were never delicate proposals. Indeed, there was little in Leroy's makeup that was subtle. In his late twenties, he was a large man with stringy blond hair and wide flat features. He had not shaved this day, and coupled with a worn pullover jacket and rumpled chino trousers, he presented a slovenly appearance. His grey eyes broadcast his personality – hard and restless.

He and Emily were in the Sanctuary near a small wooden bridge that spanned a stream – their usual meeting place. Leroy had just delivered a half-ounce of cocaine and was awaiting payment. It was dusk, still light enough to see, but rapidly getting dark. Overhead, trees outlined in the twilight had become hulking grey forms, parties to the transaction.

As he waited for Emily to count the money, Leroy appraised her body. What a shape. No doubt a terrific pair of tits, although it was hard to tell with her jacket. He'd know real soon, though. He'd made up his mind. Tonight he was going to do more than talk. He was horny, his senses sharpened by a line he'd done in the car. Soon he'd have her on her back.

The thought made him increasingly impatient. 'You hear me? I can save ya some of that bread. Let's go back there and have a snort.'

Emily continued to ignore his remarks, counted out his

money and handed it to him. 'Twelve hundred. This better not be cut or you can forget about coming back.'

'I'm not comin' back.'

She didn't speak, but he knew she'd picked up on his threat. 'I don't think you're listenin'. I told ya, tonight I'm gonna give ya a chance for a little discount.'

'No, thanks.' Emily moved around him to pass over the bridge, but he moved in front of her.

'Not so fast. We're not finished. The price just went up. It's gonna cost ya another fifty . . . make it a hundred.'

Leroy ignored the dark eyes focusing on him. His thoughts were now focused. One way or another he was going to have her. He'd try a little more talk, if she didn't come around he'd belt her a few times.

It was their fourth meeting in the Sanctuary. He figured she must live nearby. He'd never seen a better-lookin' chick. Probably society. Maybe important. She had a sister. He knew that from the phone call. Probably that's why she didn't want him to come to her house. He knew people in the Hamptons who snorted the stuff right in their pool.

No, she had to be special. That face, that body. He'd tried to check her out with his wholesaler in Queens. They knew from nothin'. Else they weren't talkin'. Too bad. He could've shook her down. Who'd know the difference? He was gone, man. Tomorrow night he'd be in Mexico. That's why he'd bang her tonight. Nothin' to lose. Perfect spot for it. Even if she reported it, he'd be gone. Not much chance of her going to the fuzz. What would she tell 'em? She was buyin' coke from some guy in the woods and he banged her? C'mon. No, nothin' to gain, lots to lose. She wouldn't be meeting him in this fuckin' wilderness unless she was worried about anyone knowin' . . .

'That's the deal, Baby. Another hundred if ya want to

143

keep that stuff, or . . .' he shrugged, 'we have some fun and we're all even. It's your call, Honey.'

Emily wrenched her arm free. Her strength surprised him, but it was okay. He liked spunky chicks. More kicks whippin' a bitch that put up a fight than some broad that rolled over and played dead.

'You can have it back,' Emily said evenly. 'First, give me back my twelve hundred dollars.'

'You already spent the twelve.' Leroy smiled but his eyes were deadly. 'That's my expenses.'

Emily regarded him for a moment and then moved towards the bridge. Leroy struck her on the side of her face. The blow sent her to the ground. It had not been a hard punch by Leroy's standards, just enough to let her know he meant business.

It was not the first time Leroy had struck a woman. It was a familiar sight as he looked down at the form on the ground. The difference was that the woman looking up at him was not hysterical, not cowering, not even crying. To the contrary, the unblinking dark eyes were locked on him; neither enraged nor defiant, but rather emotionless. Instinct told him they were not the kind of eyes he should turn his back on. Obviously, she needed more softening up.

He stepped forward and kicked her in the side. She gasped, writhing on the ground. Kneeling, he grabbed her by the hair and pulled her face towards his groin. Still no tears. Nothin'. Just those fuckin' eyes. Tough chick, man. Real tough. He slapped her across the face. It felt good.

'That's for starters. Now you're gonna do it real good, right? And if I feel your teeth once, I'm gonna knock every one of the fuckers out of your head. You understand what I'm sayin', huh?'

It was quiet as night closed in. Suddenly a shriek pierced the silence of the forest – an animal mortally wounded as a paroxysm of pain shot through Leroy's loins to his stomach, to his very heart. He collapsed to the ground, rolling over and over, clutching the place where blood spurted from his groin. And then he was numb, bordering on shock. He felt for his genitals. Then came the awareness. 'Oh, *no*. Jesus, *no*.'

And there she was, standing a few yards away. He staggered to his feet and lunged for her. But she was moving. Through the woods. He tried to follow, moaning, incoherent with rage. He was in a clearing. He stopped. Where was she? There, standing on the other side of the clearing. He'd cut her off. He rushed forward. Suddenly there was something under him. Moving. It was water. No, it was alive. It had him. Sucking him down. He struggled but the sand moved in with crushing force. Slowly the earth swallowed him.

Emily watched from the edge of the clearing as the mouth of the pit devoured him. Then holding her side, she moved through the forest to the pond. Here in the light of the pale moon she washed out her mouth and wiped the blood from her face. Then she went to the bench, where she sat down, exhausted. The throbbing pain in her side was intense. She pulled up the jacket of her jumpsuit and felt the area gingerly. There was some swelling but it did not appear as serious as she had feared.

She rested her head against the trunk of the tree and closed her eyes, breathing deeply. She needed the cocaine badly but she would have to wait a few minutes until she had reviewed everything in detail. Ensure there was no evidence. Unlikely, there would be. By prearrangement Leroy had left his car in town and walked to the Sanctuary. Her only concern was if someone were waiting for him, someone who knew he was going to the Sanctuary.

The pain in her side worsened. Taking the white powder from her pocket, she spilled a small amount into the crease between the thumb and forefinger of her left hand and sniffed it deeply. Once again she rested her head back against the tree. Soon the throbbing in her side diminished. She listened to the night sounds around her, relieved to be free of the pain. The cadence from the forest grew louder. She tapped her fingers on the bench in time with the beat, concentrating on the rhythm. It was a trochaic beat that pulsated relentlessly in the side of her head where she had been struck.

Suddenly, above the pond, an image. Was it her father. He had appeared to her before during drug trips. She watched anxiously as the features of Louis Morrow formed in the grey light. Slowly the apparition moved towards her over the water, stopping a few yards away. The colourless face looked down at her, a face of sadness. Then the mouth moved, forming words, and a low modulated voice seemed to fuse with the lyrical beat from the forest. 'Come my child . . .'

> Come dissever life forever,
> Leave this dreaded dark endeavour
> Where ill-fated phantoms lurk and loom.
>
> With availing winds prevailing
> Come we'll find incessant sailing,
> Sailing in our yellow-striped balloon.

The apparition turned and moved off into the night, beckoning her to follow. In the wake of its departure she was gripped by a terrible loneliness. She looked out over the pond, a slick ebony surface that stretched off into the darkness. With one plunge she could pierce the gossamer of life and join him and the other blue phantoms lingering in the vapours. But not yet. Not until she had seen her novel published. *The Sanctuary* must live.

She sat listening to the sounds from the forest. The pain

in her side had returned. With it came thoughts of Leroy, and a deep sense of loathing. But Leroy was gone. Most of him, that is. Part of him was still out there on the ground somewhere near the bridge. In the morning she would recover it. Perhaps she'd keep it. It must have been his most prized possession. Yes, she would preserve it . . . a memento of Leroy.

Chapter 23

A barrage of lightning illuminated the smoking clouds. Incoming rounds of surf boomed offshore as a driving rain of fire ricocheted off the battlements. The heavy artillery of the elements was laying siege to Bayrock.

Not since the summer of '38, when natural forces recaptured much of the south shore of eastern Long Island, had there been an assault of such fury. The attack had come with little warning at the most unpropitious time. It was Saturday, the night of Bayrock's summer revel, its most important social event of the year.

Fortunately, although the onslaught had left the Bayrock staff reeling, actual damage was confined to a few broken windows and some torn canopies. After consultation the dance committee directed that the gala should proceed as planned.

Richard was delayed by the storm, as were many of the guests, and Emily had told him she would meet him at the club. As he drove up the winding entrance to Bayrock, he felt unsure about the evening, his pleasure at being with Emily tempered by the uneasiness he felt about what she had in mind regarding his application.

Alighting from his BMW in the parking area, he looked up at the towering clubhouse. Strains of music emanated from the brilliantly lighted interior, signifying to arriving guests that all was shipshape. But in spite of its festive glow, the turreted structure had a forbidding gothic look. From out at sea where the storm had moved, he heard a low ominous rumbling in the heavens – Bayrock forebears, he thought, fulminating against his presence.

Inside was a great foyer with panelled walls and a high ceiling from which hung an immense crystal chandelier. Many of the arrivals were congregated here, exchanging greetings. Richard hesitated, looking for Emily. Not finding her, he made his way through the crowd to a room on the side that housed the club library.

The reading room, so-called, was a large square area furnished with oriental rugs and antique pieces from the Tudor and Stuart periods. Panelled walls, similar to those in the foyer, stretched from floor to ceiling and supported several oil paintings, one of which was of Louis Morrow. On shelves throughout the room were numerous volumes of books attesting to the members' erudition.

Richard stepped inside the entranceway to avoid the flow of traffic from the front door. Here, he stood nervously fingering his tie, observing the milling guests.

They were a patrician group, silver-haired and soft-spoken, elegantly attired in stylish gowns and black dinner jackets. Although predominantly middle-aged, their ranks were occasionally infused by younger Aryan types.

One, a handsome blond woman in her early thirties, glanced at Richard as she brushed past. Anticipating that she was going to greet him, Richard smiled graciously. However, she appeared not to notice and glided confidently away through the crowd, chin raised, her uninterested blue eyes on some elusive distant object.

It was an awkward encounter. Richard readjusted his tie as he returned his attention to those in the foyer. Many of the members spoke with the Received Pronunciation dialect characteristic of London's upper class. (RP, as it is known in England; an accent in which the preconsonantal or postvocal r is often omitted and replaced with a lengthened vowel.)

> *Oh, thah* you ah . . . How *ah* you? . . .
> Wasn't the *staum* dreadful? . . . *Haven't*
> seen anything like it in *fauty yeahs* . . .

But in spite of the distinctive, at times, affected delivery, the restrained persiflage flowed through the room as gently as a rippling brook; the easy banter of urbane personnages accustomed to gracious social living.

Richard was so absorbed in the surroundings that he did not notice the tall man who approached.

'Hello, Richard.'

He turned to see Steve Sawyer, whose greeting, although reserved, seemed reasonably pleasant.

'Oh, hello there, Steve.'

'Nice to see you,' Steve said. 'Not a good day for tennis.'

'Wouldn't affect my game,' Richard said. 'My overheads always come off as if they were hit in a hurricane.'

'You're looking for Emily, I suppose. She asked about you a few minutes ago.' His voice was formal, polite.

'I'm late, the traffic was backed up on 27.'

They made small talk, then Steve said, 'Emily said something about you joining the club.'

Richard was thinking of a good way to answer when he was saved by a voice from the foyer.

'Richard, you made it.'

He looked up quickly to see Emily moving towards him through the crowd. She was wearing large blue-tinted glasses, and for a moment he was struck by her resemblance to Lydia . . .

'I was beginning to worry about you,' she said, smiling brightly and holding out her hand.

Richard took her outstretched hand, leaned forward and kissed her lightly on the cheek.

She drew back quickly. 'Sorry, Richard,' she said apologetically. 'I got hit by a tennis ball.'

Richard glanced self-consciously at Steve, back at Emily, and then noticed the reason for her glasses – a slight swelling of her cheek near her eye. 'With the glasses, well, you remind me of Lydia.'

'Come with me,' Emily said, ignoring the remark and taking his arm. 'Mr Rodgers, the membership chairman, is here and I want you to meet him before he goes. He usually leaves early . . . thank God. Would you excuse us, Steve?'

'Of course,' Steve said. 'Good luck.'

Richard glanced at Steve. Had he rolled his eyes at Emily when he wished her luck? He felt his stomach constricting as he followed Emily into the interior of the club.

Inside was a large ballroom, decorated for the occasion with flowers and red, white and blue bunting. Several large crystal chandeliers glistened coolly from the ceiling. Tables were arranged in ranks on the periphery of a highly-polished dance floor. A number of elongated windows, tapered at the top, stood on one wall like poised missiles.

In addition to providing space for social gatherings, the room served as a forum for more solemn purposes. The club's annual meeting, for example. Lending importance to these meetings was a stage at one end from which the Bayrock fathers delivered pronunciamentos on important matters such as the list of candidates for club membership. On each side of the stage was a standard, one bearing the American flag and the other the Bayrock coat of arms. Atop each standard was a gold bald eagle with piercing eyes that scrutinized the congregation.

Emily paused inside the door. 'I want to be sure you meet this person,' she said, surveying the room. 'Oh, there he is. Mr Rodgers,' she called as they approached several people. 'Excuse me.'

A man looked towards them, hesitated, then excused himself from the group. 'Yes, Emily?'

Kenton Rodgers, membership chairman of Bayrock, was a large heavyset man in his late sixties. He had a pink bald head that glistened, even in the amber glow of the regulated lighting. Between two remarkably tiny ears was a horseshoe-shaped fringe of white hair. As he spoke to Emily he adjusted horn-rimmed glasses on a pointed nose and peered down at Richard as though examining an unusual specimen. Richard's first impression was that he bore a striking resemblance to the eagle above the Bayrock flag he had noticed in the corner.

'Mr Rodgers, I'd like you to meet a friend of mine, Richard Fox. Richard is the publisher of Hollard House. I believe Lydia may have mentioned him to you. He does her books on ornithology.'

'Yes, of course.'

'I believe you know Richard's going to be proposed for membership – '

'Yes. Well, I'm afraid there's a waiting list, Mr Richards.'

'It's Fox,' Emily said. 'Richard Fox. And I wasn't aware of any waiting list – '

'I believe I covered it all with your sister. Perhaps you'd like to discuss it with her. By the way, I haven't seen her about recently. It would be nice to see *more* of Lydia . . . Well, if you'll kindly excuse me.' He turned to Richard. 'I trust you'll have a pleasant evening with us, Mr Fox.' With a look at Emily, he returned to his group.

Richard shoved his hands in his pockets. 'Emily, about this membership business, I'd rather we dropped it for now. Okay?' He noticed people watching them from the other side of the dance floor.

'I really can't stand that man,' she said. 'Let's go out on the terrace, it's getting warm in here.'

He followed her outside to a large terrace overlooking the ocean. The storm had moved out to sea, leaving a splendid evening in its wake. A soft breeze blew from the ocean. Overhead a white moon rode high in the heavens, illuminating the endless stretch of sea.

They walked to the edge of the terrace, where they rested their arms on the balustrade and looked down at the rolling surf expiring in white spray.

Emily let out a long breath. 'What a night. Who would've thought with that storm a few hours ago we'd be standing here.'

Richard agreed, then said, 'I just hope I didn't embarrass you with Rodgers – '

'Oh, that man infuriates me. I'm sure you realize what he's doing.'

'Having read *The Sanctuary*, I'd be pretty obtuse if I didn't. But I honestly don't give a damn. What's important to me, is that *you* want me to be a member. Emily . . . Well, I've grown quite fond of you these past weeks. I consider you . . . a very good friend . . .' He would have liked to have said more, but decided against it.

Emily continued looking out at the sea, without responding. Richard shifted slightly, and his arm came in contact with hers on the balustrade. Her closeness excited him. He longed to put his arm around her, to draw her close. He didn't think he could take her rejection. Still, when would be a better opportunity? She hadn't moved her arm. Was she giving him a signal? From inside drifted music from the orchestra. It quickened the beat of a romantic heart, inspiring lovers to action. Impulsively almost, he reached around Emily's waist and drew her towards him.

'Oh, my God, be *careful*,' she exclaimed moving away, holding her side.

'Sorry, excuse me,' Richard mumbled, mortified.

'No, no, it isn't your fault.' She grimaced, still holding her side. 'I hurt my ribs, you touched a tender spot – '

'God, I'm terribly sorry, Emily. I had no idea . . . what happened?'

'It's nothing, really. I twisted something . . . When I was playing tennis on the coast.'

'I'm very sorry,' Richard said, blushing. First her cheek, now her ribs. It sounded more like she'd been playing football than tennis.

'Here, let me fix your tie,' she said, recovering and smiling. 'It's all askew.'

After straightening his tie she turned again towards the sea, once more quiet and withdrawn. The many moods of Emily Morrow, he thought. It wasn't easy adjusting to them. This time he wondered if he were responsible . . . 'You seem awfully quiet. I hope I didn't – '

'No, no, it isn't that. It's just . . . well, sometimes I get these dreadful headaches.' She lowered her head, placing the tips of her fingers to her temples. 'I let that man in there get me all upset. I should've brought my pills.'

'Would you like me to go over to your house and – ?'

'No, I'll give Lydia a call. She can bring them. She won't mind as long as she doesn't have to come in. I can meet her there in the lot.' She nodded towards the parking area just beyond the terrace. Then turning, she moved towards the door leading inside the club. 'Would you excuse me a minute while I call her?'

'Of course,' Richard said. 'I'll wait here.'

He watched her go inside, admiring her figure. Then turning he lit a cigarette and looked out at the sea.

When some ten minutes passed and she had not returned, he began to worry. Maybe she hadn't been able to reach Lydia. If so she probably went for the pills herself. Or maybe she'd been diverted by someone. Steve, for example.

Suddenly a voice came from the stairs leading to the parking lot. 'Are you there, Richard?'

It was Emily. Relieved, he walked quickly to the other side of the terrace and looked down over the balustrade into the darkness. She stood near the base of the steps. 'Emily? I was beginning to worry about you.'

'It's Lydia, Richard.'

'Lydia? Oh, nice to see you. Just a second, Emily's inside. I'll go – '

'No, she's home, Richard,' Lydia said quickly peering up at him through her large glasses. 'She's really a wreck with that headache. She wanted me to come over and ask you if you'd mind terribly if she stayed home. Believe me, Richard, she's not up to it. These headaches she gets are devastating.'

Richard stood for a moment looking down at her. 'I hope she's all right. Please tell her not to worry about me. Just a second . . .' He moved towards the stairs. 'I'll come down and – '

'Oh, that isn't necessary, Richard.' She moved as though to go. 'Emily just wanted me to tell you how badly she feels about leaving you like this. She hopes you'll understand . . .'

'Well, sure . . .' He paused at the top of the stairs, looking down at her. She was wearing a nondescript skirt and sweater and her blonde hair was slightly tousled, as though she might have been rousted from a nap to run the errand. Still, she was attractive in the dim light that spilled from the building.

'It's nice to see you, Richard.' She smoothed her hair with her hand as she spoke, and he had the feeling that she might be sensitive about how she looked in the context of the formal doings in the clubhouse.

'Well, it's always a pleasure to see you, Lydia. Please tell Emily it's okay, I understand.'

'Yes, I will. By the way, Richard, be careful driving home. There's a bad curve down here at the end of

Forsythia Lane. There was a terrible accident there recently.' Although she moved as though to leave, there was something about her manner that suggested she maybe would have liked to linger.

'Goodnight, Richard,' she said quietly. With a little wave of her fingers she was gone.

Richard stood for a moment peering into the blackness where she had disappeared. Then turning, he walked back to the other side of the terrace overlooking the ocean. Resting his arms on the balustrade, he looked down at the rolling white surf, thoroughly frustrated. Nothing seemed to be going right. Had Emily really developed a headache? Was it an excuse? Was she bored with him? Had he embarrassed her? Looking out over the water, he felt the loneliness of the vast, empty sea.

PART THREE
Old Hampton
July

Chapter 24

'I *cannot* believe it!'

Kenton Rodgers dropped his racquet, placed his hands on his hips and glared reproachfully at the net, which had just intercepted one of his volleys. It was tournament time on the grass courts at Bayrock. The club singles championships were underway. Steve Sawyer, Kenton's opponent, waited patiently at the other end of the court.

It was the first round of the tournament, and Steve's main concern was to end the match as gracefully as possible. There was no question of the outcome. He would continue to win his matches easily. That is, until the semifinals. Here things would become difficult. His conversion to the two-handed strokes had not been altogether successful and would not hold up against the talented younger players. In previous years he had sailed through the quarters and semis, and only occasionally had anyone tested him, even in the finals. But that was before the accident.

Mr Rodgers was approaching the net now, limp hand outstretched, the defeat furrowed on his brow. 'You played well,' he murmured. 'I don't know what happened to my game. I couldn't hit a thing.'

Steve shook hands with his left hand. 'Thanks, Mr Rodgers. It was great fun.'

After a closing amenity, Steve walked to a table next to the court, picked up his spare racquet, and proceeded towards the veranda overlooking the courts. During his match he had noticed Emily among the spectators. She had been with Richard Fox, an association he had observed with disturbing frequency.

'Have you seen Emily?' he asked Ron, the pro, who stood near the entrance to the courts next to a large bulletin board where the results of the matches were recorded.

'She was sitting on the porch a while ago,' Ron said. 'She may have left with her guest, Mr Fox.'

Steve concealed his disappointment and continued walking towards the clubhouse, trying to balance his concern about Emily and her new associate with the knowledge that their dealings – at least from Emily's standpoint – was an intellectual affair based on her novel. And – as she kept telling him – the process should be completed soon.

As he stepped inside the clubhouse a figure came towards him. For a moment, it resembled Lydia. As his eyes adjusted from the sunlight to the interior he saw that it was a younger member with whom he had a casual acquaintance. He smiled, allowing her to move by, and then passed through an interior door that led upstairs.

On the veranda, he looked about for Emily among the members, hoping that Ron had been wrong about her having gone. There was no sign of her. Disappointed, he proceeded towards a table overlooking the courts. For a moment he watched the matches on the courts below, but soon lost interest. He sat, head bowed, hands in his lap, rubbing the thumb and stump of his right hand musingly. Glancing beyond the terrace, he noticed the young woman who had reminded him of Lydia, walking across the parking lot.

With thoughts of Lydia came the usual frustration and worry . . . their previous relationship and his own responsibility for what had happened. In retrospect, he didn't really see what he could have done differently. He hadn't

160

planned it, God knows. He'd just fallen deeply and irreversibly in love with Emily. Lydia must have suspected it was happening, but no one would have known from the way she acted. Never once had there been any break in her composure, not even when he had finally told her . . . That dreadful night a summer ago . . .

Lydia laughed. It was a delightful spontaneous laugh. A short high-spirited trill that rolled easily from her lips. Virtually anything one might say bordering on jest would evoke it – another mark of Lydia's good nature. Steve loved her laugh. As a joke he'd suggested maybe she and Emily should arm-wrestle and it had provoked her laugh.

'*You* do it,' she said. 'But I warn you, she'll probably beat you. She's strong as an ox, and she just doesn't like to lose, at *anything*.'

Steve and the two sisters were seated around a fire on the beach behind Number 12. They had just finished a dinner of steamed clams, lobster and potato salad prepared by Lydia. A gentle breeze was blowing from the ocean. Offshore, a rumbling surf erupted at intervals while overhead an orange moon sailed in the black sky.

'C'mon, Emily,' Lydia urged. 'Show him.'

Emily, in a yellow bikini sitting cross-legged, eyes fixed on the fire, did not seem to hear. A beach towel she had used earlier to dry off following a swim with Steve was looped over her shoulders. It was an incident that happened during the swim that had prompted Steve's half-facetious comment about arm-wrestling. Emily had submerged in the dark water, and then surfaced directly behind him, and pulling him under. He had been amazed at her strength, and it had led to his mention of arm-wrestling.

When Emily didn't answer, Lydia said, 'She's off in her private world. Emily, wake up.'

161

Emily startled, turned to them.

'Steve wants to arm-wrestle you – '

'I don't want to do anything of the sort,' he said quickly, leaning back on the blanket, one hand cradling his head. 'I said I'd watch *you* two. Besides, my shoulder's killing me. I played six sets of tennis today. The way I feel Mrs Feddyplace could beat me.' He was referring to one of the elderly women at Bayrock.

'You overhit,' Emily said, 'particularly returning serve. You don't have to destroy the ball every time. Put more spin on it. All right, c'mon I'll wrestle you.'

'Not on your life,' Steve said.

'I think he's afraid,' Lydia said winking at her sister.

'Of course he is,' Emily agreed. 'Like tennis, men can't bear to have a woman beat them. C'mon, Steve, I dare you.' Her eyes were alive, her face animated.

She moved to an adjoining blanket and sat cross-legged behind a large red cooler, positioning her elbow on top of the chest, hand raised, ready. 'Well, Doctor Sawyer?'

Steve found her confidence provocative and exciting. Like everything else about her, it was seductive . . . the lush black hair, wet from the saltwater, glistening in the firelight; the haunting, intense eyes, the remarkable body. From the moment he had met her at the yacht club with Lydia, he had felt himself charmed. During the days that followed he had become increasingly attracted to her, even though he had resisted the feeling. She was, after all, Lydia's sister. But the attraction had grown. And Emily had done little to inhibit the relationship. Finally, the day before, it had happened . . .

'C'mon, Steve,' Lydia said, interrupting his thought. 'I never thought I'd see the day you'd be afraid of a woman.'

'Yes, I'm shocked too,' Emily said, looking at him with unblinking eyes, her sensuous mouth half-smiling.

Steve, in spite of himself, wished he were alone with

162

her, the way he had been the afternoon before. After tennis at Bayrock he'd suggested . . . or had she? . . . they go for a swim and then a walk down the beach. What had then happened seemed inevitable. In a remote cove, beneath the blue summer sky, they had made love. He had *not* planned it, not even anticipated it. But it had happened quickly and as irresistably as the tumbling surf beside them. Though later remorseful, he knew nothing else in life would be comparable.

'I never thought I'd see the day Steve Sawyer would turn into a jellyfish,' Lydia was now saying.

Steve looked at her, misgivings clouding his thoughts. She must have some idea. He'd been spending more and more time with Emily. Most of it had been on the tennis court, but still, it would have been noticeable to most people. But Lydia was different, so igenuous. The thought increased his guilt feelings.

'Look at him. He's green with fear,' Lydia persisted.

'Okay, that does it.' Steve rolled into a sitting position across from Emily. 'Even a jellyfish has a breaking point.'

He positioned his elbow on the chest and took her hand. Her warm flesh excited him. Even a casual touch . . .

'Now, don't hurt her.' Lydia crawled over on the blanket and knelt down next to them. 'Remember, she's my little sister.'

'Oh, now she's your *little* sister,' Steve said. 'What happened to that ox you were talking about?'

Lydia laughed putting her arm on his shoulder and kissing him on the cheek. Steve looked straight ahead, avoiding her eyes.

'You can start us, Steve.' Emily adjusted her elbow on the chest. 'Just say "one, two, three, go."' She screwed herself into a starting position and tightened her grip on his hand.

'Ready? Okay, one . . . two . . . three – '

He never had the chance to say 'go'. Emily, jumping the gun, slammed his hand down on to the chest. The lightning-swift manoeuvre brought a squeal of laughter from Lydia. 'What did I tell you, Steve? After watching that, I don't think you should take Mrs Feddyplace too lightly.'

'Hey, I wasn't ready.'

'You started it,' said Lydia.

'All right, we'll do it again. This time, wait till I say "go."'

Emily nodded, placing her elbow back on the chest.

'One . . . two . . . three . . . go . . .'

This time he held his ground. But he marvelled at her strength. The black eyes locked on him as he contained her power.

With passing seconds, he felt her weakening. Applying pressure gradually, he forced her arm downward. When it became obvious she was going to lose, he noticed a change in her expression, particularly in the eyes. There was a strange, almost lupine gleam.

He would force her arm down a bit farther, he thought, then call the match a draw – no chance. Suddenly he felt a sharp pain as her long nails sank into the flesh on the back of his hand. He wrenched his hand free and squeezed it under his left arm in pain.

'What *happened*?' Lydia exclaimed. She took his arm, trying to look at his hand.

Steve was bewildered. It must've been an accident . . . but the look on her face . . . He glanced down at the wound. He was bleeding from four deep scratches.

'Good Lord,' Lydia said. Then turning to her sister, 'Emily, how *could* you?'

Emily said nothing. She sat unmoving, her eyes shifting in the firelight, like a cat that had been rebuked.

'It's nothing,' Steve said quickly. 'I twisted her hand, she couldn't help it.' He looked at Emily. Her face showed no emotion. All at once, she stood, and without a word stalked off into the darkness towards the house.

Steve folded his arms, concealing the wounded hand. Sure, it had been an accident . . . her long nails . . . She could have done it inadvertently in the heat of the contest. She was a hell of a competitor. Still . . .

'Steve, I'm so sorry.' Lydia put her arm around his shoulder and kissed him. 'It's my fault, I egged you on.'

'No, it's nothing.'

'Nothing? Lord, it looks like . . . like claw marks. Come on, we'll go up to the house and wash it off.'

'No, it's all right. See, it's even stopped bleeding.'

'I don't know what to make of her sometimes.' Lydia shook her head. 'She does such crazy things.'

'Wasn't her fault,' he said, explaining how their hands were interlocked. 'The way I was pushing her hand down she couldn't help it. She's very competitive – '

'She's that,' said Lydia with a sigh. 'Really, Steve, sometimes I wonder about her. She used to have these spells . . .'

'Spells?'

'When she was a child. There'd be times when she'd sort of forget things . . . I told you how she discovered my father in the Sanctuary. Maybe that's what started it. She won't talk about it now. She'd be furious if she knew I told you.'

'You mean she had some sort of breakdown that – '

'Oh, no, nothing like that. It's just that . . . well, the things she does. That taxidermy stuff, for example. How could *anyone* get involved in such, such repulsive . . .' Her voice trailed off and she shook her head.

Steve shrugged. 'Well, it's just a hobby, Lydia. She's interested in animals. Lots of people – '

'Do lots of people go prowling around alone in that Sanctuary at midnight?' Lydia's tone was unusually sharp. 'I don't know what she does in there. Henry Todd once told me that he saw her there one night years ago when she was a teenager wearing one of those wolf-heads that Indians used to wear over their heads. Where or how she ever got it, I'll never know. She said she was communicating with the other animals. Do you think lots of people do *that*?'

Steve smiled uneasily. 'That sounds like Emily, I guess.'

'Honestly, Steve, I don't think it's funny.' She took off her glasses and rubbed an eye with the back of her hand. Then, looking closely at him said, 'What's the matter?'

'Matter?'

'Yes, you were looking at me kind of funny.'

'Oh, nothing, I'm always amazed at how much you two look alike. Without your glasses, that bandana over your head, you really do look just like her.'

'People have always said that.' She put back her glasses. 'Sometimes I thank God for these glasses.'

They were silent for a while. Then Lydia said, 'Steve, do you mind if I ask you something? I hope you won't think I'm silly.'

'Go ahead.'

'Well . . . I know I'm going to be sorry later that I said this, but . . .' She paused again.

Steve tensed, sensing what might be coming. 'What is it?'

'It's just that . . . well, you seem to spend quite a bit of time with Emily. I realize you both like to play tennis and . . . well, I thought I'd mention it . . . Do you know what I mean?'

He looked into the fire and didn't answer. The only sound was the surf offshore. Finally he turned to her, started to speak, then didn't, agonizing over what to say.

166

Lydia looked at him curiously, then gave her nervous little laugh.

'Did I ask something I shouldn't?'

Steve was quiet for a moment and then said, 'Lydia . . . I've been avoiding this moment . . . I don't know *how* it happened . . . What can I possibly say?' He paused, searching for words that never came.

She regarded him for a moment, puzzled. But then the innocence gave way to awareness. The blue eyes fluttered. She swallowed.

Steve looked back at the fire, feeling the pain in her eyes.

Lydia sat motionless, stupefied, head bowed. After a moment, she straightened, brushed her cheek with the back of her hand and sighed. 'Well . . . I suppose we should go.' Rising, she gathered a few of her things and started towards the house. 'You can leave the rest there, Steve . . . I'll get it later.'

As she moved off into the darkness, Steve remained, staring at the fire, listening to the building surf. It was colder now, the shore dark. He looked down at the back of his hand, examining the wound in the firelight. His thoughts turned to Emily as he gazed out at the dark sea. He loved the sea. It was mysterious, beautiful, unpredictable.

Chapter 25

'Bob, it's a thrill for me to be working for you. You're a legend in this business. Frankly, the only reason I came here is because of you.'

Norman Kaplin, new associate publisher of Hollard House, was delivering what had started out as an oral report on *The Sanctuary* to Robert Bennett, the silver-haired newly designated president. Midway in his report he had digressed.

'I guess you probably know they wanted me over at Packard, but I told them that I had a chance to work with you. My contact there said, "I don't blame you, Bennett is one helluva guy."'

Norman felt compelled to play sychophant to compensate for his other deficiencies. In his mid-forties, he was not attractive. Dirty-blond hair clung to his head in tight curls, giving a Harpo Marx effect. There was nothing comical about his moist blue eyes, however, and a meanness in his veiled, restless look made one uneasy. Small in stature, he had remarkably long arms, which had given rise to predictable and unkind simian references.

'I think we can really do something with Hollard,' Norman went on. 'Fox has let the trade division all but fall apart. *The Sanctuary* is only the tip of the iceberg, Bob. Frankly, I'm not sure just how much time he's really devoting to the job. He has some real problems at home, you know . . .'

Robert Bennett sat at his desk regretting anew that he'd been obliged to take on Kaplin. The chairman of British American, his overlord company, was married to

Norman's sister. Kaplin's resume had reflected attendance at Harvard, and experience in a variety of positions at several small to mid-size companies. Checking it out, Bennett had determined an element of hyperbole. Norman's attendance at Harvard, for example, had consisted of a two-week corporate seminar at the business school. Norman Kaplin, it seemed clear, was a liar. Compounding Bennett's problem was the matter of *The Sanctuary*. He had received a call from his boss, the British American chairman, asking him to look into the project.

Emily, it seemed, had been overheard at Bayrock talking to Steve Sawyer about some references to the club in her novel. Some of the comments had made the rounds of the bridge circuit and been heard by Mrs Rodgers, wife of the membership chairman. It had taken Mr Rodgers only one phone call to a prominent New York industrialist who was a member of Bayrock to begin an investigation. The industrialist had contacted the chairman of British American, who phoned his new president at Hollard. Bennett, in turn, had looked to Norman to find out why *The Sanctuary* was causing such a stir.

'Norman,' Bennett said, 'we were discussing *The Sanctuary*. How can you be sure that Fox is involved with the author?'

'No question about it,' Norman said. 'Everyone here knows it. I've been discreet but I've found out plenty . . .'

Indeed, Norman had elicited much information. His position on the editorial board gave him instant access to works in progress. This, together with the desire of employees to be part of the new team, had enabled him not only to read *The Sanctuary*, but to learn the circumstances surrounding its impending publication. Norman had been quick to see the opportunity to take advantage of an old adversary.

'We can stop it before it goes any farther,' said Norman.

'No real harm done yet. But believe me, Bob, it's filled with potentially libellous material. I know the Hamptons. I've had a place in Southampton for years – '

'The book must have some merit,' Bennett said, tapping his glasses against the edge of his desk. 'A person like Fox has too much pride, too much experience, to publish a book because of – '

'I only wish that were so, Bob. To get a disinterested opinion I had a close friend of mine, the critic Arnold Seigler, look at it, on a confidential basis. He said it was hopeless.'

'Well, from what you say, the book isn't that far along. We'll discuss it at the editorial meeting on Monday and get Fox's point of view. I told the chairman I'd keep him informed.'

'Is . . . British American getting involved?'

'I don't see them involved,' said Bennett, frowning. 'They've guaranteed our editorial independence. They want to be kept informed of potential legal problems, that's all.' The president picked up a paper on his desk, indicating the meeting was at an end. 'Thanks for the report, Norman.'

It was late in the afternoon and Bennett was preparing to leave his office when another call came from his boss at British American. This time there was a note of urgency in the chairman's voice.

'Bob, our board is getting pressure on that *Sanctuary* book. I had two directors call me today. The Bayrock Club has some damned influential members. One of them owns a large soft drink company that buys most of its cans from one of our subsidiaries.'

'I'm looking into it, David. We'll be discussing the book at our editorial meeting on Monday. I should know more about – '

'They tell me it's libellous. Frankly, I'm getting pressure that I don't need right now.'

'I understand, David. I should know more – '

'How important is this book, anyway? From what you told me I had the impression that it wasn't that great anyway.'

'I understand, David, but I'm sure you realize these things have to be handled discreetly. There's nothing more important in a publisher's life than his editorial independence, and – '

'That's fine, but just remember, Bob, there's nothing more important in a chairman's life than his shareholders, and I have our annual shareholders meeting coming up in three weeks. I have all the problems I can handle for one meeting. Have I made myself clear?'

Silence. Finally, 'I understand, David. I'll take care of it.'

After the call Bennett settled back in his chair and gazed for a moment through his office window where the late afternoon sun reflected off the glass. Turning abruptly, he reached for his phone to call his secretary. After almost forty years in the publishing business, much of late with conglomerates, Robert Bennett was a realist.

'Sarah, please ask Mr Kaplin to come back up to my office.'

Chapter 26

'Steve?'

'Hi, Emily.' Steve Sawyer balanced the phone between his shoulder and ear as he placed some packages on a hall table with his left hand. 'I just got home from the hospital. I was about to call you – '

'I tried to reach you earlier but there was no answer.'

'The traffic was backed up on the expressway. I'll be over in a few – '

'Steve, would you mind if we didn't go out tonight? I have one of my damn headaches. Besides, I have to finish these revisions on my novel.'

'I thought you'd finished them,' Steve said. Having been in the city most of the week, he had been looking forward to dinner with her.

'I still have some odds and ends to handle. Sorry to cancel this late. I hope you're not upset. I tried to reach you at your office, but your nurse said you'd already left.'

'Are you sure you wouldn't like to have a quick bite? You have to eat. We could go over to – '

'No, really, Steve. I'm not even dressed. I hope you understand . . .'

'Ah . . . what about tomorrow? We could sail over to – '

'I can't tomorrow. I'm having my publisher over to review some – '

'Oh, not again this weekend,' Steve said exasperated. 'Why don't you just move in with the guy?' Although still confident Emily's interest in the publisher was fostered by her novel, his concern was deepening. He looked forward to the weekends when he could be with her, but even these interludes were becoming shorter and fewer because of the time she was spending with Fox.

'Please, Steve, try to be more understanding,' Emily said. 'This novel means a lot.'

'All right,' he said, softening his voice. Sensing she was anxious to get off the phone, he concluded the call.

After hanging up, he went to the kitchen where he took a bottle of vodka and made a martini. Drink in hand, he walked through a breezeway to an outside porch, and sat down in a deck chair.

The house was a small grey contemporary structure on the dunes above the beach in Amagansett. After his father's death he had sold the place on Virginia Street and bought this house on the shore. He used it mostly on weekends, renting an apartment in Manhattan near the hospital where he worked during the week.

A wooden porch resting on pilings, extended from the house towards the beach, offering a panorama of the sea. The last rays of the sun were disappearing, and the ocean had taken on a dark sombre cast. A solitary gull riding on a light current of air above the beach emitted a short, plaintive call; a lonely sound that matched his mood.

He sat sipping his drink, thinking of Emily. He wanted desperately to see her. Maybe he'd drop by Forsythia Lane in the morning. Maybe not. Her moods were less predictable than ever. His concern had led him to discuss her symptoms with a psychiatrist friend at the hospital, but it was of little help. Matters of the mind were difficult to diagnose through an intermediary.

After draining the remnants of his drink he lay back and closed his eyes. He was in love with a woman who was becoming increasingly unpredictable. But there was little he could do.

He stroked the four nubs on his right hand musingly, as

173

he watched the impending night close over the water. Twilight . . . It was a disturbing time of day. It evoked memories of another time, another experience with a darkening sea . . .

'It will be getting dark soon.' Steve sat in the open cockpit of the *Tempest*, his hand on the wheel, watching the sun disappear behind the Hampton Yacht Club in the distance. 'We may have to try the engine again.'

The *Tempest* was in irons, resting motionless on the flat sea. The brisk wind that had carried the vessel from port earlier in the day had dissipated, so that the jib and the mainsail were slack, reacting only occasionally to brief puffs of air.

'What if it doesn't start?' Emily, her arm around a guy wire for support, was standing on the bow looking towards their destination in a distant cove.

'No problem starting it. I'm worried about the way it's smoking.'

'Well, as long as it gets us in.'

'I have an aversion to fires on sailboats,' he said. 'Particularly one I'm on.'

'Really?' Emily glanced back towards the cockpit. 'It could start a fire?'

'Well . . . I'm not really worried about a fire. I'm just thinking of the Whitneys when I tell them we ruined the engine.' Steve looked towards the fading sun. 'I don't think we have any choice, though. We're not going to make it under sail. I'll go below and start it up. Come back and take the helm.'

'We're not even moving.'

'That's what I intend to remedy. C'mon, get back here.'

'Well, when you get us moving, I'll take the helm . . . that is, if you ask me nicely.'

174

'That's mutinous talk. The captain gives orders. He isn't supposed to ask nicely.'

'I'm going to be the captain the next time we come out. I bet if I'd been captain today we wouldn't still be out here waiting for it to get dark.' She turned and smiled at him.

He paused at the entrance to the cabin, held by her beauty. The copper tones of the evening sun reflected off her sharp, tanned features. She was wearing white shorts, a striped blue-and-white jersey and topsiders that seemed very white against her brown legs.

It had been a little over a month since he had first met her, a month of excitement he'd never known before . . . so busy that he'd had little time to feel guilty about Lydia.

'Maybe you should come down and help me with the engine,' he said. 'How can you be the captain unless you know what's going on below?'

'Not on your life,' she laughed. 'I've got a pretty good idea of what goes on below.'

He shrugged and disappeared into the cabin. There came the sound of the motor turning over, and then a low steady rumble as it caught hold.

'Sounds good,' he said, emerging from the hold. Taking the gear lever, he eased it forward, and the sloop began to vibrate and move ahead.

'Wonderful,' Emily called from the bow. 'I've renewed confidence in my captain.'

They had made significant progress towards the cove when smoke began billowing from the cabin.

'Damn it. Here, take the wheel,' Steve said, moving towards the hold. 'I'd better shut it off.'

'What do you think's wrong?' she asked, making her way towards the stern.

'Not sure.' After shutting down the engine he returned

175

to the cockpit. 'Probably the intake is clogged with seaweed. It happened once before.'

'The intake?'

'In the hull. Where the water comes in to cool the engine.' He looked towards the cove as the sloop slowed and began to drift. 'I'll have to go over and clean it out. We'll be out here all night if I don't.'

'Over the side, you mean?'

'Yes, it'll only take a second. I've done it before. Where's the safety line?'

After locating the line, he took off his shirt and secured the line around his waist. 'If it's what I think it is, it won't take long.'

'Will you be able to see?'

'I think so. It's not that dark yet. Get me one of those diving masks we used before. They were in the galley when I last saw them.'

Emily brought him two rubber masks, one all black and a small one with red trim. 'Which do you want?'

Steve took the black mask and pulled it over his head. Then, taking a small rubber ladder from the cockpit, he hung it off the stern and climbed over the side.

'Do you think I should go with you? Maybe I could help –'

'No, you stay here.' He balanced himself on the ladder. 'You handle the safety line. If I see a shark down there I jerk the line and you're supposed to pull me up real fast.'

'Don't kid.'

'Don't worry.' He adjusted the mask over his eyes and began taking deep breaths.

'What are you doing?'

'Storing oxygen. This is what the natives do in Mexico so they can stay underwater longer.' Taking a final breath, he pushed himself off into the sea.

Below the surface it was lighter than he had expected.

The white hull glimmered in the murky sea like the belly of a gigantic fish. He was surprised at the large quantity of *Crustacea* attached to the vessel, even though the *Tempest* had been pulled and scraped two months ago. Be careful, he thought. Barnacles were sharp.

He anticipated little difficulty locating the intake. He had entered the water off the stern, however, and needed to move closer to midship. With his right hand he grasped the rudder post, the vertical shaft of the rudder attached to the helm, and pulled himself towards the hull. At that instant, the vessel moved ever so slightly. Perhaps it was a gentle swell, or an imperceptible shifting in an underwater current, or nothing more than a light puff of air filling the mainsail. Whatever, with the movement of the boat came a movement of the rudder. And when the rudder moved on a forty-six-foot sloop, so did the rudder post. It moved now, crushing the four fingers on his right hand between the post and the hull.

For a moment he was aware of only a slight tug on his hand. Nerves destroyed, there was only numbness. But with the tug came the realization that he was bound to the hull. As his eyes adjusted to the dark green water, he was horrified to see his fingers wedged in the boat's apparatus, apparently partially severed.

He yanked on the safety line and tried to free his trapped hand. Almost immediately he realized that there was no way of dislodging it. If he were to survive, it would be without his fingers. He tried to tear his hand from its crushed appendages. As the seconds passed and his breath began to expire, he was gripped by terror. He was about to die –

Suddenly a form plummeted into the water next to him. Emily, wearing the red diving mask, grabbed his hand and laboured frantically to free it. Failing, she disappeared in a burst of bubbles to the surface. Once again he was alone, death imminent.

He continued to struggle, but became increasingly disoriented, enfeebled. He was about to let the sea wash into his bursting lungs when Emily was again beside him. A knife . . . his fingers . . . and then he was free, floating upward. A warm sensation, spilling into his lungs . . . Darkness . . .

Consciousness returned in the form of iridescent bands tightening about his forehead. He had lost all sense of time and place. Above him, an image. Very close. Wraith-like. Beautiful, with great flowing wings like spinnakers. Was he dead? Yes, he had drowned, his remains left dangling by his mangled hand from the *Tempest*'s stern like derelict equipment.

But then came pain. In his chest. And the spirit, very close, pressing his chest, blowing into his mouth. He couldn't breathe, couldn't move. Finally, he turned his head, coughing.

With consciousness came patches of awareness. He was in the boat, Emily looking down at him. His hand? He moved his eyes down, to the right. There, in a mass of blood was the stump, fingers gone. The image had little impact. He had no emotions left.

Where was Emily? She'd gone. He moved his eyes. There she was. On her knees, retching. But then she was beside him, applying a tourniquet, breathing heavily. 'I found some flares,' she said, 'in the emergency kit. I'll set them off. They'll come.'

He looked up at the dark sky. A solitary star, Polaris. He was back from the dead. Alive . . . Emily . . .

Chapter 27

'Twenty thousand copies? By an unknown author? There must be more to it than that, Dick . . .'

Richard squirmed. He was undergoing an orchiectomy without benefit of anaesthesia. Performing the operation was Norman Kaplin. It was the weekly editorial meeting at Hollard House. In attendance were Richard, Moseley, sales director Stanley Wharton and Norman. Presiding was Robert Bennett. At the moment, the subject of discussion was *The Sanctuary* manuscript and Norman had the floor.

'I've read it very carefully, and I must say I can't see it published successfully. What are your thoughts, Moseley?'

There was absolute silence for several seconds, and Moseley's swallowing process could be heard throughout the room. 'I think . . . well, I think it's come a long way . . .from the original submission, that is.' Moseley's eyes shifted nervously from Norman to Richard, to Norman, to the president.

When it was apparent that Moseley was not going to enlarge on his comment, Norman turned to the sales director. 'How about you, Stanley? Have you read it?'

'No, I haven't.' Relief exuded from Stanley's words.

'I talked to Grace Miller about the poetry in the novel,' Norman resumed. 'She said that while it was intellectually controlled, the energy was towards a closure of form. I believe the way she put it was there was little passion, that it didn't add to her understanding of life.'

'That bitch,' Richard thought. He'd talked to her no more than a week before on the elevator, and she'd told him the work was conceptually profound, at times brilliant. She was jumping ship like the rest of the rats. Well, if it were passion she wanted, she'd get it. Wait 'til their monthly meeting. He'd add to her understanding of life all right.

'I gave it to a friend to read on a confidential basis,' Norman continued. 'To get an independent opinion. I asked Arnold Seigler to look at it, and his opinion – '

'You gave *The Sanctuary* to Arnold Seigler?' Richard interrupted, leaning forward, his eyes blazing.

'Yes, what's wrong with that?' Norman said. 'I've had him read manuscripts for years, Dick – '

'First of all, my name isn't *Dick*.' He knew Norman called him Dick because of the vulgar anatomical connotation, and it infuriated him. 'Secondly, I don't think you had a right to show this before consulting me. It's one thing distributing galleys, and quite another giving someone an unfinished manuscript – '

'I thought it was finished,' Norman responded. 'According to this schedule the copy-editing has been completed. Look.' He held up a copy of *The Sanctuary*. 'The manuscript is supposed to go to the typesetter next week. Isn't this the time to get the opinions we're looking for?'

'No, it isn't. Lawyers get manuscripts, not reviewers.'

Bob Bennett cleared his throat. 'Pardon me, gentlemen. Richard, this morning I received a call from our lawyers. Somehow the people at Bayrock got hold of a copy of the manuscript.'

'*The Sanctuary* manuscript?'

'That's correct. Their lawyers contacted our counsel and quoted portions of the text that they claimed are libellous *per se*. They've threatened to enjoin its publication.'

'But how did they ever get the manuscript?'

'No idea,' Bennett said.

'The author was very careful. Of course, the way it's apparently been given out . . .' He turned and looked at Norman, who avoided his eyes.

'At any rate we're going to have to deal with the problem,' Bennett said. 'I have no way of knowing at this point to what extent it's libellous. I suspect the people out there may have some basis for their charges, in view of the author's membership in the club. Since the book is still in the early stages – you say it hasn't gone to the typesetter yet – I'm hoping that by making excisions and modifying portions of the text we can still salvage it. Now, Richard, I don't want to see you get bogged down in legal matters, diverted from more important matters. Therefore, I'd like to ask Norman, here, to look into the specific libel aspects with our lawyers and to report back to us. I'm sure you'll want to hold *The Sanctuary* in abeyance pending Norman's report.'

By the time Richard returned to his office, his emotions were rent, the fires of suspicion he held for conglomerate publishing fanned by the encounter. Immediately he placed a call to Emily in Old Hampton.

'I've some bad news, Emily. We've run into some difficulties with *The Sanctuary*. Somehow the management at Bayrock got a copy of the manuscript . . .'

He told her in detail what had happened at the editorial meeting, explaining his adversarial relationship with Norman Kaplin and Arnold Seigler.

'Kaplin's determined to stop publication of the book. He may well have started all the commotion out there. He and Seigler had copies of the manuscript. Either would be capable of sending it to Bayrock, if for no other reason than to make waves. They're familiar with the club, they each have a place in Southampton.'

'But what about Bennett, the new president? You said he was reasonable. Won't he – ?'

'He takes his orders from British American. If their lawyers perceive problems, they won't let it be published. In the final analysis, when things get sticky, British American will decide what we publish. It's as simple as that.'

'Really?' There was surprise in Emily's voice. 'Steve indicated that publishing companies were pretty independent.'

Richard laughed derisively. 'Only the most naïve would believe it. Sure, they'll give us all the independence we want until something develops that starts them sweating in the boardroom. Every director has a vested interest in something. If his interests are affected, then naturally he's going to react. The boardroom is his arena. That's a major problem developing in publishing. It's an insidious process, very subtle. The companies who do most of the business are owned by conglomerates.'

Emily was strangely calm. 'You think this Norman Kaplin will try to stir things up at British American?'

'I'm sure of it. He knows I'm committed to *The Sanctuary*. He'll do everything he can to exploit any problems.'

'You said he and his friend Seigler have a place out here?'

'That's right. Ocean Avenue. Arnold's gay, hangs out at Jonathan's, that bar on Market Street.'

'Is Kaplin gay too?'

'I don't think so, not the way he chases women. Arnold bought a big place out there several years ago, and there's a carriage house on the grounds that Norman rents from him.'

Another pause. 'Well, Richard, it's all quite disappointing. From what you say, this Kaplin fellow is going to be a real problem.'

'Maybe we could have lunch Monday. I can fill you in on what's happening here . . . by the way, Lydia called me again.'

'She did? What's on *her* mind?'

'Well . . . as you know, she's upset about the book, has been from the beginning. Doesn't think it should be published. Maybe you could quiet her down. It won't help things if *she* starts – '

'Don't worry,' Emily said firmly. 'I'll quieten her down . . .'

Chapter 28

'That bitch . . . !'

A loud crash had followed the words, and Emily had stormed from the house. That had been earlier in the day after Emily heard from Richard that Lydia had called him about her novel. After she'd hung up with Richard, she had reached for the closest object, which happened to be a priceless nineteenth-century iridescent tiffany vase, and had thrown it across the room, where it smashed against a 200-year-old Venetian oil.

Now Lydia stood inside the door of the downstairs study surveying the damage. She straightened the painting on the wall and tried to smooth the damaged canvas. It could be repaired, she thought, the restoration invisible to all but a trained eye. The painting would never be the same, but she hadn't much cared for it anyway – an obscure oil depicting two gondoliers on the Grand Canal.

She stopped and gathered up the pieces of the vase, which had been something she really liked. Still, it could have been worse. Like the time her sister returned home after tennis and lost her temper. She'd taken her racquet and swatted Lydia's pet parrot in flight. Later, in a characteristically strange effort at restitution, Emily had offered to stuff it for her.

Lydia carried the pieces of the vase to the kitchen and put them on the counter while she looked for something in which to store them. Possibly they could be glued, although it seemed unlikely.

After putting the remnants in a small box she stood for a moment looking through the kitchen window. It was late afternoon. A soft steady rain had been falling since morning and it was unusually dark for the time of day. A neighbour's grey Bentley drove past, its heavy tyres hissing on the puddled black asphalt of Forsythia Lane. Across the road a fringe of pink roses huddled in the rain, their colour contrasting with the lush green jungle behind.

Lydia wondered if Emily had gone to the Sanctuary when she stormed out earlier. Wherever she was, Lydia was grateful she was there and not home.

Suddenly there was a loud meow from the back of the house. Stray cats found Lydia's back door a hospitable place. She turned from the window and went to the refrigerator, where she surveyed the contents. A few liver pâté hors d'oeuvres were on a plate, left over from the previous evening. Lydia had a special fondness for liver pâté and normally would have had them for lunch but the fall-out with Emily had affected her appetite.

She carried the plate to the rear of the house and placed it on the back step. The cat, a large black-and-white tom that she called Topper softly moved in for the feast. She patted him on the head, closed the door, and returned to the kitchen. After washing and drying some utensils that Emily had left in the sink earlier, she stood for a moment looking out of the window at the rain. It would be a good day to go into town, she thought. She needed some groceries, and the stores would be less crowded on account of the weather. She went to a lavatory near the front door and freshened up, then took a raincoat from the hall closet and left the house.

Emily returned later that night, filled with nervous anticipation of what awaited her inside the house. The upstairs lights were out, heightening her expectations. After parking her car in the garage she walked to the back of the premises, intending to enter through the rear kitchen door. It was a dark overcast night but the rain had stopped. She proceeded towards a pale light that cast an eerie glow over the back door.

As she approached she noticed the plate with the remains of the hors d'oeuvres on the back step. A look of surprise came over her face. Her dark eyes took in the surrounding terrain. Then she saw it. Several feet away in an overgrown flowerbed, mouth open, eyes glazed, lying rigidly on its back.

'I'll be damned,' she said in a low whisper. 'Wouldn't you know? She fed them to the goddamn cat.'

Chapter 29

Arnold Seigler was lying on his back in the rear seat of a white Mercedes, his short legs protruding limply from the open door. The car was parked at the end of a remote sandy road in the Hamptons that wended its way down through the dunes to the beach.

It was a bright summer night and a pleasant breeze came at intervals from the ocean, the sort of night that inspired lovers. Arnold's feelings were not shared by the person with him. Standing outside the car observing a naked Arnold, disgust in his eyes, was a blond-haired man in his late twenties. He was wearing a dark blue box-like jacket, light blue denim slacks with tapered cuffs, and white tennis shoes. His clothes were baggy and unstructured, in keeping with contemporary resort fashion.

'You miserable . . . You promised you'd tell me before . . .'

Arnold, his energies spent, was only half-listening. Rarely if ever in his forty-two years had he known such a thrilling sexual experience.

His day had started innocently enough. It was Friday, and he had arrived at his office in midtown Manhattan about eleven. He was later than usual, having stopped at a Madison Avenue shop to buy a navy-blue shirt and a pair of yellow slacks that he planned to wear in the Hamptons on the weekend. The clothes described Arnold's physique – shirt, size 34; trousers, 34 waist with a 26-inch inseam. Although modest in stature, Arnold had a voracious appetite for such pleasures as food, good wine, books, the theatre, and parties. But above all, Arnold loved young men.

He was not unpleasant-looking. He had thinning sandy hair, which on occasion he had tried to lighten (sometimes with dreadful orangy results), rather plain features and round hazel eyes magnified by thick glasses. Since he'd not been in the sun for over two weeks he looked pale as he stepped off the elevator and entered his office on the twelfth floor of his building.

Melissa Trowbridge, an affable young woman who served as his assistant, looked up from her desk as he entered. 'Morning, Arnold. There're some calls on your desk. Gary Hoffman phoned a few minutes ago. He's upset. Apparently you told him a review would be in last week's issue. They wanted it for an ad.'

'Too bad,' said Arnold, skipping the morning amenities. 'I write 'em, I don't schedule them.'

Arnold's office, which more or less reflected how the management regarded him, was a narrow room with no windows. What space there was was cluttered with two desks, a file cabinet, a word processor and Melissa, who was as wide as she was high.

Arnold had to squeeze past her to reach his desk, which, classroom style, was directly behind hers. He went through the material on his desk hurriedly, anxious to leave the office so that he could beat the traffic to the Hamptons. Most of the calls could wait until Monday. One was from the head of a large public relations company he knew well. The man had cultivated Arnold's friendship, entertaining him frequently. The critic was cautious about this type of acquaintance, aware of the implicit *quid pro quo* in such relationships. After all, there was little value in promoting a bad review.

Another call was from the publicity director of a small publishing house. It was a typical call, the kind that irritated Arnold. Usually the caller would purportedly want to know if Arnold had received galleys of a book, and then try to sweet talk him.

The one message that could be important was from his accountant, and Arnold would have answered it immediately if the man hadn't left word he would be away from his office. The IRS was conducting an audit, and a sensitive item had surfaced, having to do with the disposition of hundreds of books that Arnold received regularly from various publishing houses. Since the firms sent the books for review free of charge, their ultimate destination could be an embarrassment. In fact, Arnold had an outlet for the inventory on the Lower East Side. Cursing the accountant silently for being away from his office – now he'd have to worry all weekend about the call – he looked around his desk for the material for his column.

'Melissa, where's this week's copy?' Immediately, he was sorry that he had used the word *copy*. Referring to the book synopses that Melissa prepared for him on a weekly basis as 'copy' was a Freudian slip. Arnold relied on his assistant to screen books and prepare notes for his review. He tried hard to keep Melissa's copy, which appeared in the column under Arnold's name, to a minimum.

But Arnold did read the books he reviewed. Or at least skimmed them, and he avoided using dust-jacket copy, although a little of it would creep in when Melissa was under pressure.

It was a pressured morning, so Arnold had to rely on Melissa's notes more than he would have liked. He edited the reviews she had prepared, and after hurriedly synthesizing his views with hers on one of the books that he'd read carefully, he handed the copy over his assistant's shoulder and left for the Hamptons.

* * *

It was nearly ten that night when Arnold, wearing his new navy-blue shirt and yellow slacks, arrived at Jonathan's. Jonathan's was not exclusively a gay bar. Its reputation for good food attracted a variety of people. As usual on a Friday night, the bar was crowded.

From the moment Arnold first laid eyes on the blond man at the bar, he was smitten. Long flaxen hair, a small nose, high cheekbones and a confident jaw. A small blond moustache accentuated a deep tan. He had little difficulty striking up a conversation. He had ordered a brandy, and this, following martinis and a bottle of wine he had shared earlier with Norman Kaplin over dinner, had left him in a confident, adventurous mood. After brushing off a waspish man with yellow hair, in his fifties, he moved closer to the blond man at the bar. He positioned himself in such a way that when the person moved he bumped Arnold slightly. When the man turned to apologize Arnold was gracious and forgiving. 'That's all right . . .'

Bill Summerfield described himself as an account executive with a large advertising firm. When he mentioned that he was writing a novel on the side, Arnold was quick to see the possibilities. He felt sure the person was gay. His manner, the pitch of his voice, the gestures. All were effeminate.

Soon they were talking as friends, engrossed in conversation about publishing. Did Bill have an agent? No? Oh, you had to have an agent. Would Arnold know any agents? Better than that, Arnold had a close friend who was a publisher. There was more brandy, one thing led to another, and Arnold soon found himself in what was implicitly another *quid pro quo* relationship. Would Arnold be inclined to take a ride over to where Bill was staying in Bridgehampton? Arnold was inclined.

He followed Bill outside to the parking lot, and here it was decided that since Bill had a commitment later in

Bridgehampton each would take his own car. After seeing Arnold's jeep – an ancient thing he kept in the Hamptons for beach duty – and wondering if Arnold could keep up, Bill climbed into a gleaming white Mercedes and drove off.

Once out on the Montauk Highway Arnold had to press the accelerator to the floor to keep the Mercedes' tail-lights in view. His vision, not that good during the day, was particularly poor at night, complicating matters. Canvas side curtains that once covered the jeep's chassis had long since been discarded, so that the cockpit, except for the windshield and top, was open to the elements. Now the wind whistled through the jeep, threatening to blow off the canvas top as they roared down the highway. Under different circumstances Arnold might have slowed and taken his chances on losing the other car. But now his eyes were riveted on the two tail-lights ahead, his resolution as hard and stiff as the steel spillbar overhead.

At the outskirts of Bridgehampton the red lights suddenly veered to the right. Arnold followed down a dirt road towards the ocean. Soon they emerged from some wooded pines into a remote clearing in the dunes over-looking the beach. The Mercedes ground to a stop, and Arnold pulled up along side, the cockpit of the jeep enveloped in a cloud of finely powdered sand.

If the speed with which Bill Summerfield had raced to the beach were excessive, it was no more so than his approach to the sexual interlude that followed. Arnold, dusting himself off, had barely got out of the jeep when Bill was leading him to the rear seat of the Mercedes.

'How about a swim?' Arnold began, 'I bet the water – '

'No time,' said Bill. 'I'm due in Bridgehampton in fifteen minutes. You won't let me down with your pub-lisher friend, will you?' Bill said, pushing Arnold back and removing his glasses.

'Of course not,' Arnold said, ' I promised.'

'How about a quote for my novel?' he asked, starting to unbutton Arnold's shirt.

'A what?'

'You know, a blurb. For the jacket.'

'Reviewers *never* give blurbs,' Arnold said. 'Besides, I haven't seen it. You said you haven't even finished it.'

'It's almost done. How about it? Just a few words?' He began unzipping Arnold's trousers.

'Well, we'll see . . .'

Bill hesitated.

'All right, all *right*,' Arnold said, shivering with excitement. 'I'll try to help you out . . . some way.' Leaning forward, he unzipped Bill's fly and reached inside. Although impressed by his prodigious manhood, Arnold was surprised that the man was not otherwise aroused. He felt cold, limp, indeed, almost *lifeless*. 'You . . . ah . . . don't seem very excited,' Arnold allowed.

'No time,' Bill said. He pushed the critic firmly back down on the seat. 'Relax, this is going to have to be fast.'

He quickly stripped Arnold, dropping the garments on the floor of the car. 'Just be damned sure you let me know before you do it, OK?'

Within moments Arnold's small body was a squirming dynamo of orgasmic joy. Suddenly Bill pulled away. 'Oh! You repulsive little creep.' Coughing, he backed abruptly from the car.

Arnold put on his glasses, slid from the car, kicked off his loafers and started towards the water, assuming Bill would follow. He was halfway to the ocean when he heard the Mercedes. Startled, he looked up to see the car backing into a quick turn. With a roar of the engine and grinding tyres it disappeared.

Astonished, Arnold ran back. In the road were his

192

loafers. He rushed to the jeep and looked inside. Nothing. Bill had left with Arnold's clothes in the back seat.

Arnold was suddenly sweating but he felt cold. What to do? There wasn't a thing in the jeep. His eyes travelled over the beach. It was as bare as he was. He tried to wrench the canvas top from the jeep. Having withstood twenty years of punishment from natural forces, it wasn't about to succumb to Arnold.

He climbed into the jeep, sobering rapidly, contemplating his options. Home was some fifteen miles away. In a normal car it would have been no problem, but in a jeep CJ-5 it was a definite problem. The sides of the chassis were cut very low. Driving it home would be equivalent to sitting nude in Macy's window.

As time passed and realization settled in that Bill was not coming back, he decided to make a run for it. Starting the engine, he revved the motor. He then buckled the frayed seat belt over his groin. It offered little security. Shoving the stick shift into gear, he adjusted his glasses and headed out to Montauk Highway.

Arnold might well have made it if it hadn't been for the last intersection. It was the busy corner of Route 27 and Hampton Village, little more than four miles from home, where his adventure ended. Observing a red light at the crossroads, he eased to a halt. It was then that he saw the vehicle parked in the gas station close by. A police cruiser.

For over a minute nothing moved in the jeep except Arnold's eyes, which shifted back and forth between the stoplight and the uniformed driver in the cruiser. Don't panic, he thought. Stay calm. Look natural. He casually reached up and stroked his hair. Perhaps it was the movement of his hand that caught the officer's attention. He glanced sideways towards the jeep. Arnold exchanged the look. The bored indifferent eyes under the visor focused on him, and then slowly widened in disbelief.

The light changed and Arnold, still looking natural, slipped the shift into gear and eased ahead. He got no more than a hundred feet when the cruiser, lights flashing, darted from the station directly behind him. Arnold pulled over to the kerb, heart throbbing, his world ending. He sat in the jeep, head down, eyes closed, covering himself with both hands as pedestrians gathered.

The rest was straight from one of Arnold's nightmares. From somewhere back near the flashing lights came a deep, authoritative command:

POLICE OFFICER! GET OUT OF THAT VEHICLE . . . SLOWLY . . . KEEP BOTH HANDS OVER YOUR HEAD!

Chapter 30

'I'd like to have heard the real story . . .'

'Yeah, you can be sure there was a helluva lot more to it than what he told the police . . .'

'Who'd believe that selfish little fag would ever stop to give anyone a ride . . .?'

'Unless he wanted to make a pass at him . . .'

Richard Fox's telephone was crackling. There had been coverage of the Arnold Seigler affair in the local Southampton paper. It had caused a flurry of excitement at Hollard House. The piece recounted how Seigler, a reviewer of books, had been robbed of his belongings Friday night after picking up a hitchhiker, the police report said that Seigler was driving naked when taken into custody; that the thief had commandeered his vehicle at gunpoint, forced him to disrobe and then gone off with Seigler's personal effects. The victim described the perpetrator as a large man with dark bushy hair and a beard.

Richard was on the phone, laughing to a colleague about the incident, his back to the door, feet stretched out on his credenza, when Norman Kaplin quietly sifted into his office and sat down.

'Large bushy-haired man, like hell,' Richard was saying. 'If he ever did stop to pick anyone up, it was probably a runty little fag with orange hair like himself.'

At this point Norman cleared his throat. Richard turned, surprised. 'Ah . . . Charlie, have to go, call you later.' Richard removed his feet from the rear desk and turned towards Kaplin.

'Morning, Norman, I uh . . ., I heard your friend had a rather rough time of it Friday night.'

'Yes,' Norman said, eyes flitting about the room.

'Rather embarrassing, I'd think. Losing his clothes and all. What happened?'

'I know nothing whatever about it. Look, I'd like to come right to the point of why I'm here, if you don't mind. I discussed *The Sanctuary* manuscript with Bob Bennett this morning. He's on his way to Chicago and suggested I talk to you about my findings.'

Richard moved back to his chair, the adrenalin starting to flow.

'The lawyers at British American have given their opinion. They don't think Hollard should proceed with the book. It's full of references to places, events, even people. The legal ramifications are – '

'Wait a minute.' Richard leaned forward in his chair, face reddening. 'They haven't looked at the revisions yet. I'm sure when Bob Bennett sees the changes he'll – '

'I doubt that very much. The lawyers feel that even with revisions, there'd be a residual perception that could cause problems.'

'Look, we have a lot of time and effort invested in that project, and we're not about to cave in because of some fuzzy legal opinion – '

'Frankly, I find your persistence rather odd,' Norman said. 'The book isn't that far along. Why are you so hot to publish it? Could there be, you know, any other reason?'

The remark caught Richard hard and low. Despite his discretion, he sensed involvement with Emily was the subject of conversation in the office. 'Look, Norman. There's a code in the profession I suspect you haven't heard about,' he said, restraining himself with difficulty. 'It's called editorial integrity. You can tell your people that we're under contract to publish that book and we intend to honour our agreement.'

Norman sat for a moment. 'That's your final word?'

'It is,' said Richard. 'And you can also tell your friends that we've operated pretty successfully here these past ten years without their help. Now, unless you have something else . . .'

'Fine. I'll see to it that they know exactly what your position is.' Norman stood abruptly and walked to the door and paused and looked back at Richard. 'Oh, yes, one other matter. There's an editorial assistant on the tenth floor who I understand is quite upset. Something about career promises made to her . . . Maybe we can discuss it when you're *not* so busy. Perhaps at our weekly meeting.'

When Norman had gone, Richard took the pencil he had been twisting nervously in his hand and flipped it on to his desk. He realized he had made every mistake for which Norman could have hoped.

But Sheila! That was a whole different arena. Norman would exploit her for all she was worth. He'd use anything, anybody. And Sheila was a talker. Not only that, she exaggerated almost as much as Norman. Career promises? God, she was capable of saying that she was promised Mrs H's job if she shacked up with him. And she'd never understand she was being used. With Norman encouraging her, it could lead to a lawyer . . . anything!

But he had few options. The position he had hoped to arrange for her at the other publishing firm was far from certain. She'd had an interview that had not gone well. In the meantime she was ticking away on the tenth floor.

He thought of Emily. He had arranged to meet her for lunch at noon at the Pastures Restaurant. The prospect lifted his spirits somewhat.

The bell on his intercom sounded, interrupting his thoughts. 'Mr Fox, Tank is on the line.'

Richard quickly reached for the phone. 'Hi, Tank.'

'Hello, Daddy. Grams said it was all right for me to call.'

'Sure. How's everything?'

'Daddy, you got a telephone call last night.'

'I did?'

'Yes, when you went to the drug store.'

'Who was it?'

'I forgot to tell you. Grams said I should call and tell you.'

'That's all right. Who was it, Tank?'

'It was that lady.'

'Lady?'

'You know, the one Grams doesn't like.'

'Miss Fielding?'

'No. Miss . . . um . . . Miss Tomorrow.'

'Oh, Miss Morrow. What did she – ?'

'I liked her. We talked a lot.'

'You did? Good. What did she say?'

'She said she was going to be late for lunch.'

'Did Grams talk to her? Let me speak to – '

'No, Grams was next door. I talked to her. I forgot to tell you.'

'Let me speak to Grams.'

'Daddy, she said I could come out to visit her. Across the street from her they have birds and ducks and all kinds of animals. She said she was going to ask you to bring me out next week so that . . . Daddy, here's Grams.'

There was the sound of the phone being dropped, retrieved, and then his mother came on the phone. 'Hello, Richard.'

'Hi, I'm glad he finally told me about the call. I was getting ready to leave to –'

'He never mentioned it till now. He just forgot about it. People shouldn't rely on children for messages.'

'Well . . . I guess you stepped away for a minute. Did she say how late she'd be?'

'Jared told me she said a half hour, but you can't be sure of anything.'

'That's all right. I can probably call her. Incidentally, I have a meeting at four. Make sure Jared knows I'll be late tonight.'

Following the call Richard sat for a moment thinking about his son's talk with Emily. How much had he said to her? Tank was a great communicator. Emily would have been thoroughly briefed on just about everything that happened in the Fox household.

He glanced at his watch. Almost 11:30. Should he try to reach Emily to find out the time of their lunch? No, she'd be on her way from Old Hampton by this time. He'd just go to Pastures and wait for her.

Standing, he went to his lavatory. Here, he wiped his face with a warm washcloth and carefully combed his hair, paying due attention to the thinning crown. From the medicine cabinet he took a bottle of cologne, dabbed a few drops on his hands, and applied it to his chin. Mustn't overdo it. Just enough for a light scent when he greeted her and brushed her with a kiss. Then he gargled with mouthwash, delivered a quick burst of deodorant under each arm and, bearing a redolence of spring, departed for the Pastures.

Chapter 31

'Hello, Francesco. Table for two, please.'

'Your name, sir?'

'Fox,' Richard replied, annoyed. The ten-dollar bill he had passed to the maitre d' the last time he had gone to Pastures had little residual value when it came to names.

'I don't see that here, Sir,' Francesco said, speaking with an accent, running his finger down a list.

'*Richard* Fox,' Richard repeated, uneasiness creeping into his voice. He never handled rejection well, and the prospect of being turned away from one of New York's most prestigious restaurants with Emily was unnerving. 'I made the reservation Friday.'

The Pastures was one of Manhattan's more fashionable literary salons, a place where notables lunched, conferred, and noted other notables. The decor changed with the seasons, and was eminently sucessful in providing a feeling of dining alfresco.

The power base of the establishment was where Francesco stood behind a podium, holding keys to the important tables. Although the seasonal decor was one of summer, there was a decided winter chill around the podium at the moment.

'I'm sorry, sir,' the maitre d' said after reexamining his list. 'I have no Mr Fox. Are you sure you made the reservation?'

'I'm certain,' Richard said, his nervousness showing. 'What do I have to do, have the damn thing certified?'

'Your name isn't Fogs?' Francesco asked, his finger stopping at a name. 'Yes, that's what happened. I wrote it down as Fogs. I'm very sorry. Come with me, Mr Fogs.'

Richard followed the man across the room to a table. After ordering a glass of wine he settled back to wait for Emily.

Half an hour passed when he noticed interest displayed towards the entranceway by the usually indifferent clientele. He turned and saw Emily following a restaurant escort across the room towards his table. She was wearing a light-blue cotton dress fully cut but gathered at the waist with a wide dark-blue belt. Her shoes and small handbag matched the belt. The clothes though simple, were stylish and gave her a girlish look.

When she saw Richard, she delivered a dazzling smile and approached him with her distinctive gait.

'I was beginning to wonder if you might be waiting for me at the apartment,' he said, standing as she came to the table. When he gave her a light kiss on her cheek, her hair brushed against his face and there was a fragrance of flowers.

After sitting down she ordered a daiquiri, and rested back in her chair. She seemed tired, and more diffident than usual. 'I'm sorry to have kept you waiting,' she said. 'Did your son tell you I called last night? I had to pick up some things in town before I left.'

'I was running late myself,' Richard said. 'It worked out fine.'

She took a cigarette from her purse and leaned forward so Richard could light it. As he did so he focused on her long slender fingers and manicured nails.

'Your son's awfully cute,' she said, leaning back. 'Jared, is it? He certainly talks well for a six-year-old.'

'No, nothing sphinxian about my Jared,' Richard said with a wry smile. 'I'm sure he filled you in pretty well on the doings of the Fox family.'

'Oh, yes. His school, teachers . . . everything, He said you're taking him to your place in Southampton for a few weeks. Why don't you bring him over for a visit? He'd love the Sanctuary.'

'Yes, he said that you'd told him about the Sanctuary. That would be nice.' Richard considered mentioning his son's disability but figured Emily was probably already aware of it, having talked to Jared about his school and teachers.

'I came in on one of those small commuter planes from the East Hampton Airport,' she said changing the subject. 'It was a bumpy ride. I began to feel a bit nauseated.'

'Well, you look great. Rewriting must agree with you.'

'If that novel had anything to do with it I'd look like Methuselah. And now, from what you've said about Kaplin and Seigler, it may *never* be published.'

Richard frowned. 'I had a meeting with Kaplin this morning . . .' He related what had taken place. 'Actually, Norman doesn't give a damn one way or the other about *The Sanctuary*. He's using it to stir up trouble between me and the new management. He's associate publisher. If I leave Hollard he's the logical one to take over.'

Emily ground her cigarette in the ashtray. 'I don't think I care for this Norman fellow.'

They ordered lunch and as they dined, Richard told her more about his longtime adversarial relationship with Kaplin and Seigler and the problems he expected working with Norman.

They had finished lunch and were having coffee when a tall, slender man passed their table and greeted Richard. 'Your friend Seigler is travelling light these days.'

Richard laughed. 'Well, you know Arnold, always a fashion plate.'

'You fellows live dangerously out there.' Then, noticing

Emily, he said, 'Oh, hello, Lydia. Didn't see you. How've you been? Any new books on the – ?'

'This is *Emily* Morrow,' Richard cut in. 'Lydia's sister. George Harder, Emily.'

'Oh, sorry,' the man said. 'You look so much like Lydia . . . Well, please tell her I said "hello".' With a final amenity, the man continued on his way.

'Who was that?' Emily asked.

'He used to be an editor at Hollard. That's how he knew Lydia. He was referring to Seigler's arrest.' Richard summarized the article about the reviewer that had appeared in the paper. When he finished he added, 'My only regret is that *Norman* wasn't with Seigler when it happened.'

Conversation stopped for a few moments, with Emily seeming to withdraw into herself. Suddenly she said, 'So you feel things would work out all right at Hollard if Norman Kaplin weren't there?'

'It would certainly be easier. I wouldn't be having the problems I have with *The Sanctuary*, that's for sure. If Norman suddenly dropped out of sight, it wouldn't bother me one bit. The same with his friend Seigler.'

Emily said nothing. She took a sip of her coffee. Over the rim of her cup, the dark eyes focused on Richard, thoughtfully.

Chapter 32

'How *dare* you call me.'

Arnold Seigler, seated at his desk behind Melissa, had taken a call from Bill Summerfield. The compact office was filled with tension.

'Please, Arnold, let me explain. You'll never know how dismayed I was to read that article – '

'*You* were dismayed? Do you realize what you did to *me?*'

Almost a week had passed since Arnold had been left clothesless at the beach, and he was still agonizing.

'I understand how you must feel,' Bill said, 'but I never realized your clothes were in the back seat. I was going to contact you to return them and then I saw the paper, and well . . . frankly, I've been reluctant to call because I knew you'd be angry and – '

'Angry is hardly the adjective. How you have the nerve to call, I don't know.'

'But, Arnold, I had no idea. I was upset that night when . . . well, you remember what happened, and I just took off. When I got home I noticed your clothes in the back seat. I drove right back to the beach, but you'd already gone. I can't tell you how sorry I am. By the way, what happened? The police apparently stopped you. You didn't actually pick up a hitch-hiker – '

'Are you insane? How could I have picked – ?' Arnold stopped, glancing towards Melissa. 'Look, I'm really not at liberty to talk at the moment.'

'May I call you back, then? I want to return your things.

Would you mind if I called you, say, on the weekend? I'd really like to see you again, Arnold.'

Arnold hesitated, memories of the pleasanter aspect of their experience surfacing. 'I can't stop you from calling, I suppose.' His voice was testy but softening. 'I'm in the local directory. I'm sorry, I have to go now.'

'Melissa,' he said when he had hung up. 'I'm going to lunch a little early.' He squeezed out from behind his desk. 'Norman Kaplin may call. He's pestering me for a confidential reaction to that *Sanctuary* novel. I told him it was terrible.'

In fact, Arnold had not read the book but was proceeding from his firmly established conviction that any novel published by Richard Fox would have to be terrible. Melissa hunched forward in her chair so Arnold could pass. With their desks aligned behind one another in the tight quarters, they were like a two-man bobsled team with Melissa's huge body the determining factor as to which direction Arnold would go.

'Also, tell Norman I'll be late getting out tomorrow. I'll pick him up for dinner about eight o'clock.'

It was early Friday evening when Arnold next heard from Bill Summerfield. He was in his house in Southampton about to go to dinner when the doorbell rang. He assumed it was Norman Kaplin and was surprised to find Bill on the porch carrying two packages.

'Hi, Arnold,' he said, 'I hope you'll forgive me for coming unannounced.'

'Oh, it's you,' Arnold said. After a moment's hesitation he opened the door wider. 'Come in.'

Although pleasantly surprised to see him, Arnold maintained reserve as he ushered his guest into the living room, and motioned to him to sit down. The living room was an open area with high ceilings and bone-white walls covered with brightly coloured abstract paintings. Oriental scatter rugs covered a polished oak floor. Hides of exotic animals were displayed on both the floor and walls, including that of a large zebra tacked above a white brick fireplace. Baroque statuary was standing, resting, leaning or hanging everywhere.

'I brought your things.' Bill put the packages on a glass coffee table as he sat down on a couch. 'I'm sorry to resurrect a bad subject, but I *must* tell you how awful I feel about your experience – '

'I suppose it could have been worse,' said Arnold, 'although I don't really know how. Let's not talk about it, all right?'

'Of course.' Bill looked about the room. 'I love your place.'

'Do you? Some people don't care for it.'

'Oh yes. It comes together so well. I particularly like those things . . . those animal skins. Nice touch. Must've been a job skinning those mothers.'

'I beg your pardon,' Arnold said, taken aback. 'Well, I certainly didn't skin them.'

'No, of course not.' Bill said quickly, his dark eyes lingering on the hides. 'It's just that . . . well, I have an interest in taxidermy. Those paintings over there are magnificent,' he continued, changing the subject.

Arnold sat observing his guest closely. The man was wearing the same dark-blue blazer and was just as handsome as he had been the other night. 'Thanks for returning my things,' he said, reaching for one of the packages on the coffee table.

'Actually, that one's my novel,' Bill said quickly. 'I hope you won't think it presumptuous of me to have brought it. You were kind enough to say that you'd give me a comment for it.'

'Oh? Oh . . .' Arnold let go of the package as though it

were hot, remembering the promise he had made when he would have promised anything. 'Would you like a drink?'

'Well, a martini? But I really shouldn't impose this way. You probably have plans.'

'Not really.' Arnold stood and walked to a small bar nearby. 'I'm having dinner later with Norman Kaplin. He's the publisher I told you about. You're welcome to join us.'

'Thanks, I wouldn't want to intrude.'

'No, we'd be glad to have you. Frankly we get bored with each other. You might learn more about publishing.'

After making the drink for his guest, Arnold made himself an extra-dry, extra-large martini. It was his first drink of the day. What better way to ease into the spirit of the weekend than with Bill and a martini?

'You'll have to come to dinner with us,' he repeated, carrying the drinks from the bar. 'I told you I'd arrange to have you meet Norman.'

'Thanks.' Bill took the drink.

'Know of any good spots?'

'There's a nice place over near the Bayrock Club. Alfredo's.'

'Never heard of it.'

'It's new. But I wonder whether I should intrude on your dinner plans. Why don't we wait and see what your friend Norman thinks?'

'Norman will do whatever I tell him,' Arnold said. 'He lives here on my grounds.' He proceeded to explain how Norman had been renting the carriage house in the rear. 'At a very nominal rate, I might add. It was nominal when he moved in and I've never raised the rent. That was *eight* years ago.' Arnold raised an eyebrow.

As they drank, Arnold became increasingly talkative, explaining his relationship with Norman. They were strictly friends, *nothing* more. He fixed another drink for his guest and himself. When Bill took out a cigarette from his jacket Arnold moved closer to light it.

'If you're sure I'm not imposing and if you decide to go to Alfredo's, I'd like to have you stop at my place for an after-dinner drink. It's not too far from there.'

'I'd like that, but I doubt if Norman would be up to it. He goes to bed early Friday night so that he's rested for the weekend. I'd like to stop by, though.'

'Why don't you and your friend follow me over in your car, then? After dinner you can come to my place. I'll give you a ride home afterward.'

'Perfect. I'll call Norman and tell him our plans. I told him I'd pick him up in a little while.'

'Ah . . . Arnold, I wonder if you would do me a favour. Would you, ah . . . would you think it presumptuous if I asked you to give me the blurb for my novel?'

Arnold took another swallow of his martini. He had no intention whatever of giving a comment. No reviewer would ever give a blurb. The most Arnold would even consider doing would be to give the manuscript to Norman, and then only in total confidence. 'Well . . . I'll try to take a look at it over the weekend – '

'Would you mind doing it now?'

'Now? You mean right now?'

'Yes, it would make me feel – '

'But how can I read it now?' Arnold asked with a mixture of amusement and annoyance. 'It will take me time to – '

'Oh, I couldn't ask you to read the whole thing. Here, I typed a little remark on the last page that I thought you could sign. He reached for the box and took out the last page of the manuscript, at the end of which was a brief statement. He put it in Arnold's lap.

'But this isn't . . . no, impossible . . . Leave the manuscript with me over the weekend and I'll show it – '

'You promised me, Arnold.'

'What? Oh, this is *too* much,' Arnold said, rolling his eyes.

'Please, Arnold. I realize I'm being forward but it would mean a great deal to me. I'd be *very* appreciative.'

Arnold paused, regarding the handsome face. He picked up the page and began to read:

I have read the foregoing novel and, in my opinion, it is one of the finest works to appear on the literary scene in recent years.

Arnold Seigler

'Good Lord, you expect me to sign *that?*'

'Why not?' Bill looked at him innocently.

'Why? Because it's outrageous. It's as though I were certifying your novel, like some notary public or something.' Then, afraid he was offending Bill, he said more quietly, 'You see, you don't understand publishing. It's almost funny what you're asking me to do. I'm a critic, a reviewer. I could never say that about *any* novel. I never *would* say it about any novel. Don't you see?'

'Well, then, write something you would say.'

'But . . . what's the hurry? I told you. I'll read it over the weekend.'

'Well, frankly, I wanted to work on the manuscript. I hadn't really planned on leaving it.'

'What? Look, Bill, honestly, don't you think you're being a bit unreasonable? I'm only asking for a few days to – '

'You're hedging,' Bill said, cooling.

'I'm not hedging.'

'You promised me a blurb.'

'But you have to be reasonable.'

'Oh, well, never mind.' Bill reached for the manuscript. 'Let's forget it.' He glanced at his watch.

Arnold panicked. He began to rationalize . . . Not many first novels were published. Chances of the comment ever being used were remote. Besides, he could always pass it off as a personal note to a friend, *not* intended for publication. Could he help it if some irresponsible . . . 'Here, let me look at it.' He reached for the manuscript.

'Oh, you don't have to bother,' Bill said, holding the box protectively. 'If you don't want to sign the comment you don't have to.'

The telephone rang. 'That's probably Norman,' Arnold sighed, standing and leaving the room. He returned shortly, confirming that it had been his friend. 'He's getting impatient. I told him you were coming to dinner with us and I'd be over in a few minutes.'

'Would you mind signing this before we go?'

'Look, Bill, I can't sign something like that.'

'Well, then, just scribble something here underneath that you feel would be appropriate.'

'Boy, you're really persistent.' Arnold took the page and wrote hurriedly, 'A fine first attempt. The author shows promise.'

'That's the best I can do for now. And *don't* show that to anyone unless you discuss it with me first, agreed?'

Bill took the page, glanced at what had been written and placed it in the box with the rest of the manuscript. 'Frankly, I'd hoped for something more enthusiastic,' he said coolly.

Arnold shrugged. 'I think under the circumstances I've been generous.' He started towards the door. 'You don't have to mention anything about that comment to Norman.'

'No, I won't. You're going to follow me?'

'Yes. I'll drive down to the carriage house and pick up Norman and meet you out front.'

After showing Bill out, Arnold drained the martini glass and entered the garage from a side door in the kitchen. He climbed into the jeep, backed it from the garage and proceeded down the narrow drive that led back to the carriage house.

Norman was waiting at the entrance when he pulled up. 'Who is this guy?' he asked as he crawled into the car.

'He's charming,' Arnold said. 'Wait till you meet him. He's written a novel. I only glanced at it but it doesn't look bad.'

Bill was standing next to his Mercedes when they reached the front of the house. Arnold eased to a stop next to him and Bill peered in Norman's side of the car.

'Bill, this is Norman Kaplin,' Arnold said. The two shook hands through the open side of the jeep. 'We'll follow you, okay?'

Bill nodded, went to his car and drove off. Arnold, in high spirits, followed closely in the jeep.

'Good-looking guy,' said Norman.

'He is that,' Arnold agreed.

'I wonder why he's wearing that wig? Do you think he's bald?'

'Wig? He's not wearing a wig.'

'The hell he isn't. Are you blind? Well, of course, you *are* blind. That guy is wearing a wig. I could tell when he bent over to look in. Anyone who could see would know it.'

Arnold, his enthusiasm tempered, fell silent.

It was getting dark when they reached the Montauk Highway and headed towards Old Hampton. The Mercedes immediately began to accelerate.

'Have you ever thought of investing in a *real* car?' asked Norman, trying to be heard above the wind and the roar of the motor. 'I would think you'd had enough of this thing.'

Arnold did not answer. The tail-lights of the Mercedes were drawing away and the jeep was at full throttle.

'Aren't we going awfully fast?' Norman asked. 'What's the hurry?'

'I'm afraid we'll lose him.'

'So, what's the difference? We'll meet him there.'

'I don't know where the restaurant is.'

His senses blunted by the martinis, Arnold cared little about speed. His attention was glued to the red lights in the darkness ahead and the promise they held for the evening.

Near the outskirts of Old Hampton the Mercedes slowed and turned off the highway. They followed closely as the car made a series of turns before straightening out on a country road.

'Where the hell are we?' Norman demanded. 'That sign we just passed said Forsythia Lane.'

'I'm not sure. We must be somewhere near the Bayrock Club. Alfredo's should be close.'

'This guy must be a member of Bayrock,' Norman said.

'Why? He never mentioned anything about – '

'I noticed a Bayrock parking permit in his rear window when we were leaving.'

The Mercedes again drew away at great speed. As the lights became distant, Arnold's anxiety mounted. 'We're losing him,' he said above the noise of the engine.

'For God's sake slow down!' Norman shouted.

But Arnold, his sexual expectations fading with the disappearing tail-lights, was not listening. He did his best to coax more speed from the jeep as they rocketed down the lane. Mansions flashed past the open cockpit, and the Sanctuary became a dark blur of vegetation.

'Didn't you see that *sign?*' Norman screamed.

'What sign? Did it say Alfredo's – '

'There's a curve ahead, you dumb bastard. It said five miles per . . .'

Norman's words were lost on the wind, as they came over a rise to find that Forsythia Lane had disappeared.

Chapter 33

The untimely deaths of Norman Kaplin and Arnold Seigler were duly noted, without emotion, by the publishing industry.

One of Richard Fox's first calls was to Emily in Old Hampton.

'I read about it,' she said. 'I guess everyone out here heard the crash. Lydia said they apparently never saw the curve. The car ploughed straight through a potato field for a hundred feet before it struck a tree in the Sanctuary and exploded.'

'At least it was quick.'

'Yes, if they had to go, I suppose that was as good a way as any,' Emily agreed quietly.

There was a brief pause – a split second of respectful silence for the departed – and then Richard said, 'At least we won't have to worry about Arnold panning your book.'

'No, in fact he gave us a blurb.'

'A blurb?'

'For the jacket.'

'Arnold? But how – ?'

'Well, I'm getting a little ahead of myself. It might be better if I finished the book before I start talking about blurbs. This rewriting is difficult,' she said, changing the subject.

'How are the revisions going? You said you might have them this week. I think Bob Bennett wants to see them.'

'I'm almost finished. I hope they'll satisfy your lawyers. There's one person we're never going to please, though.

'Only one?'

'Lydia. She's even more upset. She's going to call you again. I'm alerting you.'

'Can't you explain to her that you're changing the setting, making modifications – '

'She won't listen. She's convinced she's the protagonist. She's burned up about it, and people at the club are fanning the flames. Everyone out here knows about it now. I guess we may have to hold up your club application till things calm down – '

'Oh, don't worry about *that*. Really, forget it. Ah . . . what should I expect from Lydia when she calls?'

'She'll, of course, try to convince you not to publish it. She'll invoke my father's name, how he helped develop Bayrock, the Morrow family's reputation. You'll have to be firm, Richard.'

'Maybe when she hears what we've done to change the locales and – '

'I doubt it. Once Lydia sets her mind on something she's deceptively persistent. Oh, she'll act sweet but she could be more of a problem than you think.

'How far do you think she's prepared to go?'

'She'll do whatever she thinks is necessary to keep it from being published. First, calling you. If that doesn't work, then I imagine she'll contact our lawyers.'

'That could be serious. If another law firm starts pressuring British American . . .'

'Well, we'll see,' Emily said quietly. 'It may not come to that.'

There was a pause, and then Richard said, 'You're almost finished with the revisions? I'm coming out on the weekend. I have to drop my son off in Southampton and then go on out to Montauk. I'll be going right past your place. I could pick up the manuscript.'

'Fine. Why don't you bring Jared along? You could leave him with me while you go to Montauk.'

Richard hesitated.

'If you're thinking it's an imposition, you're wrong. I'd be delighted to have him. I told him on the phone I'd show him the Sanctuary. He'll love it.'

'Well . . . if you're sure it won't interfere with your day – '

'Not at all. That's settled then.'

They agreed that Richard would drop off Jared early Saturday afternoon, and then hung up.

After the call Richard sat for a moment thinking about Emily's invitation. It was a damned nice gesture. Not many women would give up their afternoon entertaining a disabled child. It was especially moving coming from Emily. It showed her gentle and caring side that people often overlooked.

Thoughts of Emily were displaced by the more disquieting news of Lydia's possible legal intentions. *The Sanctuary*, it seemed, was a never-ending source of heat. No sooner was one fire extinguished than another started.

The manuscript had continued to aggravate Moseley, increasingly offended by similarities he perceived between the bald editor in Emily's revision and himself. 'Look,' he had said recently, displaying the manuscript. 'She's lifted my editorial comments from the margins, and attributed them to the pornographic editor in her novel. The character no longer just looks and acts like me. Now he talks like me! Verbatim! I think she does it to be vindictive. I know the author doesn't like me.'

Richard had dismissed the editor's concern out of hand.

'Nonsense, Moseley. You're much too sensitive. The editor in *The Sanctuary* is a spineless, whimpering flunky. Absolutely no similarity there, whatever.'

Other problems couldn't be handled so easily. He sensed a growing awareness in the office about him and the author, which would come under scrutiny if the libel charge ever went to court. At least he no longer had to contend with Norman.

His relief was brief. Through his partially opened door he saw Helen in the outer office look up from her desk as someone entered and glimpsed a wisp of honey-blond hair. It showed for only a second, but that was enough. Helen fluttered in, her eyes wide with excitement. 'Mr Fox, Miss Fielding is outside and wants to see you.'

Richard picked up a paperclip from his desk, mangling it. 'I'm very busy,' he said, concentrating on the paperclip. 'What did you tell her?'

'I asked her if she had an appointment.'

'What did she say?'

'She said she has more than that. She has a *lawyer*.'

Chapter 34

Emily's mind was racing. She stood peering out a kitchen window at Forsythia Lane, smoking a cigarette, anxiously awaiting the arrival of Richard Fox and his son. They were almost half an hour late.

She had reason to be impatient. She had spent most of the previous day devising an ingenious and intricate scheme, and the arrival of her guests would set it in motion. If things went as planned, by the end of the day, the last major obstacle to her novel would be eliminated.

She looked again at her watch, leaned over the counter close to the window and looked down Forsythia Lane. Nothing. She went to the kitchen table, sat down. After a few puffs on her cigarette she jabbed it out in an ashtray, and sat drumming her long nails against the table. Then she went back to the window.

Where were they? She was sure Richard had said 1:00.

She walked into the hallway, stopped, listening for sounds from upstairs. Lydia was up in the study, and she wanted her to stay there until after Richard and his son arrived. From below came the muffled barking of a dog. She had locked Rusty in the cellar earlier to make sure he didn't interfere with her project. Little boys liked to play with dogs, and the animal could be a diversion.

She glanced down the hall towards the front door. On a table near the entrance was a large red kite, presumably there to entertain Jared. In reality, it would serve a far deadlier purpose.

The inspiration for her plan came from something that had happened years before during an afternoon when

Louis Morrow had been down on the beach behind the house flying a kite with his two young daughters. It had been a favourite pastime for the family, and the strong steady breeze blowing in from the ocean provided splendid conditions for the sport. The kite had been sailing on a long string directly over their house when suddenly it dipped behind the house and became trapped under the overhang of the roof beyond the narrow widow's walk. Her father had to go up to free it and the sight of him leaning over the small wrought-iron railing high in the air, attempting to free the kite, had made both his daughters nervous.

Memory of the incident had suggested her present scheme. Pretending to entertain Richard's son, she would take him to the beach, where they would sail the kite. At the proper time she would let the line go slack, allowing the kite to drift down on the other side of the house. She would then draw in the string until the kite was caught on the overhang of the roof. When the kite was trapped, she would have the boy go to the house to ask Lydia to go up and free it. Once on the roof, Lydia would have to lean over the small railing to dislodge the kite, as her father had done. Since the railing was more for decorative purposes than any real safety measure, Emily had found it easy to loosen the screws attaching it to the building, so that the slightest pressure would cause it to give way.

But now, anxiously waiting for Richard and his son, her mind was full of things that could go wrong. Little boys were unpredictable. What if he didn't want to fly the kite but preferred, say, to swim, or to run up and down the beach? On the phone, he seemed to have a good deal of energy.

Or what if Lydia decided to go out? Unlikely. Such a damn recluse. Probably up there scrutinizing her breasts.

Looking for lumps. Such a hypochondriac. What was a little lump? Didn't she have one on her own breast?

Suddenly there was the sound of tyres crunching on the gravel drive. She hurried to the front door and looked out. It was Richard. But rather than the BMW she had seen him driving at the club, he was in a van. Peering through the windshield beside him was a handsome blond child. Smiling benevolently, she stepped out into the sunlight to greet her guests.

'Hi, Emily,' Richard said, coming towards her. 'Beautiful day.'

'Hello, Richard. Yes, isn't it splendid? So this is Jared,' she said, moving towards the passenger side of the van. 'Hello, Jared. I'm Emily.'

Richard moved quickly beside her to open the door. Jared sat quietly propped between some pillows, his unwavering eyes focused on Emily.

'Why, he's a little doll,' murmured Emily. Then raising her voice, 'I'm glad to meet you, Jared.' She extended her hand towards him, but he remained motionless, the grey eyes fixed on her.

'Tank!' he said suddenly.

'Tank?' Emily looked to Richard, puzzled.

'His nickname,' Richard said, moving towards the front seat. 'He likes to be called Tank.'

'Aren't you going to get out, Tank?' Emily said gently, motioning with her hand.

She had no sooner said it than she noticed the wheelchair in the rear of the van. 'Oh.' She glanced at Richard again.

'I thought you knew,' he said quietly. 'The other night on the phone . . . I thought he talked to you about his school . . .'

'We're going to have a wonderful time, Tank,' Emily

said, recovering quickly and forcing a smile as she considered the implications of the boy's condition.

'He's been looking forward to coming,' Richard said, at first uncertain about Emily's reaction. When he saw her smile, he walked quickly to the back of the van. Opening the door he removed a wide board he used as a ramp and eased the wheelchair to the ground. 'We have a lighter collapsible chair, but he moves around better in this electric one.'

'How wonderful.' Emily strained to put enthusiasm in her voice, immediately realizing that it would be impossible to negotiate the chair down the narrow path through the dunes to the beach. 'There's a little stream just inside the entrance there.' She nodded towards the Sanctuary. 'We can feed the ducks.'

Richard pushed the chair towards the passenger side of the van. Reaching inside, he lifted his son from the seat, and sat him in the chair. Throughout the procedure the boy's eyes stayed on Emily.

'Wait till you see the ducks,' she said. 'They'll eat right out of your hand.'

'Hear that, Tank?' echoed Richard. 'Right out of your hand.' And then quietly to Emily, 'He'll be fine. Just has to get used to you. Believe me, once he starts talking he won't stop.'

Emily continued to smile sweetly. 'Oh, we're going to have a wonderful time.'

'I'll only be gone for an hour,' Richard said, as though sensing her letdown. 'Are you sure it isn't too much trouble?'

'Of course not. I'm delighted. He's so handsome . . . beautiful, really.' Her eyes lingered on the boy.

'This is his pack.' Richard reached into the van and brought out a small canvas knapsack that he hung by its straps over the handles on the back of the chair. 'His toys and books are in there.'

'Why don't you go ahead, Richard?' Emily patted the boy on the head. 'Don't worry. We're going to have lots of fun, aren't we, Tank?'

Tank's eyes shifted uncertainly from his father to Emily, then back to his father. 'Will you be gone long, Daddy?'

'Not long, Tank.' He cuffed the boy lightly on the cheek, went to the van and started the engine. With a final wave and smile he drove off. The boy's eyes followed the vehicle down Forsythia Lane until it disappeared.

'Well, Tank, we might as well go right over to the Sanctuary.' A sense of frustration had replaced the sweetness in Emily's voice. Gritting her teeth, she added under her breath, 'and feed the goddamn ducks.'

She guided the boy across the road into the Sanctuary, then stopped in a clearing next to a small stream just inside the entrance. 'I'd better get some bread for the ducks,' she said. 'Don't move, Tank. I'll be right back.'

As she crossed the road and entered the house she felt one of her headaches coming on. She'd have to take a pill. In the hallway the red kite caught her eye. She snatched it from the table and moved on into the kitchen. '*Damn* it.' She whacked the kite against the counter, breaking its fragile strands.

'Lydia,' she called. 'Lydia, honey, would you do me a favour?'

Chapter 35

Tank's grey eyes focused on a large hawk that floated effortlessly on a current of air high above the Sanctuary. The bird hovered in the blue sky, at times almost motionless. Once, it descended in a long graceful glide towards the clearing where he was sitting, but then with a few flaps of its powerful wings it regained altitude and resumed circling in wide concentric patterns.

Always fascinated by birds, Tank watched its manoeuvres intently. Soon he was imagining himself as the hawk, soaring across the countryside on great wings. It was typical of the daydreams in which he had lived so much of his time.

He already had an awareness of what had been lost to him in life and was constantly assessing what he could do and what he could not do. But his imagination knew no bounds, and his fantasies were his escape from his restricted world.

When his father left him he had been in a panic – which often happened when Richard left him, especially if the surroundings were unfamiliar. He had kept the feeling in check, sensing this visit was important to his father. But the day was not working out as he'd hoped. There were no ducks, no animals, no popcorn, soda . . . Even the lady was gone.

Except that he didn't mind that she'd left. She'd tried to be nice to him, but he sensed she really didn't mean it. And there was something about her that was kind of, well, scary. Her eyes. They looked a little like the black tiger at the zoo. But he could tell his father liked her. He seemed to be spending more and more time with her, time he could be spending with him. No, he didn't really like her at all.

He didn't know what to make of the Sanctuary. In a way it was like something on TV. The little clearing where he was sitting was okay but the jungle beyond was frightening. Even if his chair had been able to fit down the winding dark path that led into the forest, he didn't think he'd want to go.

It was hot in the bright sunlight, and as the time passed he thought about moving his chair under the trees near the stream. The lady, though, had said don't move. Not until she came back with the bread for the ducks. But where were the ducks?

He looked down the path that tunnelled into the dark foliage, wondering where it led. He thought again of the zoo, the wild animals. He gripped the lever of his chair with both hands.

Suddenly a yellowjacket appeared near his chair, hovering close by in the warm sunlight, oscillating between his ear and shoulder. Panic began to take hold. What if it should land on him? Bite him! He had heard about bee stings. One of his friends at school had told him about someone who had died from a bee sting. He sat rigidly, afraid to move, to breathe.

'Hello, there.'

It was a soft feminine voice. He looked from the corner of his eyes, unwilling to move his head. It was a blond lady with glasses carrying a basket and small blanket, walking towards him. Never was he happier to see anyone.

'Well, so you're Tank,' she said with a warm smile. 'I'm Lydia, Emily's sister. Emily's not feeling well. I thought we could have a little picnic.'

'Bee,' gasped Tank continuing to sit rigidly.

'What?'

'A *bee!* A *bee!*'

'Oh, that's just a little yellowjacket,' Lydia said brushing it away with her hand. 'He won't hurt you.'

Tank sighed in relief. Composure regained, he looked up at the woman wonderingly. Anything new on his scene was always the object of scrutiny. She looked a lot like the other lady except for her hair and glasses. He watched her closely, examining her eyes, hair, nose, teeth, the tiny mole on her neck, the small pearls piercing the lobes of her ears, the slender gold bracelet on her wrist.

'Shall we go over here in the shade?' she said, starting towards the stream.

Tank pushed the lever, moving his chair forward, his eyes still fixed on the woman.

When they reached the bank of the stream, Lydia set the basket down and spread the blanket. 'This seems a good spot. I brought some lemonade and cookies. Do you like chocolate chip cookies?'

Tank kept silent, his keen instincts evaluating this most recent entry in his special world.

'I think you'll like them,' Lydia said. 'Would you like to sit here on the blanket with me?'

Tank gripped the lever on his chair tightly and did not answer.

'All right, you sit there,' Lydia said, dropping down on the blanket. 'We'll have our picnic. Maybe the ducks will come downstream and we can feed them.'

'Are you making believe?' Tank suddenly asked.

'Making believe?'

'There aren't any ducks. No animals nothing. You're playing make-believe, aren't you? There's a bird, though. See?'

He pointed towards the sky, but the hawk had disappeared. 'Oh, it's gone. But there was a bird. Before you came. That's all right, we'll make believe there's a bird, just like the ducks. We have birds over at our house. They're all over the beach. Do you have a beach? I thought I could hear it before when we were over there by your house. I have a friend who has a pet bird. He brought him to school once. Do you always play make-believe . . .?'

It was nearing three-thirty before Richard returned to Forsythia Lane. He had parked in the drive and was getting out of the van when he heard Tank call him.

He turned to see Emily guiding the boy from a door near the kitchen. 'Sorry to be late,' he said waving. 'It took longer than I expected.'

'That's all right,' Emily said. 'We had a great time, didn't we, Tank?' Then, lowering her voice as she drew near, she added, 'Actually, Lydia was with him most of the time. I had one of my headaches.'

'Oh, sorry,' Richard said. 'I hope we didn't – '

'No, no. I'm fine. Won't you come in for a drink?'

'Thanks, but I think you've seen enough of the Fox family for one day.' He reached down and lifted the boy into his arms. 'I should be getting this little guy home.'

'Well, don't forget my manuscript. It's right here inside the door.' Emily turned towards the entrance. 'I'll get it.'

As she entered the house, Richard put his son in the passenger side of the van, propping him up with pillows. Tank leaned back and closed his eyes.

'Ready for a nap, Tank?'

There was no reply, and Richard closed the door.

'Here it is,' Emily said, reappearing from the house and handing him the manuscript. 'I hope the next time I see this it has a binding on it.'

'We're getting there.' Richard glanced towards the house. 'How's Lydia?' he said in a near-whisper.

226

Emily shrugged. 'Okay, I guess. That's all right, you can talk. She's upstairs.'

'Did she mention that she called me yesterday?'

'No.' Emily looked at him quickly, frowning. 'What did she say this time?'

'She wants to come in to see me about this.' He gestured with the manuscript. 'She made noises about going to your family's law firm.'

Emily pursed her lips. 'What did I tell you? I knew she'd try to involve our lawyers.'

'Maybe you should come in with her. It might be better if we both talk to her, explain how we've – '

'No, she won't talk with me around. She'd be afraid of a scene. I know Lydia. Let me think about it. Maybe you should come out here for cocktails one night. I could try to get her to join us. That way we can discuss it in a relaxed atmosphere.'

'That's fine with me. The more I think about it, if Lydia begins legal action . . . What about Steve Sawyer? He's a member of Bayrock. Maybe he could convince her that – '

'Steve? Are you kidding?'

'He wouldn't do it?'

'Oh, he might try if we asked him. But it wouldn't help. Lydia barely talks to him.'

'They don't get along?'

'Well . . . it's a long story. Forget about Steve.'

Richard shifted uncomfortably. 'Well, I'm worried about her,' he said. 'The fact that she's your sister could give a libel charge even more weight. If she gets your lawyers involved it could kill publication.'

'Listen, Richard,' – her voice was low, deadly serious – 'I've spent a great deal of time and effort on this. Nobody's going to stand in the way of its publication. Particularly Lydia . . .'

227

Emily's darkening mood signalled an end to their conversation, and after promising to call within a few days, Richard climbed into the van and drove off.

As he motored down Route 27 towards Southampton he tried to question his drowsy son about his day. 'Did you have a good time, Tank?'

'There were no ducks,' Tank told him, yawning. 'But there were lots of birds and animals in the house.'

'In the house? Oh, well, not in the house.'

'Yes, they were. And a dog. Rusty. He came over and tried to play ball with me, dropped it right in my lap . . .'

'What else did you do all that time?'

Tank's eyes closed, the motion of the car lulling him to sleep.

'Tank, what else?'

Tank struggled to open his eyes. 'We played a game,' he said, his eyes closing once again.

'A game?'

'Yes . . .,' Tank said, his words becoming less audible. 'We played make-believe . . .'

Chapter 36

Lydia was sitting on the terrace behind Number 12, her head inclined so that she could look out over the plant life next to the house. She took pleasure from the scene, preferring the wild growth to the manicured gardens of neighbouring estates.

It was a lazy summer afternoon, warm, but relieved by breezes from the nearby ocean. Lydia dressed in one of her sister's old tennis dresses gazed out at the perennials that popped their brilliantly coloured heads from the tangled mass of greenery. Black-eyed Susans dotted the scene, surrounded by profusions of Shasta daisies and phlox. Spectacular clusters of golden day lilies sparkled gaily in the sunshine. Dominating was a large mimosa tree, its vivid pink blossoms a contrast against the blue sky. Lydia closed her eyes and breathed the redolence of summer.

Rusty lay dozing on the nearby grass. The rhythms of his gentle breathing contributed to Lydia's sense of lethargy, and her mind wandered to something that happened with the dog the previous day when she'd taken over for Emily in caring for Richard's son. She and the boy had come back from the Sanctuary, and she had left him under the mimosa tree while she returned the picnic articles to the kitchen.

Inside the house she had happened to glance out a window to see Rusty approaching the child, a tennis ball in his mouth. He carefully deposited the ball in the boy's lap, and then moved back with an eager bark, waiting for it to be thrown. Tank had quickly obliged, and Rusty had scampered after the ball, returning it as before to the boy's lap. This time it had fallen to the ground just beyond Tank's reach. After straining unsuccessfully to recover it, the boy had leaned back in his chair, quietly shaking his head. Sitting there among the strands of sunlight that pierced the mimosa tree, he seemed enclosed in a sort of golden cage. She had been deeply moved by his helplessness.

Her thoughts of the previous day were interrupted by the sound of tyres crunching on gravel at the front of the house. She quickly went through a rear door leading to the kitchen, where she stationed herself behind a window and peered out. Her heart quickened when she saw Steve leave his car and walk to the front door. In his white slacks and navy-blue shirt, light hair ruffling in the breeze, he seemed especially handsome. Her usual conflicting emotions – yearning and resentment – welled up within her. She stood motionless near the window as the bell rang several times. Finally, Steve went back to his car and drove away.

She remained at the window for a moment, then turned and went back to the terrace, where she stood looking out at the ocean, her melancholy building. She lay down once again and closed her eyes . . .'

Thoughts of ending it all inched into her consciousness. It wasn't the first time. But lately they were coming more often, and she had actually considered ways of doing it. She'd decided the easiest way would be to take an overdose of the sleeping pills she'd been saving up.

Opening her eyes, she looked up at the sky. The sun had dropped below the mimosa tree, and the colour was fading from the blossoms.

PART FOUR
Old Hampton

August

Chapter 37

Enraged by Richard's disclosure that Lydia was about to involve the family lawyers, Emily now set about devising an elaborate scheme to end her sister's interference once and for all. Frustrated by recent failures, she was determined that this time her plan would be failproof.

The following Monday morning she got up early and drove to the shopping centre near Islip. She went first to the women's clothing section of a large department store, where because of her sister's preference for ready-made dresses she was able to buy a lime-green linen dress identical to one that Lydia had recently bought.

In a nearby boutique she picked up a navy-blue shetland sweater bearing the initials LM, which she had ordered under a fictitious name. She then walked to a shoe store in the same complex for a pair of beige sandals, the kind Lydia often wore in the evening. During the transactions she wore dark glasses and paid for the merchandise in cash.

She stored the packages in the station wagon and drove back to Old Hampton, where she proceeded to the commercial area of the village. The downtown business section was a picturesque square of quaint shops and trim municipal buildings. In the centre, separated from the establishments by a cobblestone street, was a postage-stamp park with shade trees, benches, a small fountain, a monument honouring Old Hampton's dead from World War I, and a tall flagpole. 'Downtown', as residents referred to it, was a tranquil area, particularly the park, where usually the loudest sounds were the chirping of songbirds and the water splashing in the fountain.

After parking the station wagon, Emily entered the park and sat down on a wooden bench near the base of the monument to think over her plan. The sunshine reflected off her beige linen suit as she took in the immaculate shops neatly arranged around the square.

A soft buzzing drew her attention to a large bumblebee that was trafficking in the nectar of some red roses at the base of the monument. She watched its black-and-yellow form moving from one flower to the next, transfixed by its movements. Suddenly she had a vague feeling of having watched the bee precisely in this fashion before, a sensation of reliving something that had happened long ago.

At the same time she felt the first stages of one of her headaches. It scared her, as it always did . . . She hoped she was not going to have one of her spells. Usually they happened at home or in the Sanctuary, where she was able to cope with them in private.

To avoid thinking of it, she took out a small white card from her purse and tried to focus on it. The card listed several additional items she would buy that day from the neighbouring shops. Although the purchases so far had required anonymity, she was confident that what she would buy locally would create no residual problems. All were components for her plan; a shopping list of innocuous items that would hold the solution to her problem with Lydia.

After studying the list for a moment she slipped it into a pocket of her jacket. Then, with a swipe of her purse, she knocked the bumblebee from one of the roses to the ground. She stood, about to grind it into the ground, but thinking of possible grass stains on her shoe, left the insect quivering at the base of the monument.

She crossed the cobblestone street, to a hardware store. As she entered, an elderly man came towards her from the rear.

'Well, well, Miss Morrow, isn't it?' he said smiling. 'We haven't seen you for some time.'

'Hello, Mr Clark.'

'Now, is it Lydia or Emily? I'm always getting you two mixed up.'

'I'm Emily. How's Mrs Clark?'

'She passed away,' he said, his face clouding. 'Over three months ago.'

'Oh, sorry,' Emily said, genuinely sorry that she had asked.

'It was for the best. A blessing really,' said Mr Clark gravely. He leaned against the wall, prepared to discuss his late wife's passing. 'You know Dr Long, don't you?'

Emily, never at her best in such situations, wasted little time on Mrs Clark. 'Do you sell those long poles with the sieve on the end for skimming the tops of swimming pools?' she asked abruptly. 'The pole comes in sections. You screw the ends together to make the handle longer. Do you know what I mean?'

Mr Clark hesitated, taken aback by her cutting him off about his wife. 'Ah . . . no, we don't carry those. Bartels might have them. They carry pool equipment.'

'I need some rope. Maybe thirty feet. Something strong.'

'Strong? What do you need it for?'

'Oh, just to tie some things.'

'How about this clothesline over here?' he said, walking towards an aisle where rope was displayed.

'Well . . . something stronger.'

'Here's a pretty good hemp.' He lifted a coil of rope from a hook. 'This is quite strong.'

'That should do it.' Emily looked past him to another

counter displaying flashlights. 'Also, I need a large flash-light. Maybe like that one over there.' She pointed towards a square red lamp with a handle on top.

'This one?' said Mr Clark, picking up the light she had designated. 'Anything else?'

'A pair of gloves. Regular garden gloves.'

'We have a selection back here.' He turned and led Emily to the rear of the store, where she picked out some gloves.

'Anything else?' he asked, carrying the goods to the checkout counter.

'No, that's it.' Emily glanced at her watch. Almost four-thirty. She'd have to move along. 'Could you ring that up quickly? I'm running late.'

Mr Clark put the items in a shopping bag . 'Here you are.' He handed her the bag. 'Give your sister my best.'

Outside, Emily walked down the square to the store that carried swimming pool equipment, where she was able to buy a long-handled skimmer. She then proceeded to the ready-cooked food section of a nearby grocery store and bought five pounds of barbecued spare ribs.

Back in the car, she carefully stored the packages in the rear compartment, and after checking to be sure she had everything, she slammed the door.

Turning, she focused on a shop on the far corner of the square. She did not like the store. She had never gone in without sensing hostility. Not only from the owner, but from the other inhabitants as well. Still, she had to go. It would be her last purchase – the most important.

236

Chapter 38

The brass bell attached to the front door of the Old Hampton Pet Shop jangled, announcing a customer. Immediately a thousand small eyes turned and focused on the entrance-way. The shop, usually alive with chattering sounds, was all at once still, the keen primitive instincts of the occupants suddenly alerted.

Emily again sensed the hostility. At the rear of the store a woman regarded her from behind a large desk. Emily avoided her cool eyes and proceeded down the aisle lined with cages and glass cases, observing the variety of pets.

The shop inventory was broad, containing a range of birds, fish, puppies and snakes, as well as a frightening assortment of insects, including a large, hairy tarantula. Nothing in the shop was quite as unnerving to the naked eye, however, as the creature that occupied the last glass enclosure at the end of the aisle. It was an amber-coloured scorpion over three inches long. Two eyes peered from behind a pair of menacing pincers. Extending behind the tiny eyes was a curved segmented tail that terminated in a poised deadly stinger.

Emily brushed quickly down the aisle towards the figure in the rear, giving the menagerie only passing attention, except for the last enclosure containing the scorpion. Here, her eyes lingered.

At the rear of the store she stopped. 'Mrs Osterman, I'm Emily Morrow. I called yesterday about – '

'Yes, I know.'

Wilma Osterman, proprietor of the Old Hampton Pet

Shop, was gentle with her animals, less so with her customers. A strong-willed, hard-working widow, she lived for her business. Her concern for her store was evident in the neat rows of cages and their well-kept occupants. Nothing provoked her Teutonic temper more than patrons who displayed a frivolousness towards her merchandise. It was natural, therefore, that annoyance had crinkled her features when she glanced through the front window a few minutes earlier to see Emily Morrow approaching her shop.

Her displeasure with the Morrow sister was deep-rooted, going back over twenty years to a day when Louis Morrow came, chagrined, to the pet shop to return a rabbit he had purchased for his daughter the day before. Such returns were not uncommon, particularly with rabbits, where the novelty wore thin quickly as awareness set in that someone had to *care* for the pet.

Mrs Osterman would have accepted the returned merchandise without comment if it hadn't been for its damaged condition. Mr Morrow had explained sheepishly, that his daughter had started to give it a haircut, as a child might do, and, well . . . she simply got carried away. Emily, it seemed, had cut off not only the rabbit's hair but most of its ears as well. The father's assertion that he did not want a refund, indeed – wanted to pay to help rehabilitate the poor animal – had done little to appease Wilma.

But it was a more recent transgression that truly embittered Wilma and resurrected the first incident. It seemed Lydia Morrow had purchased an expensive Amazon parrot from the shop. Wilma had prized the bird for its beauty – it had spectacular red and green plumage – but even more for its extraordinary vocabulary, which it used constantly. She had parted with the bird reluctantly, but with confidence that Lydia's background in ornithology would insure it a good home.

She was shocked and infuriated by a subsequent rumour that Lydia's *sister* had become irritated by the bird's nonstop loquacity, had wrung its neck, and then *stuffed* it.

Now, yesterday's call from Emily asking about a specific item had rekindled Wilma's hostility. Although she carried the item, she disapproved of it and had never recommended it to a customer. The call had reinforced her misgivings about Emily, and although she had acknowledged she had the product in stock, she had done so with cool reservation. A coolness much in evidence now as she addressed Emily.

'You're the one who wanted the dog-trainer. I was just about to close. Wait here, please.'

She turned and walked into a back room, and almost immediately reappeared carrying a leather case that she put on the counter.

'This is it.' She opened the case and took out a leather dog collar to which a small boxlike device was attached. 'And this is the hand-control. It works on batteries.' She removed a chrome cylinder some eight inches long that resembled a flashlight.

'Seems simple enough,' Emily said, picking up the collar and cylinder. 'I just put the collar on the dog, and when I want him to respond I shock him with this.'

'There's more to it than that, Miss Morrow,' Wilma said. 'Frankly, I'm not enthusiastic about this method of training a dog.'

'The article I read in the magazine said they're very effective, that you can teach a dog to do all sorts of things in only a few days.'

'Oh, they're effective all right,' Wilma said. 'It's the overall effect on the dog that I'm worried about.'

239

'How do these buttons work?' Emily asked, pointing at two knobs on the cylinder.

'This one transmits a warning signal when you want him to perform.' Wilma pushed one of the buttons and a slight buzzing came from the instrument. 'If he doesn't respond, you push this other button and it triggers the electric shock. Say you're in the house and you want to call the dog home. You give him the warning and if he doesn't come, you deliver the shock. It's brief. It feels like when you hit your elbow, but I – '

'How far away can the dog be?'

'Maybe a quarter of a mile.'

'Will it work in the woods? You know, where there's dense vegetation?'

'Oh, yes. But it should be used with restraint. As I said, the overall impact on the dog – '

'How much do I owe you?' Emily said curtly.

As they concluded the transaction Emily's eyes returned to the deadly-looking occupant of the glass enclosure at the end of the aisle. 'I'm not sure,' she said, picking up the package, preparing to leave. 'I may want to buy that scorpion.'

'I'm sure it will be here,' Wilma said. She watched as her customer left the shop and sauntered across the square, her earlier feelings about Emily Morrow confirmed.

It was almost six when Emily arrived home. Rusty was lying in his usual place in a shaded bed of pachysandra near the kitchen door. He climbed stiffly to his feet as the station wagon came into the drive.

'Hi, Rusty,' Emily called from the car. 'I brought you some spare ribs.'

She eased the car into the garage next to the Mercedes.

After removing the packages containing the clothes and spare ribs from the back, she walked from the garage and entered the house through the kitchen door.

In the kitchen she put the packages with the dress and shoes on the table and the meat in the refrigerator. Then picking up the other packages, she went upstairs. She passed Lydia's room as she went down the hall towards her bedroom. The door was closed.

'I'm home, Lydia. I don't suppose there were any calls for me.' Not waiting for a reply, she added, 'You never have any calls for me. Sometimes I think you don't even bother to answer the phone.'

She went to her bedroom, stored the packages in the bottom of her closet. Then raising her voice: 'Lydia, I've invited Richard over for cocktails on Saturday. We're going to discuss the changes that we've made in my novel. You're welcome to join us.' There, she thought, that'll give her something to stew about.

After changing into a warm-up suit she went downstairs to the library and spent several minutes looking about the room, carefully noting the position of the furniture and the precise location of the windows. Then she left the library and began a procedure she would repeat every night that week.

First, she went to a hall closet where she kept her tennis equipment and found a yellow tennis ball that she put in a pocket of her warm-up suit. She then went to the kitchen and took out a portion of the spare ribs from the refrigerator. Breaking off some meat, she fed it to the dog, who devoured it in one swallow.

Carrying the meat, she led the dog from the house to the station wagon, removed the gloves, flashlight, dog collar, rope and pool skimmer. Next, with Rusty close at her heels, she crossed the road and entered the Sanctuary.

Chapter 39

'Steve's not here, John,' Lydia's voice was exhilarant. 'I have no idea where Emily is either. I just came in.'

'Oh, I see . . . When I talked to Steve earlier he said he was going to stop by to see Emily. I'm supposed to play tennis with him tonight. If you see him will you tell him I'm running a bit late?'

'Yes, of course, John. Ah . . . by the way, thanks for sending the cash disbursement report for the trust. It came this morning.'

'Good. You should receive the investment analysis in another week or so. We thought it had been sent to you a few months ago.'

'Thanks, John.'

Lydia liked John Collier. A close friend of Steve's, he was a Hampton bank executive who handled the local aspects of the Morrow family trust. She always liked talking to him. But there was another reason for her good cheer. It had come in the form of several glasses of punch at a Bayrock cocktail party. It was rare for Lydia even to attend a cocktail party, rarer still for her to have a drink, but it had all happened accidentally. One of the club matrons attending a small reception for the benefactors of a local charity had spotted Lydia passing through and insisted that she stop in for a drink. The affair had been held in the club reading room, with some thirty women there. Apparently someone had mixed more gin in the grape juice than was prescribed in the recipe. The punch had been a solid hit, and the party had taken off. Rarely had the staid reading room been the scene of such unrestrained laughter.

No one had found the punch more appealing than Lydia. It had eased the self-consciousness, that she always felt at such gatherings, and caused her to forget for a moment her troubles. Her ebullience had showed, the old station wagon was ticking over forty on the short ride back to her house.

At home and faced with the solitude of Number 12, she had decided to prolong her good feeling, and had mixed herself a vodka and orange juice. No sooner had she started to drink it than John called, becoming the beneficiary of her euphoria.

'I'll make sure Steve gets the message if he stops, John. Bye-bye.'

She carried her drink out to the terrace and sat down in an old wicker porch chair. It was twilight. Orange-tinged clouds streaked the darkening sky. Although she had seen many such sunsets from this very spot, none had ever seemed quite as lovely. Indeed, everything about the evening seemed wonderful, enchanting.

She sat sipping her drink, thinking of Steve, and the thoughts stirred up by mention of him in the phone conversation – feeling further stimulated by the alcohol. Inhibitions that normally closed about her during such thought were absent.

Suddenly there was movement in the bushes. Rusty appeared. The dog walked to the chair, proceeded to nuzzle her. Realizing her party had delayed his dinner, she drained her drink, and followed by the dog, which now waved its tail in anticipation, she went to the kitchen.

She fed Rusty with left overs from the refrigerator, then began tidying up the kitchen. She was about to return the vodka bottle to the cupboard, then hesitated. Deliberately, she poured a substantial amount into her glass. After adding some orange juice, she took a quick sip and, humming a few bars from 'Waltzing Matilda', she ascended with her spirits to the upstairs study.

Dusk was enveloping Number 12, but Lydia's mind was bright with thoughts of the impending evening. She sat in an easy chair, drinking her screwdriver, contemplating what she would do. Her usual evening activities – reading, writing, sewing – all at once didn't interest her. She had to get out of that drab study, do something different. Perhaps she'd go downtown, do some shopping, go to a movie . . . It'd been a while since she'd been to a show. Actually, the last one had been with Steve. A silly movie, as she recalled, but fun. It had always been fun with Steve, no matter what they did. At least for her.

Thinking of Steve, she glanced at her watch. He'd be coming later looking for Emily. She took another drink, a long one. She'd have to remember to turn on some downstairs lights. In fact, maybe she'd go downstairs when he came. They'd talk, perhaps she'd offer him a drink while he was waiting for Emily. Well . . . that might be awkward after having avoided him for so long. Still, why not? It was her house. She lifted her glass.

As she continued drinking, vague thoughts flickered in her spinning brain. Images of the past. Steve . . . sailing . . . making love on the sofa . . . Suddenly an idea – what if she impersonated Emily? Wait for Steve in the library. She put it quickly from her mind. What a crazy notion, must be the alcohol. Still, it was delicious to fantasize.

After finishing her drink she rose awkwardly and went to her bath down the hall, where she took off her glasses and wiped her face with a hot cloth. It felt refreshing. She stood, steadying herself against the washbasin, regarding her reflection in the mirror. Just like Emily, she mused. Except, of course, for the hair. Again came the earlier thought. Ridiculous, but this time, she did not dismiss it.

Instead, she kept studying her reflection, and as she did so, the eyes narrowed, the chin tilted, the expression slowly changed to one of inimitable disdain.

Abruptly she left the bath and walked into Emily's bedroom, where she snapped on the light. She took a bottle of expensive perfume from a vanity and dabbed a bit behind each ear. From a closet she got a turban, then went back to the vanity and sat down in front of the mirror, pulling the turban over her head. Carefully she tucked the blonde strands up underneath so that none showed.

She sat for a moment staring at the dark eyes that peered at her confidently from the mirror. Standing abruptly, she left the room and walked unsteadily towards the stairs.

Chapter 40

'You're not quitting, are you?' The voice from the darkness beyond the net rang with alarm.

'I can't see the ball,' Steve said. 'It's too dark.'

'Too dark? It's five-three,' protested the voice. 'I'm serving for the match.'

'The match has been called due to darkness,' Steve said, walking towards the table at the side of the court.

Steve was having his annual match with John Collier, a balding, genial-looking man in his late thirties, who challenged him once a year to a one-set singles match. Although John had never won a set, sometimes by means of a mixture of his bad calls, bad conditions and Steve's generosity he would come close. Tonight was such a match.

When John had told Lydia earlier that he would be late for his match with Steve, he had not really been concerned. In fact, he was counting on the fading light to help his chances. But now, he saw his opportunity slipping away . . . 'I can't believe you're doing this.'

'You came close. Maybe next year,' Steve picked up his sweater from the table and started towards the clubhouse.

'Well, let's go upstairs. The least you can do is buy me a drink.'

'I can't, I'm supposed to be over at Emily's at nine.'

'I called there earlier to tell you I'd be late. I talked to Lydia. How's she doing? She doesn't come into the bank much anymore.'

'Okay, I guess,' Steve said uneasily. He experienced a

sinking sensation whenever someone said they had talked to Lydia. 'I haven't really seen that much of her myself.'

'Yes, well, I've been trying to contact her about some trust matters. Have you talked to her? I mean, actually seen her?'

Steve glanced at him quickly, then looked away. 'No, I haven't,' he said with a touch of sharpness.

Steve regretted his abruptness. After all, he and John often talked about personal matters, their friendship dating back to when Steve was himself a beneficiary of the Morrow Trust, via his father. The question was one John might naturally ask. But because of his own uncertainty about Emily, and especially Lydia lately, he found almost any question about them hard to handle. 'I see very little of Lydia,' he said. 'She avoids me, as you can imagine. Why do you ask?'

'Well . . . it's kind of a sensitive thing. I was going to call you about it.'

Steve waited.

'Obviously this is between us, Steve . . . A few months ago we started getting some inquiries at the bank about the Morrow sisters – unpaid bills, that sort of thing. I checked Lydia's accounts – she handled most of their bills – and found little activity. I called her but Emily said she'd gone away, that she'd be back soon. Sometime in the spring, wasn't it?'

'Yes,' Steve said uneasily, 'she went to Europe.'

'That's what Emily said. Anyway, several weeks passed and when the accounts still weren't being handled properly, I called again. This time I talked to Lydia – I thought it was Lydia – and she said that she'd just come back and that she'd take care of things. Well, she never did, so about a month ago I called and asked her to stop by my office. She never showed up. Last week I called her again and tried to discuss the accounts with her, but she wasn't knowledgeable about even the most rudimentary things. It was damn odd. Lydia was always so fastidious, so conscientious about fiduciary matters.'

He waited for some response from Steve, got none. 'Frankly, the call made me a little suspicious so I pulled the accounts myself. When I reviewed the records, it became apparent that Emily was forging Lydia's cheques. Then I began to think about those phone calls with Lydia. Both of them sound almost the same, as you know. So a few days ago I called Lydia, feigning an annual review of the trust, and asked her some leading questions. This sounds far out, Steve. Frankly, I think Emily was impersonating Lydia . . .'

John paused. 'Of course I don't know all the factors. These domestic things . . . could be Lydia's given Emily some power of attorney.'

Steve said nothing as they approached the clubhouse, his anxiety building. If John's suspicions were real . . . well, it would be the most serious indication so far of Emily's emotional instability? And what about Lydia? He hadn't seen her since she came home. Still, others said they had . . .

It was after nine when Steve drove his Porsche into the drive at Number 12. The light in the kitchen was burning brightly, as were those upstairs. He had noticed coming up the road that the light in Emily's room was also on. It lifted his spirits. Maybe they could go for a walk on the beach, and he could check out what John had said.

As he approached the house he noticed the front door was ajar. He rang the bell, pushed the door open, and stuck his head inside. 'Hello.'

No answer. He rang the bell again, waited, and then went into the house. It was dark in the foyer, the only light spilling from a partially opened door to the butler's pantry beside the kitchen. The sound of soft music drifted from down the hall near the entrance to the library.

'Anybody home?'

When there was still no answer he moved quietly down the dark corridor. It was unusual for Emily not to greet him – maybe she didn't hear the bell or was preoccupied . . .

He paused at the entrance of the library, peering inside. The only light was from a solitary lamp on a table against a far wall. He was about to turn back into the hall when he saw a figure in the shadows at the other end of the room, on the sofa where he often sat with Emily. The quiet form sitting in the dim light startled him. As his eyes adjusted to the darkness, he saw that it was a woman wearing a turban, sitting primly, holding a glass.

'Who's that?' Steve asked, straining to see.

The woman swayed slightly and raised the glass to her lips. 'Hi, Steve,' she said. 'It's . . . It's Emily.'

Chapter 41

'She was here this afternoon with – '

'Dr Sawyer. How could he associate with her after – '

'Well, if anyone needs a doctor, it's that Emily. A psychiatrist would probably be more – '

The four women huddled over the bridge table on the Bayrock terrace had fastened on the subject of Emily Morrow. It was between hands, a time when random thoughts tumbled on inattentive ears. The 'Bayrock Four' had long since become so bored with one another's comments that rarely could one finish before the others jumped in. News of the Morrow novel had done much to stimulate their lives, though it had been worked over to the point that it was losing some of its original appeal. The Four, nevertheless, were devouring it as the best from a warmed-over meal.

'I hear Lydia's on the verge of a nervous break – '

'Poor thing. No one ever sees her any more since – '

'No one ever saw her much *before*. She was always a recluse living – '

'They say Henrietta's in the book.'

'You don't say.'

'Oh, yes. She's a deer or something in an orgy in the Sanctuary. She – '

'To think Emily has the gall to come and play tennis here after – '

'Listen, there's someone still playing now.'

The light, hollow popping sound of a tennis ball came from the distance.

'Isn't it rather late for tennis? It's getting dark.'

'Maybe it's Emily.'

'Could be. Probably the only time she can get someone to play with her . . .'

But Emily was not on the Bayrock courts. Although her tennis bag was slung over her shoulder at that very moment, she was in the Sanctuary pursuing a deadlier game. She was on the path just inside the entrance, her new flashlight in her gloved hand, preparing for the dress rehearsal of a routine she had been going through all week.

Rusty, his new training collar around his neck, was tied to a nearby tree with the rope from the hardware store. She had secured him there earlier in the evening, as she had done on the previous nights. Using the training device, she had disciplined him so that he would sit quietly and patiently by the tree until a specific moment, whereupon he was induced to bark by electrical impulses transmitted by Emily from the house.

Emily had triggered such an action from the kitchen a few minutes before, and the dog was now barking loudly as she approached. She set her duffel bag on the ground, took off her gloves, and untied Rusty. Immediately he bounded off into the forest. Emily glanced at her watch. It was 7:55.

She picked up the bag and flashlight, continuing down the path. Soon she reached the pond, where she walked to the bench and sat down, setting the bag on the ground.

She thought again about Steve, who had called earlier in the evening from Manhattan, remonstrating about some nonsense that had supposedly happened the previous night. She hadn't the foggiest notion what he was talking about and told him so, whereupon he had replied that that was understandable since she had been drunk. It was true . . . well, it was just another one of the incidents

251

in her life when time had come and gone without her knowledge. Such episodes were happening to her more frequently of late.

Airily dismissing the matter, she'd told him to call her at eight the next night so they could have dinner. She had also assured him that they could discuss another of his concerns – something John Collier had mentioned about the Morrow trust.

After sitting for a moment, she bent over and removed the cylindrical training device from the bag. She waited for a moment, checking her watch, her finger resting on the shock button of the cylinder. At precisely 8:10 she pushed the button. Immediately, from deep in the forest, came the yelping of a dog. She returned the cylinder to the bag, and picking up the articles from the ground, proceeded in the direction from which the barking came.

It was 8:16 when she reached the clearing surrounding the quicksand. Standing on the other side of the pit, barking loudly, was Rusty. His attention was riveted on a yellow tennis ball that rested in the centre of the quicksand. Using the swimming-pool skimmer, Emily had placed the ball there that afternoon. At the same time she had used the skimmer to groom the surface of the pit with pine needles, leaves and other covering to ensure that it blended with the surrounding ground.

Rusty did not try to retrieve the ball, having learned the treacherous nature of the quicksand earlier in the week when he attempted to fetch it while on the end of the rope. After the frightening experience of becoming mired in the quicksand and having to be extricated, he was careful not to repeat the mistake.

When the dog saw Emily emerging from the woods into the clearing, he began wagging his tail and prancing about in excited anticipation. At the edge of the pit she took out a slab of spare ribs from the bag and gave it to him.

Having been fed sparingly during the week he devoured it ravenously.

Emily again noted the time. It was 8:18, darkening, but still light enough to see the tennis ball. She was right on schedule. Bending over, she took the skimmer lying nearby, carefully scooped the ball from the pit, carried ball and skimmer to the woods and put them behind a tree. Then, Rusty at her heels she started home.

As she walked back through the forest, she reviewed once more the plan she would activate the next night. Everything was ready. The only variable was the weather. She had checked the forecast and it was favourable. Should it rain, the project would have to be postponed. Other than that, she felt confident. Rusty had proved dependable, performing as predictably as Pavlov's dog.

As for Lydia's part, Emily was not at all worried. If anything, Lydia was probably even better trained than Rusty. Yes, good old dependable Lydia. When Emily rang the right bell the next night, Lydia would perform exactly as expected. And this time, there would be no mistakes.

Night had fallen as she proceeded back home through the Sanctuary. With darkness came the nocturnal sounds from the forest, sounds fusing into a steady beat. Strong, confident. Alongside the path blue phantoms floated in the mist above the bogs, nodding approvingly.

Chapter 42

The flags above Bayrock hung limply from their staffs, a sagging guard silhouetted against a still evening sky. Although most of the day had been clear, with the approach of dusk there was a subtle change in the weather. A light breeze that had been blowing cool air from the ocean had passed, and there was a heaviness in the atmosphere that portended rain.

It was Saturday. A short distance from Bayrock, Emily Morrow, dressed in black chiffon that matched her dark hair, was having cocktails with Richard Fox in the library on Forsythia Lane.

'Yes, you're right it feels like rain,' Emily said, 'although the forecast was for good weather tonight.'

She was speaking in an above-normal register, wanting to be sure that Lydia could overhear her. She was confident that her sister was eavesdropping at the top of the stairs – a vantage point from which they had listened to conversations in the library since childhood.

'You can't depend on them,' Emily went on, her voice taking on a querulous tone.

'I beg your pardon.'

'The weather bureau. I called no more than an hour ago and they were still saying it was going to be clear tonight. But it's already clouding up.'

'It's difficult to forecast the weather at the shore.'

'Well they could at least look out the window and see what's happening. I'm sure if I called right now they'd still be saying clear skies, even though most of Long Island is probably in fog.'

The weather was the lone imponderable in Emily's meticulously prepared scheme. The uncertainty of the forecast heightened the tension that she had felt building all day.

Suddenly from the study down the hall came the ringing of the telephone. Emily waited while it rang several times, then stood. 'Would you excuse me, Richard? It seems *I'm* the only one around here who answers the phone.'

She went quickly into the hall towards the study but then, changing her mind, went to the kitchen. Less chance of being overheard by Lydia or Richard.

The call was from Steve. 'How you doing with your manuscript?' he asked after initial greetings.

'Fine. Actually, Steve, we're in the middle of things right now. I didn't expect you to call until eight. Would you call back then?'

'Sorry,' he said quickly. 'Ah, how about our dinner? After you finish your – '

'Please call at eight?' Emily repeated. 'We'll see how it goes. I can't really talk right now, Steve.'

Ringing off, she left the kitchen. As she passed through the hallway she thought she heard a creak at the top of the stairs. Lydia repositioning herself, she guessed. Glancing at her watch, she moved quickly towards the library. It was time to set things in motion.

'I suppose we can use the rain,' she said, entering the library. 'Our flowers are all dying.'

It was the first of a number of comments she would make in a carefully designed plan to antagonize her sister. Earlier in the week she had neglected to relay a message from Lydia to the local nursery about watering certain plants in the absence of Henry Todd.

'Yes, well, we've had good weather,' Richard said. 'It must have been great at the beach this week. Of course, you probably haven't had much time for that, working on your manuscript.'

Emily pounced on the comment. 'I'm glad you mentioned the manuscript.' It was important to begin talk about the novel early. There was nothing like the topic of *The Sanctuary* to keep her sister fixed to the stairwell.

'Richard, we may as well get to the point of the evening. I've tried to explain to Lydia what we've done with the book. The modifications we've made. But she's just not willing to listen.'

Richard, startled by the abrupt switch from weather amenities to the sensitive issue of the novel, fingered his tie, and brushed some lint from the sleeve of his blazer.

'I hope you'll point these things out to her, Richard,' Emily went on. 'She's already contacted Stanley Barnett's office – our family lawyers – and reviewed the matter with them. Apparently they're going to call you next week.'

Richard crossed his legs, moving his suspended foot nervously. 'Well, as you said, our own lawyers are going through the manuscript very carefully. Lydia may be sure nothing will be printed that's libellous.'

'There's *nothing* libellous in the book. Lord knows, I've spent enough time rewriting the . . .' She hesitated, her attention turned towards a window at the front of the house.

Richard looked at her questioningly. 'Is something wrong?'

'No, I thought I heard Rusty barking, I told Lydia yesterday I found him tied across the road inside the entrance to the Sanctuary. He sometimes wanders down the road and bothers the neighbours. We have a leash law, you know. One of their handymen probably did it.'

'I didn't hear anything.'

'I may have imagined it,' Emily said with a smile.

She had, indeed, imagined it. The only reason for

saying it was to plant in Lydia's mind an awareness of and concern for Rusty in the Sanctuary. 'But as I was saying, I've rewritten so much of the book I simply can't understand what all the fuss is about. Particularly Lydia. We've changed the protagonist, if that's what she's worried about. Frankly, I don't think that's what's bothering her, anyway. It's not the book.'

Richard looked at her questioningly.

'It's something else. Something personal. I probably shouldn't mention it.'

Richard glanced uneasily towards the door leading to the hall.

'Something she wrote that I happened to read . . . inadvertently, of course.'

Emily was sure her sister was glued to the stairwell at this point, and positively livid in anticipation of what Emily was about to say.

She looked at her watch. Three minutes to go. Next she would make her carefully prepared statement, something so shocking and upsetting to Lydia that it would drive her from the house.

Chapter 43

From the moment Richard entered the house on Forsythia Lane he had sensed tension. Although Emily had greeted him graciously, she had also seemed strained. He suspected she might have been arguing with Lydia.

Their conversation in the library confirmed his feeling, and now he was becoming more and more uncomfortable as Emily attacked her sister about the novel. It was the dark side of her that he'd heard about but rarely seen.

'She's like all the others,' Emily was saying, 'she hasn't even read the book and she's ready to condemn it.'

Richard remained quiet. He wondered if Lydia were going to have cocktails with them. Emily was speaking loudly. It was possible that her sister had overheard some of her caustic remarks. If so, it was unlikely she'd come in.

When there was a pause, he asked if Lydia would be joining them. This had been the original intent – to hash things over in their home rather than the office.

'Probably not. She's upstairs in her bedroom. She hasn't been feeling too well.'

Emily glanced at her watch, stood abruptly. 'Would you excuse me for a moment, Richard? I have to go upstairs. I won't be a minute.' With a smile that seemed incongruous with her previous remarks she left the room.

After she left, Richard settled back in his chair, sipping his drink, reflecting on the evening and his first visit to the Morrow residence. He had been in reasonably good spirits before coming. Although Lydia was apparently creating more trouble with *The Sanctuary*, other problems had been cleared up. Norman and Arnold were gone. And hadn't Moseley only yesterday reported that Sheila had been seen lunching with an editor whom Richard had arranged for her to see about a job? And if they were already lunching, she'd probably forget about her lawyer. It looked good. Who knew better than he that few men could watch Sheila manoeuvring her assets over a lunch table without being impressed with her career potential.

He looked about the library with its expanse of panelling and leather-bound books. Although orderly and furnished with antiques and oils collected by Louis Morrow, the room had the mustiness of disuse. Somehow its atmosphere went with the strangeness he sensed in the house.

A noise in the hall. Then nothing. Sounds of an old house?

It was then he noticed the small birds. They were in a dark corner suspended by thin wires. Looking closer he saw other stuffed animals on shelves against the wall. Mounted on small bases, they were lined up row after row like trophies. Apparently these were the animals his son was talking about after his recent visit. An unusual assortment of relics, anomalous in the otherwise tastefully decorated quarters. His uneasiness grew as he thought of the bizarre stuffed objects in Emily's novel.

He went across the room to inspect them and in so doing came closer to the door leading to the hall. The sound of Emily's voice came from upstairs. She was talking to someone, presumably Lydia, although he couldn't hear Lydia's voice. If anything, Emily sounded even angrier than before.

'All of this supposed concern for the people at Bayrock,' she was saying, 'their delicate feelings and reputations. Don't you feel like a hypocrite? You see, Lydia, *I* happen to know the real reason you're so against my novel. It's because it's coming between you and something you've wanted so badly . . .'

There was a pause and then Emily's voice again. 'You see, Lydia, I know you're jealous. And I don't mean about Steve. You can't *bear* to have Richard working with me on the book. It's all right there in your diary. *You're in love with Richard . . .*'

Absolute silence. Richard was stupefied.

'Go ahead,' came Emily's voice, much lower now. 'Go to the Sanctuary. Who gives a damn!'

Chapter 44

Emily was alone in her bedroom, smoking a cigarette. Her sister had just passed from her life.

For a moment she was seized with uncertainty, remembering a time long ago when Lydia, her blue eyes wide and frightened, had waved goodbye through the train window as she left for boarding school. A fragmentary sensitivity, quickly overwhelmed by more brutal emotions.

Snuffing out her cigarette in an ashtray, she strode from the room downstairs to the library. Richard was standing inside the door observing her animal collection. He did not look at her immediately, and she sensed he was embarrassed.

'I guess you heard our little spat upstairs,' she said, walking across the room and dropping into a chair. 'I'm sorry for that. It was rude of me.'

Richard made a wry face, started to speak, paused, then said, 'Emily, I think I'm intruding. I don't want to get into a family affair, I mean – '

'I know . . .' Emily's voice softened, a smile appeared. 'I guess I sounded pretty severe, but that's the only way I know to deal with Lydia. One has to be firm, or there's no point in even talking to her. That's her nature, I guess. She'll be all right, though. She went for a walk on the beach to unwind. I'm really sorry to be putting you through this, Richard.'

'Please don't worry about me,' he said, returning to his chair. 'How about dinner?'

'Well, if you don't mind, Richard, I'd like to wait until

Lydia comes back. Emily gripped the arms of the chair, and her long strong nails dug into the soft fabric. 'I'm afraid I lost my temper and upset her. I'm sort of worried about her.' She lit a cigarette, inhaled deeply, and exhaled a long stream of smoke through her pursed lips.

She went on with small talk for a while, then, glancing at her watch, said, 'I'm really getting worried about Lydia. Would you mind terribly going down to the beach and checking on her while I freshen up? Since she was upset with me, it may be better if you go. I know she'd appreciate it, and it will give me a chance to get ready.'

'Ah . . . okay, but are you sure she didn't go to the Sanctuary?'

Emily's stomach tightened. He must have overheard her mention the Sanctuary when she was talking to Lydia. 'I heard her go down the back stairs. I'm sure she went to the beach. There's a path behind the house. You can't miss it, just follow it down through the dunes. It's deserted this time of night so she'll no doubt be the only one there. She usually walks down on the right towards the jetty – the large rocks that go out into the water.'

She started towards the hallway. 'It's eight. We should probably hurry if we're going to dinner.'

In the pantry leading to the kitchen she paused, listening. When she heard Richard leave and the door close behind him she breathed easier. She turned and walked quickly into the kitchen, where she sat down at the table.

Had she overlooked anything? She had made a mental checklist. Should something go wrong with any part of the procedure, she had prepared for contingencies.

But the backups should be unnecessary. The practice sessions had worked to perfection. Everything was on schedule. Everything but Steve, that is. He was supposed to have called at eight, the time Richard had left for the beach, so that there would be a confirmation of her presence at the house. It was almost five past eight. Should he fail to call, her backup was to call him and then give some reason for him to call back. This she would do if she didn't hear from him in the next few minutes.

Lydia . . . by this time would have discovered Rusty on the path in the Sanctuary where Emily had tied him earlier. It had been unnecessary to signal the dog to bark with the training collar. The barking was her backup to entice Lydia into the Sanctuary if Emily hadn't succeeded in driving her there with comments about the diary.

Her sister would have untied the dog by now, and he would have raced to the quicksand pit to be fed. Lydia would be on her way to the bench by the pond, where she usually went. In precisely six minutes Emily would push the buttons on the training cylinder. It was the critical part of her plan. The electrical charge would jolt the dog into barking as he had been trained to do, whereupon Lydia would go to see if he were in trouble. When she got to the clearing around the quicksand, she would see him barking at the ball, and try to retrieve it for him. Finally, Lydia would be out of her life.

If suspicion were ever directed at her, there was no way she could be implicated. Yes, she had argued with Lydia, but she had not left the house after her sister had departed, a fact that Richard and Steve could verify. She would have managed Lydia's death without any overt act on her part. As far as explaining Lydia's disappearance, Richard would be taking care of that right now . . .

As she sat smoking, she noticed a small painting on the far wall – a watercolour depicting a kitchen scene done by Lydia when she was a child. Their father had had it mounted and placed there years before. Throughout the kitchen were other examples of her sister's art: the dried flower arrangement in the corner, the needlepoint fabrics on the backs of the chairs. Until that moment Emily had given them little attention. Soon, she would have them removed. Like their creator, they were objects of the past.

She looked at her watch. Six past eight. What had happened to Steve? She went to the kitchen cabinet and carefully removed the training device, taking pains to avoid touching the buttons. Four minutes to go. Then she would jolt the dog. It would be the final stroke. She placed the cylinder gently on the counter as she looked out the window at the heavy foilage across the road. The stillness of evening had settled on the Sanctuary. Deep in the woods, beyond the shadows, the final drama would soon unfold.

As she stood gazing through the window, the tension she had been feeling throughout the day seemed to intensify. Then came the first faint sign. A heaviness in her head. She knew the feeling well. Soon it would be an intense headache, a blinding pain that would settle in the region of her temples, where it would pulsate relentlessly.

But it was not the pain that worried her. She could tolerate that. It was the other possibility . . . it could be the beginning stage of a spell – the one contingency for which she had not prepared.

Damn. She closed her eyes as the pain mounted. Again, she glanced at her watch. Two minutes to go. There was still time to take a pill. She took up the cylinder and went into the hall, intending to go upstairs. At the base of the stairs she hesitated. Turning, she placed the cylinder down on a hall table, walked to the front door and went outside. On the front step she paused, shaking her head. Then, her hands pressed against her temples, she crossed the road and entered the Sanctuary.

Chapter 45

Richard paused at the edge of the dunes overlooking the ocean and took a breath of night air, relieved to be out of the house. Then he started down the winding path to the beach.

He wondered what he should say to Lydia. Would she suspect that he had overheard Emily's comments about her diary? If so, it would be awkward. Emily's remarks had come as a big surprise. His contacts with Lydia had been few. Never had there been anything to suggest a romantic interest.

When he got to the beach he paused to survey the shoreline. It was getting dark, but the sky had cleared farther out, revealing a small pale moon that glimmered across the black sea. An empty expanse of white sand stretched off into the darkness. There was no sign of Lydia.

It was cooler on the shore, and the night breeze from the ocean caused him to turn up the collar of his jacket as he walked. In the distance he saw the outline of the large boulders that formed the breakwater Emily had mentioned.

He had gone only a short way when he came upon a small bundle on the sand above the high waterline. At first he scarcely noted it, assuming it was a patch of seaweed. As he came nearer, though, he saw the garments – a green dress and navy-blue sweater. Moving closer, he saw a pair of women's sandals. Left behind by a beach-goer, he thought.

He glanced up and down the beach for some trace of

Lydia. It was then that the monogram on the sweater caught his eye. Standing out in white letters were the initials *LM*. Lydia's? His eyes shifted out over the water, straining to see. Had she gone for a swim? Not too likely. Then what? As he stood looking out at the dark sea, concern crept over him.

He gathered up the clothes and started back towards the house. Lydia was probably already home. Maybe she hadn't even gone to the beach. Still, his pace quickened as he climbed the path up through the dunes.

The door was ajar at the house when he arrived. 'Emily,' he called, moving into the hallway.

No answer. The library was empty. He looked into the study, then the kitchen. No one there. He moved down the hall to the stairs that led to the second floor. 'Emily? Lydia?'

Returning to the library, he sat down, putting the garments on a nearby table. Had Emily gone looking for him? But he would have seen her if she'd gone to the beach.

As he reflected on the clothes, his apprehension increased. What if something *had* happened to Lydia? She was upset when she left . . .

Suddenly there was a noise from above, towards the rear of the house. He went into the hallway. Maybe Emily was upstairs and hadn't heard him come in. She could be on the telephone . . . a closed door . . . He called again, then, reluctantly, started up the stairs.

At the head of the stairs he hesitated, looking down a hallway. 'Emily?' Nothing. He moved slowly down the hall.

Several rooms were located on each side of the passageway. A storage room, laundry, linen closets, a small room with a sink that appeared as if it might be the quarters for an upstairs maid, and a large study. Near the end of the

266

hall were stairs that led down towards the rear of the house. Next to it was a room with a closed door. Directly across was a large bedroom with the lights on.

He looked into the room. It was apparent immediately that it was Emily's. Tennis trophies stood on a shelf near the door. On a desk was a typewriter, and next to the typewriter, sheaves of paper. A large four-poster bed occupied a far wall.

Again, a sound. This time from downstairs. He went to the hall and called loudly. 'Emily. *Emily*, is that you?'

Silence. He was about to go downstairs when the closed door opposite Emily's bedroom caught his eye. Lydia's room, he assumed.

He rapped softly on the door, waited a moment, and then grasped the knob and opened the door.

It was dark inside, and there was the mouldy odour of a long-closed room . . .

As the light spilled in from the hallway and his eyes adjusted to the darkness he could see that it was, indeed, Lydia's room. On the bureau was a large photograph of a young blonde girl in a cap and gown, presumably Lydia graduating from high school. But it was a room ridden with dust and cobwebs.

Puzzled, he was about to move into the room for a closer look when a shrill ring from a telephone in the nearby study split the silence. He hesitated for a moment as the ringing continued and then went to answer it. The phone was on a large desk by a window overlooking the ocean. As he lifted the receiver he noticed a thick ledger lying open on the desk in front of him. It appeared to be an old journal. He thought of Emily's earlier comment about Lydia's diary. He glanced at it as he lifted the phone. The call was from Steve Sawyer, looking for Emily.

'This is Richard Fox, Steve. It seems no one's here.'

'Oh?'

'Actually, I'm sort of worried. I just came back from the beach . . .' He related how Emily had asked him to go for Lydia, and how he'd found the clothes. 'When I came back there was no one here.' He paused, and when Steve didn't reply he said, 'Emily said that Lydia was very upset when she left. You don't think she would ever . . . you know, do anything crazy?'

'No, of course not,' Steve said quickly. 'She must've been at the beach earlier in the day and left the things. Why don't you sit tight? I'll come by. I'm here at Bayrock. Shouldn't take me long. Emily probably just stepped out for a minute.'

Richard detected an uneasiness in Steve's voice. 'Yes, I'm sure you're right,' Richard said. 'I'll see you in a while.'

Putting down the phone, he looked more closely at the diary. He was about to turn to leave when he noticed a recent entry bearing his name:

Emily determined to nominate Richard for membership at Bayrock. Wants me to propose him . . .

He now started flipping through worn pages. Though aware that this was an invasion of privacy, he felt a measure of justification because of his concern for Lydia. He was nearing the end when he stopped. Strange, the handwriting seemed different in the earlier entries. He held it up to the light. No question, the script was a consistent style until earlier in the year, when the entries stopped. They started again in late spring, but the writing was different, as though by another hand . . .

There were numerous references to him, particularly to the last few months. It seemed Emily might have been right about Lydia's being jealous of her relationship with him. In the more recent entries Lydia, it seemed, was clearly becoming suspicious about her sister's activities. An entry made just the day before was especially revealing:

Richard coming for cocktails tomorrow. Emily acting odd. Said if I come down I should wear my new green dress so I won't clash with her black chiffon. She's up to something. Don't know what. Wouldn't put *anything* past her, though.

He heard a car coming up the drive and hurriedly replaced the diary on the desk. Leaving the study, he returned to Lydia's room to close the door. As he looked into the dim interior, the headlights from the car shone briefly through the windows on the far side of the room. Steve? Emily? He made his way across the dark room to the front windows and saw Steve get out of the car and start towards the entranceway.

He turned quickly from the window, intending to go downstairs, and bumped into a large screen, knocking it over. He was groping in the darkness to retrieve it when his hand came against a pliable leathery object. He looked down and was astonished to see what appeared to be a woman's leg. As his eyes adjusted to the dim light he made out the form of a woman lying on a chaise. Shocked, he stood motionless for an instant before realizing his mistake. What he'd at first thought to be a woman was apparently a life-size dummy. A mannequin for fitting dresses, he thought.

He recovered the screen, straightened it around the chaise and made his way from the room. In the hallway he paused outside the study, then went in and picked up the ledger from the desk. Diary in hand, his confusion mounting, he went downstairs to greet Steve.

Chapter 46

Night had fallen on Old Hampton. It was very still. One by one the lights blinked out in the mansions along Forsythia Lane as residents prepared for the end of another day.

In the library of the Morrow residence Steve found Richard even more anxious than he had been on the phone regarding the whereabouts of Emily and Lydia. Richard had told him what had taken place earlier in the evening: the sisters arguing; discovering the clothes on the beach; returning to the empty house, and then going upstairs and finding the diary. He had given it to Steve, who reluctantly flipped through it.

The recent entries reflecting the marked change in handwriting left Steve as bewildered as Richard, adding to the questions that had been building in his mind since he had heard John Collier's suspicions.

'From what you've said, you never actually saw Lydia tonight, did you?' Steve asked. 'You only heard Emily talking to her about – '

'That's right . . . I wonder if we should call the police. They have those radio cars they use to patrol the beaches. We could ask them if they'd take a run along the shore to see if – '

'No . . . I think we should wait a bit. Emily should be back soon, she wouldn't appreciate a big thing being made over nothing . . .'

'*Nothing*. Lydia was obviously very upset . . . I find her clothes on the edge of the ocean. You think she always goes down and takes her clothes off on the beach at night?' Richard sat back in his chair, recrossing his legs and folding his arms about his chest. It was a singular movement, characteristic of him when he was upset, as if harnessing his emotions with his limbs in a self-imposed strait jacket.

Steve realized that he would be unable to put off Richard much longer, but he saw the need to protect Emily, especially after what John had told him. When a few minutes later Richard pressed him about calling the authorities, Steve decided he had no choice but to divulge what he'd learned about Lydia.

'I think I understand how confused you must be,' Steve began, 'and frankly I don't know any more than you do about what's going on here tonight. But I don't think we have to be worried about Lydia going to the beach. Emily's the one we should worry about.'

'I don't understand. What are you holding back? I'd appreciate it if you'd – '

'There are some things you should know about Emily and Lydia,' Steve cut in, 'and I'm going to confide in you because I know you'd want to be helpful to Emily.'

'Of course.'

'I've been very concerned about Emily the past couple of months. I suspect she may be having some psychological problems.'

Richard shifted in his chair, a mixture of surprise and concern on his face.

'I'm sure you'll keep this confidential,' Steve went on, 'at least until I can convince her to get some help.' Taking a deep breath and exhaling slowly, he settled back in his chair. 'This isn't my first encounter with that diary. I became aware of it a few months ago. I came here one evening to see Emily' – he paused, sorting out the memories – 'we'd planned to go to dinner . . .'

* * *

'Hi, Steve,' Emily said at him through the doorway. 'You're late.'

'Sorry,' he said, moving into the hallway. He was relieved she and not Lydia had answered the door. He'd mistaken her for Lydia through the kitchen window when he'd approached the house. 'I forgot my wallet, had to go back.' He glanced towards the kitchen.

'Don't worry, she's not here,' Emily said.

Embarrassed that he'd been so obvious, he followed her down the hallway into the library. Actually Lydia's absence was no surprise . . . he'd barely talked to her since the night he had confessed his feelings for Emily. She would go on avoiding him, he knew. Nor had Emily talked about her. Her reticence in this regard was understandable. He was a little surprised, therefore, when she mentioned her as they sat down.

'No, Lydia isn't here, Steve' – she hesitated, her eyes flat on him – 'I might as well tell you, you'll find out eventually anyway. Fact is, she's gone.'

'You mean she . . . she's moved out?'

'Yes.' For an instant, there was dead silence, and then she added with a shrug, 'She probably wanted to get away.'

Before Steve could react, Emily said, 'Excuse me a minute, I want to show you something.' She left the room and reappeared carrying what looked like a ledger. 'Here, I may as well show you this while I'm at it.' She opened to a bookmark and handed it to him. 'This is her diary. Read that entry. Go on, don't be embarrassed.'

Steve took the book reluctantly, balancing it on his knee as he read:

I miss Steve terribly. My life becomes increasingly empty. I don't see how I can stay here in Old Hampton.

'A few weeks later she said she was leaving.' Emily shrugged. 'That's the last I heard of her.'

'And she left?' Steve's voice was barely audible, aware of his own responsibility.

'I was going to mention it sooner only . . . well, so much has happened these past months. You were recovering from the boat accident, my novel . . . Frankly, I thought she'd be back by now.'

'But it's been weeks. Hasn't she called, written? People must wonder where she is – '

'No one's missed her. Not even you. Hardly anyone around here ever saw her except you and that old care-taker Henry Todd. And he could never tell us apart, forever calling her Miss Emily and me Miss Lydia. She spent most of her life away at school or in New York City. Besides, even when she was here she was always a recluse, writing those bird books . . .'

Steve sat quietly, balancing his guilt about Lydia with relief that she was gone.

'Frankly, it's just as well she left,' Emily was saying. 'We haven't been getting along too well, as you probably know. To be honest, it's been one long continuous fight. But there are other things to consider, now that she's gone.'

'What do you mean?'

'Well, her inheritance . . .'

Emily proceeded to explain how a trust created by her father had been arranged so that the proceeds would be distributed to his daughters when they each reached the age of twenty-eight. A touch of bitterness showed when she added, 'The trust is really too conservative, Steve. Apparently we had an aunt who squandered her inheritance when she was young and our father over-reacted to it. We just started receiving Lydia's cheques last year. I think it's not only unfair but impractical that I have to wait longer for mine . . . The government's already taken almost everything else through inheritance taxes. People think we're so rich, they don't realize that our trust was set up over twenty years ago. What was provided for us to live on until we come into our inheritance isn't that much. Now with inflation, taxes. I just don't know how I'll manage without Lydia's cheques.'

'Cheques?'

'Her inheritance cheques. Don't you understand? No Lydia, no money. I won't get my share of the inheritance for a couple of more years.'

'But shouldn't you try to find her?'

'How? I've no idea where she went.'

'You could ask . . . well, there are people who special- ize in that sort of thing.'

'Why get anyone else involved? I don't think I should make a big fuss. There could be some kind of investiga- tion, then after we've created the brouhaha, in walks Lydia from Europe or God knows where. I think I should just go on the way I have for a while. She'll probably come back soon.'

Steve shook his head. 'Well, I'm suprised you haven't heard from her by now. I'd think she'd notify the post office of her change of address if she doesn't plan on coming back. I feel bad about all this . . .'

Emily rose and came to him. Dropping to her knees beside his chair, she took his maimed right hand and squeezed it gently. 'Really, Steve,' she said softly, nestling beside his leg, 'don't worry about it. It's a family matter . . . between Lydia and me. I'm sure she'll be back soon. Let me handle it. Okay? Believe me, no one's going to miss Lydia.'

Steve paused, reached for his brandy, avoiding Richard's eyes, he did not wait for the questions that he knew must be building. 'It turned out that Emily was right. No one did miss Lydia. I kept telling myself that it was a domestic matter, like she said, that Lydia would be back soon. Then several weeks ago I was relieved when Emily told me that Lydia had finally come home from Europe. I never saw her, but other people said they've seen her in town and over at the club. I assumed she was avoiding me. Then earlier this week I learned some very disturbing things . . . I can't be sure, but I suspect that Lydia never did come back. Emily may be impersonating her in order to get Lydia's inheritance cheques.'

Steve paused, the strain evident in his face. 'Yesterday I discussed her condition with a psychiatrist friend. He's agreed to see her on Monday. The problem will be to get Emily to keep the appointment.'

Richard, recovering from his astonishment, was about to say something when suddenly there was a sound from the rear of the house. 'Did you hear that? It sounded like a door closing.'

'Probably just the house,' Steve said. 'It's so old, filled with noises like – '

'No, I'm *sure* it was a back door. I think someone – listen . . .' There was the distinct quiet tread of footsteps on linoleum, then the low shuffling sound of someone mounting the rear stairs. 'Hear *that?*'

'It must be Emily,' Steve said. 'She came in the back way. I'm sure she knows we're here. She'll probably come down in a minute . . . Look, I wouldn't mention anything we've just talked about . . .'

They waited a few minutes, and when Emily didn't appear Steve became restless. 'I'm sure she knows we're here. I'll give her a call.'

At the doorway he stuck his head out into the hall. 'Emily.' There was no answer. 'Emily?'

He turned to Richard, shrugged. 'Apparently she's not there. Maybe we imagined – '

'No, I'm sure I heard someone.' Richard went to the door and both stepped into the hall.

Steve called her name again. Silence. He moved down the hall towards the base of the stairwell, calling again, louder. He stopped, listening. There was a sound at the top of the stairs.

Suddenly a blond figure with glasses appeared and quietly began to descend the stairs. It was Lydia. But the face . . . not round, the eyes dark rather than blue.

'Emily,' Steve exclaimed. 'What in God's name are you doing?'

She paused, and it was then that Steve saw the pain in the dark eyes. As she peered down at him, he felt a chill.

'I'm sorry, Steve,' she said coolly. 'Emily isn't here.'

Chapter 47

'Lydia hasn't been in Old Hampton since last spring,' Steve said. 'Any contacts you *thought* you had with her were with Emily impersonating Lydia.'

Richard sat in the Morrow library listening to Steve, who was speaking in a numbed monotone about Emily's condition. The two had reacted with shock, disbelief, and finally, utter bafflement when Emily had revealed her dual personality earlier on the stairs.

At the time, Emily, believing herself to be Lydia, had apologized to Richard for her lack of hospitality, explaining that she and Emily had had an argument and that her sister had gone to bed. She was going to find Rusty and would return soon. There was no doubt that she was convinced she was Lydia. Richard and Steve had heard her leave the house shortly thereafter. Now, with the awareness that the Hampton sisters of preceding weeks were, indeed, one person, they found themselves emotionally devastated.

Steve sat with the journal open on his lap, perusing the entries, searching for answers. 'You can get a pretty good idea of what happened from what's here,' he said, soberly. 'There aren't any entries during April and May, which was *after* Lydia left home. But then they start again in June – in *Emily's* handwriting. Apparently that's when Emily began having these spells, confusing herself with Lydia. After Lydia left she got a wig and started impersonating Lydia, apparently in order to keep the inheritance cheques coming. The conscious impersonation probably helped bring on the switches in personality that she couldn't control.'

Richard sat shaking his head. 'When I think of the times I thought I was talking to Lydia . . .'

Steve nodded. 'I once treated a child who had a similar condition. In psychiatry it's classified as a dissociative disorder. Each of the personalities has its own behaviour patterns, two different people in the same body. It's an amnesiac situation that leads to fugues – '

'Fugues?'

'Psychological amnesia – times when the person lives another life, but after coming back to normal can't remember what happened. An escape from reality. When she's in a fugue, Emily's convinced she's Lydia. And given the similarity in appearance, and Emily's acting ability, it's no wonder we were fooled.'

Richard crossed his legs and folded his arms tightly over his chest, his mind full of questions and uncertainty, images of the soft-spoken Lydia clashing with those of the outspoken Emily.

An antique clock in the corner of the room began striking the hour. It was a tall-case English clock, standing almost eight feet to the tips of its interestingly carved finials. Its chimes, unlike the bell-like tones from the imitation clock in the upstairs hall, were flat and disonant, contributing to the sense of illusiveness in the room.

'It's remarkable,' Richard said. 'I mean their voices and looks being so close, it all made the switch so convincing . . . And to think of her up there in her study writing in her diary as though *she* were Lydia . . .'

'Well, the diary also helped her . . . provided her with an intimate look at Lydia's thoughts and feelings. From some of these notes she made referring to earlier entries, you even get the feeling looking at those that she'd reminisce over the previous entries as though they'd actually been her own experiences.'

278

'Well, what now?' Richard said. 'You're a doctor . . . What's her prognosis, can she be cured?'

'I'm not a hell of a lot better off than you, Richard. What little clinical knowledge I have is from a few patients I was treating for unrelated illnesses.' He went to a front window, his shoulders slumped. 'Obviously, she needs long and extensive treatment. Maybe therapy can help lead to personality integration. But I'm no expert about the extent of her condition. I'd suspected that she was having some problems, but this . . .'

'I heard her talking upstairs earlier,' Richard said, 'just as if Lydia were right there.'

'The little girl I treated carried on conversations with her alter ego too.'

'What brings on these spells?'

'Pressure of some kind, generally. The fugue is an escape. When Emily can't cope as Emily, she reverts to Lydia. Lydia the good sister, the one *nobody* criticized.'

'Yes, she even went so far as fight against her own manuscript. You say she avoided you when she was Lydia?'

Steve looked especially uneasy. 'As Lydia she had reason to. She felt jilted. She'd have nothing to do with me, you saw for yourself out in the hall. She was very cool, hostile. Exactly the way Lydia should react. The first time I really saw her as Lydia was there on the stairs.'

Richard shook his head. 'Most of the time she was very normal . . . delightful.'

Steve shrugged. 'Other than that she's convinced Lydia is there in her bedroom behind the closed door, she's rational – except, of course, when she's in one of her fugues as Lydia.'

Richard was silent. His look drifted about the room, coming to rest on the relics Emily had chosen to preserve. For an instant it was as though time had suddenly stopped.

The room seemed an eerie photograph, birds fixed in flight, motionless objects staring from the shelves.

As he gazed at the strange menagerie, a certain suspicion almost subliminal at first, began forming in his mind. 'Steve, don't you think it's strange that nothing's been heard from the real Lydia?'

Steve shrugged. 'She was very upset . . .' He paused, then added, 'You'd think, though, she would have contacted John Collier or someone at the bank.'

The comment strengthened the ghoulish thought pressing for recognition in Richard's head. He struggled to put it from his mind, but it persisted, expanding, an embryo that took horrifying shape with passing seconds. 'I went in Lydia's room earlier,' he said, shifting uneasily. 'In fact, I even *thought* I saw her . . . it was a mannequin.'

'Mannequin?'

'You know, one of those dressmaker's dummies . . . Maybe she thinks, somehow . . . you know, that the mannequin is Lydia . . .'

His voice dropped off. The room was very still. Suddenly, from the corner the clock sounded the half hour, the solitary stroke falling lifelessly amid the rigid rows of unblinking eyes. As he looked up at the weird relics, a tingling sensation crept down the back of his neck into his shoulders.

'Something *wrong*?' Steve said.

Richard shook his head. 'It's just that . . . well, I had a crazy notion. No, it's too . . . forget it.'

Steve continued to look at him curiously for a moment, then turned back to the window.

Finally, dismissing the thought, Richard stood up and joined Steve looking across the road at the dark vegetation comprising the Sanctuary. 'Do you think she went in there after she left us?'

'Hard to say. If she's Lydia, I mean in a fugue, she's doing whatever Lydia would do . . .'

Richard felt warm; the closeness of the room was oppressive. 'I think I need some air,' he said, turning and walking towards the doorway. 'Maybe I'll go into the Sanctuary and see if I can find her.'

'Are you serious?' Steve said, turning and looking after him. 'You'll never find her in there at night. She may not even be there.'

'I need some air, anyway.'

In the hallway Richard noted the training cylinder that Emily had left on the table earlier. Mistaking it for a flashlight, he picked it up and casually stuck it in the pocket of his jacket.

A soft breeze drifted down Forsythia Lane. The night air felt refreshing as he crossed the road to the Sanctuary. At the entrance he looked down the trail that tunnelled through the dark vegetation. A heavy fog lay over the path. All at once there was a slight movement in the mist. Startled, he looked closely, straining to see what looked like forms undulating in the vapours . . .

Reaching into his pocket, he took out the dog cylinder. He realized quickly that it was not a flashlight as he'd thought. He looked back down the trail, the forms had vanished . . . eerie, like the phantoms in Emily's novel.

He inspected the dog cylinder, turning it curiously. Seeing the two buttons, he automatically pushed each one. A low buzzing sounded in the device. Puzzled, he returned it to his pocket.

From deep in the Sanctuary came the muted barking of a dog.

The sound contributed to the forlorn setting. He stood for a moment, breathing the night air, reflecting on the extraordinary condition that allowed Emily to withdraw from a troubled existence into the gentle life of Lydia. It was, in a way, an escape like Tank's reveries that took him off to toyland. He thought of Tank's recent visit with 'Lydia' in Old Hampton. They had, it seemed, shared a world of make-believe . . .

He turned and walked slowly back across the road to the house.

Most lights were out now in the mansions. Forsythia Lane was enveloped in quiet darkness. Yachting flags on top of the Bayrock Club fluttered in the light breeze, tired ensigns in the black sky. From a nearby residence came the subdued conversation of guests leaving a late dinner party, their voices hushed, considerate of neighbours. The only other sounds were from the soft wind, and the waves that whispered beyond the dunes. Nightfall, like everything, arrived gently in Old Hampton.

Epilogue

The Sanctuary in Old Hampton has been the scene of strange sightings for over two hundred years. Mostly by town folk, a hardy breed, many of whom trace their ancestry back to the 1700s when talk of spirits and witchcraft was more prevalent. Sightings have been less frequent in modern times and most have been dismissed by local meteorologists. Nothing more than miasma, they claim. Foggy exhalation from the decaying organic matter that forms the bed of the Sanctuary.

Nevertheless, the sightings continue. Wavering forms of a bluish-greyish cast floating above the bogs.

Richard Fox had had such a sighting earlier in the evening, but like the atmospheric scientists, had passed it off as a fanciful image. Had he continued down the winding path he might have seen more. They were there, waiting. The dead of night . . .

Dark shrouds of vaporous clouds draped the Sanctuary. A stillness had settled over the wild as spirits of the departed moved with the mist, deadening sounds of living things.

It was a disparate band of phantoms, lost souls aggrieved with their lot, all having suffered premature passings at the hands of the mortal who now rested below them on the bench by the pond. The lost souls drifted in the vapours, complaining bitterly in voiceless whispers while searching through sightless eyes for scraps of immortality.

First came Lydia, looking for her journal, and for her lost love. Then Henry Todd, searching for his dog Bart. Close behind, not too comfortable with their present company, were Arnold Seigler and Norman Kaplin, proceeding cautiously, looking for Alfredo's. Trailing was Leroy Taylor, forever combing the underbrush for his irrecoverable manhood. Bringing up the rear was a host of lesser creatures – victims seeking the elusive refuge the Sanctuary promised.

They mingled in the mist, a parade of revenants deprived of their corporeal rights by the individual below. This person now impersonating the departed Lydia *all* knew to be Emily. They had learned her deceptive ways.

The spirit of Louis Morrow was also present. But he stood off by himself in the damp shadows, observing his daughter's lonely form sitting beside the steaming black pool. He was wrapped in nostalgia, reflecting on Emily as a child playing with ducks beside the pond, forever dancing, whirling and tripping in eurhythmic movements with the sounds from the forest.

The other witnesses were less sympathetic. They had watched throughout the week preparations for Emily's elaborate scheme, and took satisfaction from the dramatic irony about to unfold.

Leroy Taylor was especially pleased. No shrinking violet, Leroy, he had been immensely proud of his missing member. To have had it become the subject of Emily's taxidermy, and then used by her as an artifice in a homosexual encounter with Arnold Seigler, was more than any manly spirit should have to bear.

And Henry Todd, having been dispatched in the quicksand, could certainly see the justice in Emily's self-destruction. Norman Kaplin and Arnold Seigler were, of course, pleased. Norman, as a publisher, had an instinctive dislike of authors, and Arnold a book critic, had killed off a few aspiring novelists himself in his day.

And who would deny Lydia a measure of satisfaction, having succumbed to Emily's taxidermy?

With the barking of the dog there had been a flurry above the pond. The grey cast of shapes, sensing the end was near, had gathered over Emily. The barking was now agitated, persistent. The shapes hovering in the mist waited. Finally Emily rose, and, trailing the grey spectral procession, disappeared into the forest towards the quicksand.

The barking continued for a few minutes before stopping abruptly. Then it was quiet. Quiet, that is, except for a faint lyrical beat. It started far back in the forest, gaining intensity. The song of the Sanctuary. Creatures of the night beating out their dark rhythm for a form that now danced endlessly in the vapours steaming from the bogs.